Legacy of Gray

The Jed Gray Series Book Three

Jodi Walter

THIRTEEN PAGES

To You, My Reader,

With deepest gratitude, I dedicate this book to you. Thank you for choosing to journey with me through Jed's story and for embracing the world I've humbly shared.

If there is one message you carry from these pages, it is this: Our pasts do not dictate who we become. Each of us holds the power to change our lives' course, to rise above what once was, and to shape a better future. We can all make a meaningful impact on the world—if we choose to.

Thank you for being apart of this journey.

CHAPTER 1

___

IT WAS ONE OF those days.

Jed was leaning lazily against the leather backrest of his chair, his eyes traveling out the window and landing on the pavement right beneath his building. He watched as the sea of bodies constantly shifted, swelling and flattening in unending tides—men hoisting briefcases and striding briskly, women cradling cups of steaming coffee in their arms as they rushed to their appointments, and little children tottering alongside their parents, their large schoolbags sagging against their shoulders.

How many of these people have ever gone to therapy? Jed wondered. *How many of them will need it later in their lives?* The answer, when it came, did not cheer him. Although Jed derived a great satisfaction from helping people, from bringing into light the wounds they had buried beneath so many useless memories, it did not come without a price of its own. You did not simply get to heal others' pain without letting some of it rub off on you.

Today, thankfully, was not one of those busy days. Jed's office had remained mostly silent and peaceful since that morning. The telephone on the desk had also rung only twice—the first a call from the receptionist downstairs to sort out some paperwork, and the second one from Ruth, one of his newer clients, who had just been in a chatty mood. Since then, Jed had been idle, staring contently down at the unaware people below him, trying to tackle the conundrum he was facing.

The conundrum was simple: Should he call Christie for lunch or not? It seemed terribly frustrating to Jed that, while he had solved quite a few tricky mysteries in his career as a consultant for the police, something as simple as a lunch date had him at a loss. He just could not decide what to do. It wasn't as if he had never asked her before. He had, of course. They had gone on numerous friendly dates in the interim between finishing a case and not being assigned a new one. But all those dates had been on the weekend, well past working hours. That was the problem.

Will it be appropriate if I ask her to join me for lunch? His fingers drummed on the desk. *On one hand, we've gone for lunch so many times while working, it really shouldn't be that big of a deal. On the other hand, it's a weekday and still noon. It could seem a bit strange if I call her out of the blue and ask her to grab a bite with me during her working hours. That's not something friends generally do. That's something people who are more than just friends do.*

Jed sighed, running a hand through his soft brown hair, which he had let grow for the past couple of months. The chair beneath him let out a startled creak as he rose abruptly, deciding that he would just grab something from the hotdog stand near his office. A dollop of all those delicious sauces smeared on a fresh, toasted bun would definitely improve his mood.

He had only made it to the door of his office, though, with his hand on the knob, when the phone rang for the third time that day. Jed sighed and took a few steps back toward his desk before realizing it was not his office telephone that was ringing but his cellphone.

He stuffed his hand into his pants pocket and took it out. A light and fleeting wave of nervousness rolled through him as he read the name flashing on the screen in bold black letters. It was Christie.

"Hello, Detective," Jed answered, putting the phone against his ear.

"Howdy, partner." He couldn't see her, but Jed could sense the grin resting on Christie's face as she uttered those words.

"Is that what we are?" he asked with a small laugh, plopping back down on his chair. "Partners?"

"I mean, if you prefer the word colleague, I can use that, too." Christie's voice turned half-serious and half-teasing. "Is partner too intimate a word for your stoic aura?"

"My *stoic aura?*" Jed stared out the window, grinning himself. "Wow, someone's clearly been using the dictionary in their spare time."

Now, it was Christie's turn to laugh. "Well, even if I have, that spare time has come to an end." She cleared her throat, turning suddenly serious and businesslike. "You're wanted down at the station."

Finally. Some work, he thought, and then felt an instant stab of guilt at being excited about what was most certainly a murder or some other form of catastrophe.

"I'll be there in 15 minutes," Jed answered, rising back up from his chair, bidding a forlorn mental goodbye to the hotdog he had been picturing in his mind.

Twenty minutes later, Jed was in a sort of conference room inside the police quarters, with Derek and Graham by his side. Derek was fixing the screen at the back of the room, and Graham was deftly organizing a pile of papers on the table, removing all unnecessary ones and throwing them in the bin in a crumpled ball.

"What is this about, exactly?" Jed asked the two men, just as the door swung open.

"It's a murder," Christie told him, entering. "Happened last night, and I was informed of it this morning." She paused and looked at Jed for a moment. "I think we could use your insight on this one, so I asked the chief if we could bring you in on it."

Jed stared at Christie, momentarily rendered wordless by her appearance. She was dressed in a cream-colored sweater and charcoal pants, with her tawny hair dangling behind her in a tight ponytail. It had been a few days since he had last seen her, not that much time by any means, but it felt like an eternity had passed.

"Detective," Jed began with a soft smile, unable to tear his gaze away from her, "while I have always appreciated the value you place in my deductive skills, is there something about this case that crosses into mental health or addiction?"

Christie shrugged, now looking just a bit embarrassed. "We don't know yet. I was looking over the case this morning but couldn't shake the feeling that I was missing something. Thought an outside perspective would be useful. And who better than my partner, who I haven't worked with in almost a month?"

I'm not the only one keeping track of the time. She has been, too. The thought pleased Jed, but he didn't let it show.

"I'm thrilled that you think so highly of me," he commented, "but please don't be too disappointed if I'm not able to provide you with any enlightening insights. This is not exactly my forte, but I will do whatever I can to help."

Any further conversation between them was cut off as the video whirred to life, casting a single picture on the screen. It was a woman, probably in her mid-thirties, with olive skin and curly hair.

"That's Janet Simmons," Christie informed him. "She's thirty-two, lives on Madison Avenue, and works as a mortgage banker. Or, rather, she used to do all those things."

Jed peered closely at the face, which was marked with stern lines and a long, prominent nose. "I take it that's our victim.

"Correct." Christie motioned toward one of the men, and they pressed a button on a remote, moving the frames forward. Now, Jed was looking at another image—this one of a rusty red Chevrolet in the basement of some building's parking lot.

"Janet was found here last night, propped upright in the driver's seat of her car." Christie added in a clipped voice, "She had been strangled to death, her purse and wallet stolen."

"So, it was a mugging, then?" Jed inquired, looking carefully at the car and the surrounding area.

"That's what I think, yes. But I want *your* opinion on it. Your own, unfiltered take on what might have happened here."

Jed turned to Christie. "Why?"

Christie paused for a moment, struggling to find the right words. "I have this… feeling. This ominous, nagging feeling that won't go away no matter what, and it's been pestering me. I feel like I'm missing something… essential."

"And you want me to find it for you," Jed finished, turning back to the screen before him.

"Yes. I'll send you Janet's file containing her background details, and if you want to talk to the witnesses where she was found, we can arrange that as well."

Jed pursed his lips, eyes still fixed on the picture. It looked quite haunting now, considering that when it had been taken, the insides of that car had contained a fresh corpse.

"Where is the car parked?" he asked.

"It's the entrance to a shopping center," Christie told him. "Janet had gone in and purchased two packs of laundry detergent and a face wash before exiting. We found them on the passenger seat of her car."

The last purchase of her life. She had no way of knowing that at the time. An uneasy disquiet stole over Jed as he continued to inspect the picture before him, waiting for some hidden insight to strike him. But none did. He turned back to Christie.

"I'm going to need to speak to the person who found her. I also need to know the time and cause of her death."

Christie nodded somberly. "Got it. The coroner will have the time of death for us soon. In the meantime, we can go to the scene right now. The employee who found her will be starting his shift soon. Derek, why don't you stay in touch with the medical examiner and let us know if there are any new findings of interest? Graham, try and see if you can locate the victim's family and friends. We need to know if she had any enemies or was involved in suspicious activities of any sort."

Graham nodded, and Derek grunted in acknowledgement. Jed motioned for Christie to exit the room first, and she did, with him behind her, Derek and Graham trailing behind them both. Christie led Jed through a snaking corridor toward the building's backside, where her black Ford Explorer waited outside.

"You know what? We actually have some spare time before the security guard begins his shift," Christie stated, buckling her seatbelt and turning the ignition. She gave Jed a sidelong glance. "You want to get something to eat? I'm famished."

Jed's eyes gleamed with amusement. "I thought you'd never ask."

Twenty minutes later, they were at one of the joints they often frequented, a small but cozy sandwich shop squeezed between two laundromats. Jed was having his usual double-layered wasabi beef sandwich and Christie had gone for a croissant stuffed with tarragon chicken.

They sat together in a companionable silence and enjoyed their food, watching the cars and people pass by outside. This had become a kind of routine for them, in the month they had spent without working together. Since there had been no reason for them to meet professionally, they had used their shared love for food as an excuse instead, visiting the most popular culinary spots in the city and catching up on each other's lives.

Now, here they were again, the vacation over and a case in their hands. Jed looked at Christie as he chewed slowly, noticing the slightly distracted look in her eyes. She always got like this when starting a case; for the first few hours, it occupied all her attention.

"Penny for your thoughts, Detective?" he inquired softly, snapping her from her reverie.

Christie looked at him and blinked. She returned his smile with a sheepish one of her own. "I guess you already know them, Gray."

Jed nodded, popped the remainder of his sandwich into his mouth and dusted the crumbs from his hands. "I wouldn't be much of a therapist if I didn't. You're worried about the case, mentally going over the details again and again, wondering what you missed."

Christie did not object. She spread her hands before him in surrender. "I can't help it. Unsolved puzzles drive me crazy."

Jed cocked an eyebrow. "Is that why you seem to be so helplessly drawn to me? Because of my mysterious aura, which you just can't seem to decipher? I guess I should cherish our time together. Once you figure me out, you will have no use for me."

Christie rolled her eyes, but there was a reddish tinge to her cheeks. She finished the rest of her croissant and dabbed her lips with a napkin. "It's the case's mystery that has more of my attention right now, Gray."

"That's simply unacceptable." Jed rose from his seat, before placing a five-dollar tip on the table. "Let's go. We must solve this case at once, so your attention can return to me, where I like it."

Christie rolled her eyes at him again, but blossoming scarlet on her neck and face belied the gesture. Jed bit back an amused smile as he walked with her outside.

Forty-five minutes later, they arrived, parking the car in the underground parking lot where the incident had taken place. Jed opened the door and stepped outside. An eerie sensation gripped him immediately as he looked around, his skin prickling. They were in exactly the same place as the picture he had just seen, the only difference being that Christie had parked them in a different spot.

Jed stared at the blank slab of concrete where the red Chevrolet had been not very long ago. His gaze drifted to the flickering amber light in the overhead ceiling, and he wondered if spirits really did stick around after a violent death, waiting for justice to be served. A shiver went through him, and he wiped a hand across his sweaty brows. It was warm here, uncomfortably warm and humid, and Jed could already feel his armpits beginning to dampen.

"God, this place gives me the creeps," Christie shuddered, jamming her hands into the pockets of her pants. "Come on. Let's go and talk to the security guard who found Janet."

Moments later, a large, bald man wearing wire-rimmed spectacles and sporting a thin mustache approached them. His name was Avery, and his brows seemed set in a permanent scowl. Noticing his jittery movements, Jed surmised that the trauma this discovery had caused the man would take a while to heal.

"Avery," Christie began gently, "could you tell my colleague, Jed, how you found Janet? Please don't leave anything out. You never know what small detail might be the key to solving the case."

Avery nodded, his head bobbing up and down like an egg in turbulent water, his forehead shining with beads of sweat.

"I—I saw her on my last walk-through of the morning," he began, wringing his hands together. "I think at around 4:40-ish AM, or something. My shift ends at five, see, but I had taken off slightly early because my replacement had arrived by then." He regarded both Jed and Christie sheepishly and with a hint of fright, as if expecting them to chastise him for not completing his full working hours. Upon receiving no such scolding, he continued.

"I came into the garage, and that's when I saw the Chevrolet, parked in the middle. It was the only car in the lot. We don't usually get visitors so early, see, so it looked suspicious to me—that caused me to walk toward it. And that was when I... I... I s—saw what I saw."

"What did you see?" Jed prodded gently. "Can you tell me?"

"It was the w—woman. She was dead." Avery swallowed deeply multiple times, his entire face covered with a thin sheen of sweat now. "Her eyes were wide open, and God, they were so glassy. Like marbles, just staring off into nothing. There was a dark red line around her throat, probably where she had been strangled, I'd reckon. I saw her, and I screamed at the top of my lungs, scrambling backward like a madman. I grabbed the car's bonnet to support myself, and the metal was striking hot. Then I tumbled to the floor. Once I gathered myself, I called the police. The rest, I guess you already know." Avery exhaled in relief upon finishing the story and then looked at Jed and Christie, waiting for their reaction.

Jed didn't give him one. He was lost in thought, deep thought. There was something about Avery's story which had struck him… something he couldn't quite put his finger on.

"Thank you, Avery," Jed said abruptly, straightening. "You've been a great help."

They both turned and left, Christie walking by his side.

"Any insights forming up there yet?" She gestured toward Jed's skull.

Jed grunted softly. "Not yet. But I have a feeling something will come."

CHAPTER 2

IT WAS EARLY MORNING. Jed sat in his office with his brows furrowed, his mind on yesterday's events, especially what Avery had told them. He tried to remember what the security guard's exact words.

Her eyes were glassy, staring into nothing. A red line around her throat from where she'd been strangled. Then I stumbled backward. I grabbed the car's hood before falling to the floor.

Jed's mouth was set in a pensive line. Every now and again, he would make a dissatisfied clicking noise with his tongue as whatever key detail it was that was evading him continued to remain at the periphery of his mind. It was like an infuriating ghost, appearing in corners when he wasn't looking, dissipating into nothing if he so much as glanced its way.

Christie was right. There was more to this case than the details indicated. Jed could feel it deep in his bones. He didn't normally act this way, allowing his gut feeling to guide his behavior. Jed had always been a man of cool, calm logic, analyzing every situation with a detached curiosity because that was how you got to the heart of any mystery. He had learned it over the course of many addiction counseling sessions. The one thing addicts suffered from the most was an impaired sense of judgement: their illness coupled with their heightened emotions always made them see things unclearly. It led them to make rash decisions and give up hope at the slightest fallback. The trick was always to step back from the turmoil of your feelings and cast an objective eye over the matter at hand, the way an outside observer would.

But this case… something smelled fishy. That was all Jed could really say with certainty. He let out a weary breath and allowed his mind to drift from the subject, enjoying a moment's rest.

His phone rang right then, cutting his peace short. Jed picked it up from his desk and stared at the screen. It was Max calling, surprisingly punctual for their regular Friday appointment. "Hello, Max," Jed greeted the young man. "How are you doing?"

"Ah, I'm getting by, Mr. G." Max's drawling voice filled his ears. "You know how it is."

"I do, but why don't you still fill me in on how your week has been?" Jed uncrossed his legs and leaned back in the seat. "Any new developments I should be aware of?"

"Nah, not really. Same old, you know," Max paused, and Jed knew the boy had just thought of something. "Actually, though, there is one thing."

"I'm all ears."

"My ma." Max's relaxed tone tightened up a notch. "There's some beef... between her and Shanice."

"Beef?" Jed repeated thoughtfully. "Meaning your mom and your girlfriend aren't getting along very well."

"Nah, Mr. G—it's not Shanice that's the problem. It's my ma, you know? She j—" Max broke off and sucked in a frustrated breath. "My ma just don't seem to dig Shanice very much, Mr. G. Everything my girl does pisses her off. Now it's gotten so bad even Shanice has started noticing. Every time Shanice comes over to my crib while my ma is hangin' there, too, my ma goes away somewhere to hide so she doesn't have to meet her. Once or twice, I managed to spin some lie, but Shanice ain't no fool. She knows she's not welcome."

"I'm sorry to hear that." Jed's voice was sympathetic. He knew the boy already had enough to deal with. "Have you spoken to your mother about it, asked her why she's behaving this way?"

"Yeah, man. She started acting all innocent and stuff, said I was goin' nutty, imagining shit." Max sniffed angrily. "Like I could imagine that. She's doin' it all on purpose, to hurt my girl, and she won't even tell me why."

Jed pursed his lips, deep in thought, trying to figure out the cause for such behavior.

"Man, she really crossed the line!" Max continued hotly, letting it all out now that someone was listening. "I mean, Shanice and I went to a small music show last week. There was this really rad Columbian rock band singing near one of the ghettos—one we really digged. The show started late, so by the time I was walking back home, it was early morning. Ma was waiting for me by the time I got back, of course."

"I'm guessing she wasn't very happy with your late-night adventure," Jed commented dryly.

"Not at all. Ma was all but spittin' fire, Mr. G." Max let out a disbelieving chuckle. "Guess why? She said I was putting myself in danger, coming home so late! That I could have been mugged, or worse! Can you believe that, Mr. G?"

Jed paused. "I don't know, Max," he began carefully. "From what you've told me, I agree that your mother seems to be acting strange. But it sounds reasonable that she's angry at you for coming home late—especially if she's worried about your safety. The crime rate is skyrocketing in this city, unfortunately."

"Oh, Mr. G," Max groaned. "You're not from the streets. You don't know how the world works at the bottom."

Jed smiled patiently. "Enlighten me."

"Muggings always happen at night, man," Max's voice was filled with certainty, "unless it's some freak thing or some weirdo who ain't got all his screws tightened. I mean, who in their right mind would out themselves when they can be seen, when there's light in the sky, you dig?" He paused, and

Jed felt the boy shaking his head on the other end. "No, Mr. G. I came home early morning, around six or seven. There was no chance of being mugged."

Jed had gone very quiet. Max's comment had lit up something within him, some hidden bulb of revelation which had been lying dark.

"Is that so, Max?" he asked softly, mind racing.

"Yep," Max continued. "You know what? The hood I was going through, that street never has muggings on it—ever. But would my ma believe me? Naw, man."

"Wait." Jed frowned. "How could you know which streets have a high chance of being mugging locations and which don't?"

Max grunted. "The street I came back through was a dead-end—no places to escape. One or two at most, I think. Muggers ain't too keen on that. They like to do their dirty deed where's there's a dozen hideouts and side alleys for them to scram to. You know, in case things go bad."

Jed did not respond. His mind was whirring madly, processing the big insights Max had just casually thrown his way.

Very few places for someone to escape. Like an underground parking lot.

"Max." Jed cleared his throat. "I would suggest that you simply try to ignore what your mother is doing. That's the only way she will stop doing it—once she realizes you're not giving a reaction. The more you fume and blow steam from your nostrils, the more she'll do it, just to get under your skin.

If you act like nothing's happening, your mother's going to get frustrated and quit her antics."

Silence from the other end. "You really think that'll work, Mr. G?"

Jed smiled. "I'm confident it will. Now, I have to go and finish off some urgent work, Max. You take care of yourself, okay? I'll speak to you later."

"Gotcha, Mr. G. Catch ya later."

Jed hung up the phone and placed his head in his palms, squeezing his eyes shut. He focused on the information Max had just revealed to him, trying to fit it all together. Clearly, from what Max had said, and from what his own intuition had been yelling at him, the murder in that parking lot hadn't been a mugging gone wrong. It had been something else.

But what? Jed crowded out all other thoughts from his mind and concentrated his attention exclusively on the facts of the case at hand. He thought about Avery's statement, going through it again, and then he considered the information Max had given him. He tried to connect the two in some meaningful way that would finally reveal what had been bothering him.

The seconds ticked away, turning into minutes. Shadows falling on Jed's desk lengthened and contorted, morphing into strange, ogre-like shapes that seemed to be reaching for him. The automatic water cooler next to the door let out a small gurgle as bubbles of filtered water rose inside it. Still, Jed did not move, continuing to sit stone-still in his seat, his face buried in his hands. Finally, when he broke out of his trance, it was with a small, muffled sound of irritation.

The answer just wouldn't come to him. He had tried and tried, straining his mind to its very limit, but the riddle had remained unsolved, dancing teasingly in front of him. Jed let out a tired whistle from between clamped lips and rose from his seat. Perhaps a walk would help. The fresh air would certainly clear his mind, if nothing else.

He had only scooted back his seat and picked up his cell-phone when it vibrated in his hands. Jed looked down at it, seeing the smiling face of his mother blinking on the screen.

"Hey, Mom," he greeted her, settling back down into the chair. "You've chosen a good time to call."

"Why? Are you finally free from that girlfriend of yours, the one you've secretly disguised as just your partner?" his mother teased.

"She's not my—forget it." Jed pinched the bridge of his nose and closed his eyes, trying to fight back the smile that threatened to spill across his lips. "Anyway, tell me, how are you?"

"I'm doing okay, son," Laurie hummed with contentment. "Finally making some headway with that book I started writing."

"Really?" Jed sat up straight in his seat, interested. "Which novel is this? The sci-fi one?"

"Oh no, that's still on the burner. This is the gothic horror novella I'm writing," Laurie stated, adding a tinge of mystery to her voice. "Trust me, when the world reads it, they'll be swept straight off their feet."

"Oh, I'm sure they will." Jed laughed. "How much did you write?"

"Four chapters," his mother answered with pride. "And that's only in the last two days. I even made myself some hazelnut-chocolate donuts yesterday. A whole batch."

"Mom," Jed groaned, rubbing his stomach. "You know how much I love those. You could've called me."

"I did!" his mom protested. "Thrice, I called you. But you didn't pick up. I assumed you were neck deep in your work, as always."

"I was," Jed answered, his mood dampening as his thoughts returned to the case. "Anyway, how were your donuts?"

"Oh, absolutely scrumptious!" his mother gushed. "They were quite literally oozing with the thickest, most decadent chocolate! I ate them right after I made them, too, when they were hot and fresh!"

Jed did not respond. His hand had suddenly tightened over the phone. His eyes were fixed at a random spot on the floor.

"Jed? Hello, Jed?" his mom called out. "Am I making you jealous by talking about the donuts? I can always make another batch, sweetie."

But Jed still did not respond. His mind was fixed on his mom's last statement, on the last words she had uttered.

When they were hot and fresh.

Hot and fresh.

"Mom, just give me two minutes," Jed stated slowly. "I have an urgent work-related call I need to make. I will call you right after that, I promise."

"Oh, alright, Jed. I'll be waiting."

Jed hung up the phone and dialed Christie's number. She picked up after only two rings.

"Jed? What's up?"

"Christie," Jed began speaking in that same, slow voice, "I think I may have a lead on the case."

CHAPTER 3

CHRISTIE LEANED FORWARD OVER the desk, crossing her elbows. "Okay, now explain what you mean."

They were in her office. It was thirty minutes after Jed had called and told her he might have made some new inroads into the case. Christie had told him to hang up and arrive at the station right away. Such things were better discussed in person.

Now, here he was, sitting at the same mahogany desk as her, two steaming cups of coffee resting between them. Jed took a long breath, gathered his thoughts, and began to speak.

"Something had been bothering me ever since we had that conversation with Avery. It was something he said, something that my subconscious mind had detected, but I still couldn't put my finger on. Then I was on the phone with my mother when she told me something, and it clicked instantly."

Christie sipped her coffee, her curious eyes disappearing behind a wisp of steam. "What clicked?"

Jed placed his palm on the desk and tapped it softly. "The hood. The car's hood, Christie."

"What about it?" Christie frowned.

"Think back to what Avery told us. He slipped backward and put his hand on the hood to steady himself. He said it was hot underneath his touch. *Hot.*"

Christie's eyes widened as she made the connection. "Which means—"

"That the car had been recently running," Jed finished for her.

Christie put her coffee back down and leaned against her chair, brows knotted in thought. "But that doesn't make any sense. Why would she sit in her car until the morning, waiting to be mugged?"

"Because she wasn't mugged," Jed stated firmly. "She was sitting in her car until dawn *having a conversation with her murderer.*"

Christie's mouth formed a long O of surprise. "The killer knew who she was!"

"Exactly. He not only knew her, but he knew her intimately. Think about it. What kind of people do you usually sit in your car with in the parking lot of some mart, talking all night?"

"A romantic partner—or a very close friend," Christie answered instantly, making the connection.

Jed nodded. He picked up his own coffee and took a tentative sip, grimacing in satisfaction at its bitterness. "Now all that remains to be discovered is whether Janet had a boyfriend, or someone else she was closely involved with."

"That should be easy enough. I had Graham talk to some of Janet's co-workers and relatives. He managed to find out that she had one really good friend, someone she would speak to often. Efficient as he is, Graham immediately found out her contact details and sent them to me." Christie picked up her phone and dialed a number before putting it on speaker and placing it in the middle of the table.

Jed listened patiently to the warbled ringtone as it repeated again and again. Finally, someone picked up. A distorted, disgruntled female voice answered from the other end.

"*Hello?*"

"Hello, ma'am, this is Detective Christie Jamieson from the New York Police Department." Christie's voice had changed instantly. It was no longer the low, friendly tone she used when speaking with Jed or someone else. Now, her tone had gained the iron-hard flatness of authority. She spoke like a person not used to being disobeyed.

"Am I speaking to Megan, Janet's friend?" Christie asked.

"*Yes, this is her. What is this about?*"

"I wanted to ask you a couple of questions, Megan, that pertain to our investigation of Janet's death. Do you have the time?"

"*I—yes, I do, sure,*" the voice answered awkwardly. Jed got the feeling that this Megan woman didn't have the time, but Christie's magnetic introduction had forced her into talking.

"Great." Christie's fingers played deftly with her golden strands, coiling and uncoiling them repeatedly. Jed found that he had to force his attention back to the phone call; it kept drifting toward those shiny locks of hair.

"Megan," Christie began, "could you tell me whether or not Janet had a boyfriend?"

The voice did not take long to answer. *"Uh, yeah, she did. Barry was his name. Real piece of work, too."* A snort sounded on the other end. *"Can't believe Janet took as long as she did to break up with that swine."*

"Is that so?" Christie's brows rose in mild surprise. She turned to regard Jed, who was already staring at her with grim understanding. "Could you tell me this Barry's full name, Megan?"

"Barry Collins," the voice answered, distaste practically spilling from it through the speaker. *"I think she was breaking up with him this week."*

"Would you happen to know his address?"

"I do, as a matter of fact. Had to pick up Janet once from his place. The guy's crib was a total wasteland, have to say. Dirty dishes everywhere and crude posters on the wall."

"Where was his place?" Christie repeated patiently.

"Maple Avenue, 11th street. Two buildings away from the fish shop." The voice then added hesitantly. *"Did that sonofabitch do something to Janet?"*

"We cannot make any comments regarding an ongoing investigation, Megan." Christie said briskly. "But we thank you for your help. Take care." She disconnected the call and looked at Jed with arched eyebrows.

"Well, that explains a lot," Jed sighed, leaning back and massaging his temples with both hands. "It's always the crazy ex-lovers, isn't it?"

"Yep," Christie answered cheerily, and then spoke again in a weird, guarded voice. "Love has a way of making people do crazy things, you know."

Jed halted midway through squeezing his temples and stared at Christie from between his fingers. "You okay? Why that strange tone of voice?"

"Oh, nothing." Christie averted her eyes from him, a reddish tinge coloring the base of her neck.

"That doesn't look like nothing to me, Detective," Jed observed with a grin. "What's the matter? Thinking of a crazy ex-lover from your own past? Care to share it with me? I promise, I can handle it."

Christie turned beetroot red. Jed saw her shocked expression and laughed, despite himself.

"I'm just messing with you, Detective," he told her. "Trying to lighten the mood a bit."

"Right. Well, now that the mood has been lightened, let's get back to work, shall we?" Christie sounded flustered and slightly out of breath. "The next step now is having a talk with Barry and seeing what he has to say." She picked up her phone again and called another number, giving instructions for Barry to be brought to the station for interrogation.

Jed began to rise slowly from his chair, hearing the springs creak with relief as his weight lifted from them. "Well, you let me know when you need me for the interrogation, if at all. I have some pending work of my own that I need to complete. Call me when this Barry guy is dragged in."

"Are you just leaving?" Christie asked, and then her mouth clamped shut immediately, as if she regretted what she had said. The reddish tinge on her neck deepened, expanding to the edges of her jaw.

Jed paused where he was standing and stared down at his partner. "I can stay if you want. It's not a problem at all. All you have to do is admit your undying affection for me, which you've been hiding all this time."

I'm not hiding it, Christie thought sourly. *You just don't see it. Or maybe you're pretending not to see it.*

To Jed, though, she simply said, "Do you want to grab some lunch before you leave?"

Jed chewed his lips in thought. He did have quite a bit of work backlog that needed to be cleared. On the other hand, an afternoon with Christie was one of the few things he truly looked forward to; it always left him feeling refreshed and energized, with a warm, buoyant feeling in his stomach.

"Sure," he finally relented. "Let's go eat something."

They went to a local sushi bar this time, upon Christie's stubborn insistence. Jed was not really a sushi person; he never had been. He enjoyed simple things, like beef and chicken cooked with skill, and also the occasional lobster, if he was feeling fancy. But Christie wanted him to try something new, and she was adamant that he would love it. When she gave their order, prattling off a few names from the menu that Jed could barely pronounce, let alone understand, his expectations were low. But when the order finally came, some fifteen minutes later, Jed looked at the plates before him with a raised eyebrow.

"Huh." That single word was an admission of his mistake. The sushi did look good—quite good, in fact. The Maki rolls had been artfully decorated and presented, their tops coated with dynamite sauce and another red, syrupy substance. Jed picked up a piece using a pair of chopsticks and popped it into his mouth, chewing thoughtfully.

"Hmmm." He made a low smacking sound with his lips and looked at Christie. "This is… *absolutely delicious.*"

Christie grinned at him, picking up a piece of her own. "See? I told you. You had no reason to doubt me."

"I definitely did not." Jed popped another piece into his mouth and closed his eyes while savoring the burst of vibrant, tangy flavors. "You are my favorite food buddy, by the way. From now on, whenever I want to try something new, you're the person I'll contact. Because your choice is impeccable."

Christie's face glowed at the praise. She stared at Jed with a small, tender smile while he was busy with his own food, wondering how she had been lucky enough to get a partner as smart, perceptive, and fun as him.

But he's not just your partner, is he? You don't go to lunches like this with your partner. Your heart definitely doesn't somersault the way yours just did when your partner compliments you.

"Shut up," Christie muttered to herself, softly, under her breath.

"Pardon?" Jed looked up at her, his chopsticks hanging midair. "Did you say something to me?"

Christie shook her head, lips parting into another small smile. "No. Nothing."

They finished their lunch, fully content, and then got back into Christie's vehicle and started making their way to the police station. They had just arrived at the station, Christie pulling up the handbrake, when she received a message telling her that Barry had been brought into the station.

"He's here," Christie stated to Jed, unbuckling her seatbelt. "Let's find out what he knows—and what he did."

Barry Collins was a tall guy, over six feet, with dark skin and eyes that were beady and wrinkled, like squashed raisins. He had a mouth that permanently seemed to be trying to inch its way upward from one side, like it had been designed for scowling. His hands were long and spindly, his fingernails crusted. Jed took one look at him and could tell that even if this boy was not guilty of murder, he was not the city's most upstanding citizen.

"Barry Collins," Christie began, lacing the fingers of both her hands together and giving the man opposite her a hard, unflinching look, "do you know why we've called you here?"

"No, but then you people don't really need a reason to drag anyone here, do ya?" Barry practically snarled, his sunken eyes flaring with anger.

"We called you here regarding the recent death of your ex-girlfriend, Janet Simmons," Christie told him, continuing past his outburst as if it had never happened. "What do you know about that?"

Jed had been watching Barry closely when Christie spoke Janet's name. He was behind the two-way glass observing the interview. From his many years as a therapist, Jed had been trained to identify even the tiniest flicker of emotion that raised its fleeting head. And when Christie said Janet's name, he definitely saw something change in Barry's expressions. A ripple traveled through his angry, sulking face—a ripple that smoothed over before Jed could deduce what it was. But it had been there.

"I know that she died recently," Barry answered Christie in a flat voice. "One of my friends told me."

"Where were you on the morning of Janet's death," Christie asked, "between approximately three and 5:00 AM?"

Barry's face was a ceramic mask placed over boiling water. If Jed looked hard enough, he could peer past that cold veneer and spot the turbulent emotions brimming underneath.

"I was at home, sleeping," Barry answered in a gravelly voice, "like most sane people were, during that time."

"Is there anybody who can verify that you were at home?" Christie pressed.

"I live alone, so no," Barry grunted. "Are we done?"

"Almost." Christie grinned pleasantly at him. "I just have one last question for you."

Barry stared at her. "What?"

"Why did you kill Janet?"

The move so well-executed, so smoothly pulled off, that Jed had to resist the urge to applaud. Christie had used her intelligence and caught Barry perfectly off-guard. In that moment, the mask slipped off his face entirely, and Jed glimpsed the fury, guilt, and terror crawling inside him like worms.

"I—uh, what the hell do you mean?" Barry cried. "You're blaming me without evidence!"

The pleasant, victorious smile never faded from Christie's face. "I'm not, Barry," she uttered softly. "See, the mistake you made was choosing the location of your crime. You were smart enough to choose a parking lot without cameras, but what you forgot was the store inside the parking lot." Christie paused for a moment, letting the tense silence hang in the air. "One of those store's cameras is pointed at just the right angle, Barry, so that when we zoom in on the edge of the frame, we can see you fleeing the place after committing your crime."

Barry's eyes were bloodshot. His breathing was harsh, erratic. He began shaking his head violently, muttering to himself, his fists coiling on the table.

Is he going to take Christie's bluff? Jed wondered dimly. *Or is he going to call it?*

But Barry was not a master criminal. And Christie's unique interrogation style had already put enough cracks in him. It did not take long before his entire body sagged and he looked up at Christie with hollow, defeated eyes.

"She broke up with me! I wanted her to give me another chance," he murmured in a ghostly whisper, his eyes staring at nothing. "She said I was good for nothing, and that she could never have a life with me." A violent shudder took over his body and Barry almost fell from his seat, catching himself at the last moment. "I had to do it," he finished, looking at Christie pleadingly, as if begging her to understand. "I had to do it; do you understand? I had to make her pay!"

Christie's voice was emotionless. "Thank you, Barry. I need you to write down everything that happened." She pushed a pad of paper with a pen across the table toward Barry. "I will leave you alone to get your thoughts out on the paper."

Jed watched as Christie left the room and closed the door behind her while Barry picked up the pen and started writing. He was in awe.

CHAPTER 4

DUSK HAD FALLEN OVER the city. Streetlamps on every corner were slowly flickering to life, readying themselves for their nightly shift while the sky above darkened to a sullen, gray slate. The sun was a ruddy omelet half-eaten by the horizon, about to be devoured entirely.

It was amidst this fading twilight that Jed strolled the city's shadowy, cobbled streets, his hands in his pockets. Quite a bit of time had passed since he had gone on one of these walks of his, walks which were not really walks but more of an escape that gave him time to reflect and ponder.

A jumble of mixed thoughts crossed his mind as he strode past a dimly lit bakery, feeling the cool wind caressing his face, carrying with it the hearty aroma of fresh bread and cookies. Jed thought back to the interrogation, reimagined the stricken look on Barry's face as he had been escorted away by the two constables. No matter how much Jed tried, he couldn't move past that frozen, helpless gleam that had shone out of Barry's eyes in his last moments with Christie. He had looked like a deer caught in headlights, one that stands frozen in the middle of the road, watching its impending death approach at breakneck speed, unable to do anything.

Why do people do the things they do? Jed wondered, knowing this was not the first time he had asked this question and that no easy answer awaited him. In fact, part of the reason Jed had become a therapist in the first place, apart from his personal past, was that he had always been intrigued by how people functioned. He had always been curious as to what motivated all the psychopathic killers and eccentric criminals in the world. What went on in their minds, in those moments when they were committing crimes of madness?

Barry was the latest example. Jed knew the man had murdered an innocent woman—one he loved. She had been strangled her in her car, and yet he still couldn't help but feel a tiny prick of sympathy for the man. He had looked so crushed, so terrorized, as the police offers had hauled him away. If truth be told, Jed believed deep within himself that people like Barry had something inside them that had been broken, a wire that had short-circuited or a switch that had turned faulty. If the mistake could simply be found and rectified, then such people could be saved. Perhaps that's what the job of a therapist was, really, to find the brokenness in someone and try to patch it up.

A noisy chorus distracted Jed from his thoughts, and he looked up, finding a group of teenage boys goofing around in front of him. The boys were all in a festive mood, playfully jostling and wrestling each other, cracking crude jokes. Jed felt a slight wistfulness take hold of him as he stepped to the side and bypassed the laughing gang. He had never had a childhood as carefree and simple as this. It had always been challenges, more challenges, and then even more challenges that he felt he needed to tackle on his own.

He passed a liquor store right then and glanced inside, seeing at least half-a-dozen men milling around, eyeing the racks of bottles greedily.

How many of them are alcoholics? Jed wondered, shivering slightly as his own days of using came back to him. Addiction was a terrible, terrible thing—almost like being possessed by a demon. No matter how many times you purged and exorcised yourself, there was always a fear that the beast might return to haunt you in your weakest moment, stronger than ever before.

Sucking in a large lungful of air to get rid of those nasty thoughts, Jed jammed his hands further into his pockets and increased his pace, turning onto an empty, lit street. His thoughts came to rest on Christie.

Jed smiled as her face appeared in his mind. She was his partner, and a brilliant one. Her latest interrogation had been a testament to her abilities. But she was more than a partner, too. She was his friend, someone he enjoyed spending time with apart from work. There were not very many people Jed could say that about. He was a closed-off man, he knew—someone who kept to himself and liked keeping what was happening inside him even more secret.

But Christie was different. She was changing him, too, Jed knew, as he spent more and more time with her. Christie's warm, relaxing presence was slowly loosening Jed up, causing him to expose parts of his personality that had been bottled up for ages. It was both an exhilarating and terrifying feeling. Part of Jed wanted to run away from any such intimacy and remain in hiding forever. Another, larger part of him yearned to be let free. He did not yet know which part would win. If he continued to spend more and more time with Christie, however, then the choice was obvious.

What is it about her that disarms me so easily? Jed pondered. He did not know. Or, perhaps, he did but didn't want to admit it to himself.

His strange train of thoughts came to an end, then, as his phone vibrated in his pocket. Jed fished it out, checked the incoming ID, then put the phone to the side of his ear.

"Hello, Mom," he uttered the greeting softly, continuing to walk.

"Jed…" Laurie's voice came from the other end, and Jed stopped instantly in his tracks, his heart lurching. Something was wrong. It was in his mom's voice, as visible as the moon on a cloudless night.

"What is it, Mom?" Jed asked sharply, his hand tightening on the receiver.

"Jed… I—I have some news for you," his mom spoke slowly, and then he heard her swallow.

"What news?" Jed had to make an effort to keep his voice calm. His mind reeled in a hundred different directions at once, imagining and playing every terrible scenario that could have his mother so shaken.

"It's your stepbrother, Jed," his mother whispered. "Alex. He's... H—He's dead."

Alex? Jed frowned. An image rose in his mind—a boy in his teens, with a brooding, angled face, and a shock of straight black hair hanging over his forehead.

"Alex is dead?" Jed repeated, trying to digest the news and the strange concoction of emotions he was experiencing. Sorrow was not at the forefront, surprisingly. He had hardly known his stepbrother, having not seen him since he was fifteen years old. Instead, what Jed felt was a distant shock and a feeling of dull regret, similar to having missed out on something.

"Jed? Are you there? Are you okay?" His mom sounded worried.

Jed blinked twice, reorienting himself in the real world. "Yes, I'm fine, Mom, Don't worry," he stated quickly, his eyes scanning the road for a place to sit. He found a lone wooden bench situated not far from him and began heading toward it.

"How did he die?" Jed asked.

"I—I don't know the details. Your uncle James called and told me, you see." His mom sniffed. "They said something about him falling onto a rake or something… and it pierced his chest. God, it sounds horrible."

"It's okay, Mom." Jed spoke automatically, finding himself slipping into his role as consoler. "I'll be there as soon as I can. Just need to find a cab." Then he added, curious, "When did this happen, by the way?"

"This morning," his mother told him.

"Are you okay?" Jed's voice was grim. He bypassed the bench and changed his course toward a pack of taxis that were clustered around the street's end, their drivers loitering idly on the sidewalk. "I'll be at your place in ten—fifteen tops. Hang tight until then." He shut the phone and hurriedly strode to the cab drivers, his face clouded and his mind brimming with thoughts.

Ten minutes later, Jed was in his mom's apartment, sitting next to her on the couch. To his surprise, Laurie had recovered quite swiftly from the shock of the news. She sat cross-legged on the couch before him looking mostly like her old self, with a barely-used tissue box lying next to her.

"God, it's such a shock," Laurie said for the hundredth time, shaking her head in disbelief. "That poor boy. He had his whole life ahead of him. How tragic…"

Jed nodded in somber agreement. "Can you tell me again how he died? What you told me on the phone didn't quite make sense."

"It didn't make sense to me either," his mother replied. "When James called and told me, he said something about it possibly not being an accident… something relating to homicide."

"Really?" Jed was sitting straight up now, his mind on high alert. "What exactly did he say? You think you can recall that, Mom?"

His mother nodded, her eyes somewhere far away while recalled the memory. "There was something…. about the statements of other bystanders," she began uncertainly, pursing her lips before continuing. "A heart attack or something… then he stumbled, falling upon the rake… God, I can't recall anything else, no matter how hard I try." She shook her head in disappointment.

"That's okay," Jed said quickly. His mind was whirring. "I'm sure we'll find out later." His gaze drifted to the window in the living room, and Jed saw the street outside, lying darkened and empty. A sudden unease gripped him then, an unease whose source he couldn't quite pinpoint. It made the hair on the nape of his neck prickle with wariness. Something about Alex's death was giving him a bad feeling—a really bad feeling.

Jed hoped it was just his nerves and nothing else.

CHAPTER 5

THERE WERE TWO SHARP raps on the door.

"Come in!" Jed called out, swiveling his chair around. The doorknob turned, and the door swung open with a muffled whine. Max stepped through it, wearing a pair of baggy cargo pants and an oversized white t-shirt.

Jed gestured toward the chair opposite his desk. "Have a seat, Max. I have to say, I feel quite thrilled that you finally agreed to meet me in person."

"Well, you seem a cool enough dude, Mr. G. The phone calls were giving me a headache, so I decided I'd come by and chat with you face-to-face." Max dragged the chair back and plopped down on it, facing Jed. His eyes were the same as he remembered from their first meeting at the detention center: sharp and alert. But the rest of his face had changed since their last meeting, Jed noticed. There were light, weary lines crisscrossing Max's temples and outlining the innermost parts of his cheek, right before his lips began.

This is what happens when your life is a constant struggle, Jed thought with sorrow. *When you're born outside the system, with no one to care for or fend for you.*

He forced a smile on his face and extended his hand over the oaken desk. "How have things been going, Max?"

"Ah, I'm getting by, Mr. G." Max returned his smile with a tired but honest one of his own. "Taking it one day at a time, you know?" His grip as he shook Jed's hand was firm.

"That's the best way to take it," Jed agreed. He steepled his hands beneath his chin and directed his calm, disarming therapist's gaze straight at Max. "So, tell me, Max, what's been going on in your life? What are you up to?"

Max leaned back a little in the chair, scratching his head thoughtfully. "I've started working another gig is what I'm up to—flipping burgers at a burger joint from right up to midnight. Saving up all that extra dough, you know."

Jed's eyebrows rose in surprise. "Flipping burgers? So, you've dipped your toes into the culinary world as well, now?"

Max grinned. "Aye. I got to tell you Mr. G, I make some damn tasty burgers, too, when I've got my head in the game. Manager at my place says our reviews have raved ever since I joined."

"Wow. Max the master chef." Jed shook his head, laughing softly to himself. "I'd love to try your burgers sometime. Jot down your joint's address on this yellow notepad before you leave. I'll probably pay you a visit on the weekend, if I've got some free time."

"Sure thing, Mr. G." Max beamed. "They're already talking 'bout giving me a raise, even though I've only been there three weeks."

"That's amazing, buddy." Jed regarded Max with unconcealed pride. "You're doing great, you know that? You have come a long way since we first met."

Max cast his gaze down at the carpet, embarrassed. "Just doing my best," he mumbled. "That's all any of us can do, when we are dealt a shitty hand. Pa always used to say that to me. It ain't the hand you're dealt, but the way you play it that matters."

Something Max had said earlier came back to Jed then, and he frowned. "You said you were doing the job for extra money. Are you in some kind of trouble?"

"Nah." Max shook his head, then continued in a halting, uncertain voice. "I—I was just thinking, you know," he stammered, "what if… you know, w—what if I saved some money up… and enrolled in a few courses in community college?" He added hastily, "It was just a thought, nothing solid yet."

"Max." Jed's tone was dead-serious. He leaned forward on the desk, fixing his eyes on the boy, who was staring at him intently. "I think that is a wonderful idea. You should definitely, definitely go ahead with that." Jed clicked his tongue at the thought. "A person of your intelligence and resourcefulness could do wonders in this world with a formal education. It could open up a lot of doors for your future."

At Jed's words, a light glow seemed to suffuse Max's entire face. His eyes shone forth radiantly from their sockets, alight with pleasure.

"Thanks a bunch, Mr. G." Max's voice was strained with emotion. "You don't know how much your word means to this guy. I thought you were gonna laugh at me... but I shoulda known better." Max chuckled. "I'll look into, like, what their entry requirements are."

"You do that," Jed spoke softly, leaning back against his chair. "Tell me when you've made some progress. I can help you look into grants and scholarships. In the meantime, is there anything else you want to discuss? Any other new developments in your life?"

"There is one thing." Max sighed, the liveliness fading from his face. Jed understood that they had finally reached the reason Max was looking so worn out when he had first entered the office.

"It's Shanice," Max uttered heavily. "Things aren't exactly peachy between us right now. There are some... issues."

"Issues?" Jed probed gently. "What kind? Are they related to your mother?"

Max furrowed his brows, scratching his head thoughtfully again. "Kind of. I mean, I still haven't talked to her about that yet, even though you told me to. I plan on it, though. But this new trouble between me and Shanice isn't related to that. It's different. We've just been having a lot of fights lately," he admitted. "And they're always about the dumbest things.

Like who forgot to do the dishes. Or who forgot to switch the laundry. The kinda stuff children fight about, ya know?"

"How long has this been happening?" Jed inquired before answering himself. "Since you took on that new job?"

Max looked at him, surprised. "Yeah. How did you know?"

Jed splayed his hands on the desk. "It makes the most sense. Generally, couples start fighting over mundane things when tensions run high, and when stress is a lingering occupant of the household. I would wager that with your new job and increased working hours, Shanice has probably had to deal with a sudden, unpredictable change which has caused this."

"Huh." Max drummed his fingers on the desk, making a light vibrating sound. "So, how do I fix it?"

"By just going through it." Jed smiled at him. "You've just hit a rough patch, is all. All you need to do is ride it through." He watched as Max practically sagged with relief, leaning his head against the seat as far as it would go, staring up at the ceiling. "The most important thing is to keep the lines of communication open so you can work on this together. It can be tempting to pull away and close yourself off, but that will make things much worse. Have you talked to Sharice about this? Maybe since you are working more, she might feel neglected. It could be as simple as asking her what she needs from you."

"Aww, you can't imagine how happy I am now, Mr. G." Max exhaled deeply, massaging his forehead with one hand. He then straightened up again to face Jed, looking at him with refreshed, reinvigorated eyes. "This thing had me worried sick for the past couple of weeks. Even lost a few snores over it. I should've just come to you."

Jed grinned. "My office door is always open, you know."

They talked a little more after that, discussing other relevant details from Max's life. Eventually, the boy stood up from his seat, bid Jed a hearty farewell, his face a lot clearer than when he had entered, and left the office.

Jed watched as the door swung shut in Max's wake, letting the office's customary thick silence resettle over it. He closed his eyes, then, and let his thoughts travel to the problems that had surfaced in his own life.

Alex. Alex had died. Even worse, no one had any idea how such a freak accident had occurred. Jed ran a hand through his hair and stood up from his seat in one quick motion, walking over to the window which faced the street below. Heart attack? That seemed unlikely, or was it? Alex was two years younger than Jed.

What could be done? That was the question plaguing Jed. It had been plaguing him since the previous night, when he had received news of his stepbrother's passing. No matter how much he tried, he couldn't force his attention away from it. The darn thing was like a tapeworm with hooked feet that had managed to wriggle its way inside one of the crevices of his mind and was now refusing to be pulled out, hanging on with its curling, talon-like feet for dear life. Even Jed's sleep had been affected. He'd had the strangest dream, where he had found himself standing on a pier, observing Alex as he slowly walked toward its very edge, clutching his chest with a grimace before toppling into the murky waters.

Something must be done, Jed thought. *I have to find out about the case, somehow. I won't rest until I do.*

There was only one way he could do that. There was only one person who was his source of access to the police department and its files. Christie.

He had a plan to meet her for lunch in thirty minutes, and Jed wondered if this friendly get-together could be used as an opportunity to casually slip in his request. He turned away from the window to head into his bathroom and get ready.

Thirty-five minutes later, Jed sat on one of the plush leather seats at the Mandarin restaurant, waiting for Christie to arrive. She arrived five minutes later, sashaying her way in through the front door with her eyes searching the restaurant, looking for Jed. They found him a couple of seconds later, and a large smile broke across Christie's face like the deep-golden sun of the perfect summer afternoon finally breaking through its cover clouds. In that moment, as he gazed at her smile, Jed momentarily forgot all about his worries and was only concerned with the tingly current racing through his palms.

"Hello, Jed," Christie greeted him warmly, giving him a slight side-hug before settling down in her own seat.

"Sorry for being late," she said in a breathless rush, unslinging her purse and placing it by her side. "I was neck deep in this new case that has just been thrust upon me."

Jed's breath caught in his throat. His hands that had been lightly holding the menu pressed down on it, causing creases to line the laminated paper.

Could it be? Could his luck really be that marvelous? Was it possible that Christie had been assigned the same case he was after?

Jed cleared his throat. "Which case is this?" he asked non-chalantly.

Christie waved a hand. "Oh, another accident that the police suspect might be murder." Her eyes were scanning the menu, her mind already switching off from work-mode. "So, what's good here? Any idea?"

"The tamarind chicken is the most popular," Jed answered slowly, his appetite entirely gone for the moment, and his mind as far away from food as it could be. He waited for a second or two before adding, innocently: "An accident that appeared like a murder? Can you tell me more?"

"Oh, it's nothing. There was ju—wait a minute," Christie broke off, staring at him with narrowed eyes. "Why are *you* so interested in this case?"

Jed shrugged as indifferently as he could. "It… it just sounds intriguing."

Christie's eyes narrowed further. Suspicion glinted in them. "No, that can't be it," she stated. "Because you're the one person who hates talking about work when we're off-duty. You *never* want to mention it if it can be avoided."

Jed chuckled, feeling his heart hammering in his chest. "You really have me all figured out, don't you?"

"Not all, but good enough. Now, tell me," Christie's gaze was so intense, it could have bored a hole through concrete, "what is it, Jed? What has you so worried?"

There was nothing more to do. He had been defeated. Jed bowed his head. "I think the person who died in your case was my stepbrother," he muttered.

Christie's eyes widened. Her hands gripped the menu tightly, her white knuckles protruding. "Yo—your what?"

Jed nodded grimly. "My stepbrother," he repeated.

"So that's why you wanted to meet today?" Christie asked him, hurt flowering across her entire face. Her eyes flashed with pain. "So that you could extract some information from me about this case you don't have access to?"

Jed was already shaking his head vehemently before she finished her question. "No, that was never my intent," he said firmly. "I set the lunch because I actually wanted to meet you, because I genuinely enjoy the time I spend in your company. The idea to ask about the case came later, much later." He looked at her hard, unflinching. "You believe me, right? You know I'm not like that."

After a moment of tense silence, Christie seemed to relax, nodding slowly. "Yes, you definitely aren't like that," she admitted, the hurt draining from her face and being replaced by curiosity. "But you're also not a very open person, Jed. I mean, we've spent so much time together, and I'm only now finding out that you have a stepbrother." She leaned toward him, her elbows on the table. "What is this about?"

Jed sighed. "It's a long story."

CHAPTER 6

IT WAS A COOL and windy afternoon. The park was more crowded than usual for a weekday, with families gathered in a neat little line on its yellowing grass, their children frolicking madly around a thick cluster of trees, their gleeful shrieks breaking the tranquil silence.

Jed and Christie were in another corner, strolling through a secluded patch of yellow. Jed's hands were jammed into his pockets, and there was a deeply uncertain look on his face. Christie knew why. After a long, long time, he was about to share something personal about his life with her. For others, opening up to their friends might have been a normal step in the course of a friendship. But for Jed, Christie knew it was monumental. She felt a twinge of sympathy for him, as she noted the troubled expression marking his features. But she also knew she had to let him do this. He wanted it. She did, too—perhaps more than him. But more important than both their wants, it was necessary.

If you let something fester within you long enough, Christie thought, *it turns into poison.* Jed's entire past, most of it dark and painful, had been crumpled into a tiny ball and stuffed somewhere deep inside him. Well, it was time to slowly let it out, bit by bit. If he didn't do so, Christie worried the blood running through his veins would turn as toxic as a nuclear waste dump.

So, she kept her silence, amiably walking alongside him, letting him decide the moment he would speak. In the meantime, the only sound her ears registered was of their shoes softly treading on the fallen leaves and the birds merrily chirping in the trees above them. Far away, in the distance, she could hear children laughing if she strained her ears hard enough.

They had just crossed a patch of shadow into the day's pale light when Jed suddenly cleared his throat. Christie's attention snapped back to him instantly. Her eyes traveled to his face again, and she found that some of the clouds had departed from it. His eyes looked clearer.

"My stepbrother…" Jed began in a throaty voice, looking down at the ground while he walked, "Alex, I mean. I didn't really know him. I haven't seen him since I was fifteen. We didn't get along well back then, and we never kept in touch." He cleared his throat again, and Christie saw that this was the first time in his life Jed was openly discussing this in front of someone. No wonder he was struggling to find the right words.

"Alex and I weren't enemies either, if that's what you're thinking," Jed continued, stepping back into the shade, his features cloaking with shadows. "We never talked to each other much. He was two years younger than me and his older brother. He was more of a little brother annoyance that wanted to tag along. There was more animosity between his older brother and me. With us being the same age and both of our families destroyed by my father and his mother, we had a lot going on. I don't know what Alex thinks of m—I mean, what he used to think of me… it would depend on what my father and his wife filled his brain with, I think." Jed paused, let out a long, pent-up breath, his eyes flitting briefly in Christie's direction. He saw her staring at him with complete attention, her eyes wide and focused.

"Your father?" Christie inquired with utmost gentleness. Those two words were enough of a signal. If Jed wanted to elaborate, he would.

"My father… uh, how do I put this?" Jed absently scuffed the ground with a light kick, sending a small clump of grass and dirt flying forward. "I am not exactly close with my father, Christie—actually, cross that. I have *no relationship at all* with my father. I doubt that he cares a hoot about me, and I only wish I could say the same."

Christie bit down on the urge to lay a tender hand on Jed's shoulder. She knew such a gesture would only embarrass him. He didn't want anyone's sympathy, and especially not anyone's pity.

"I think that's it for now." Jed shuddered with a mixture of relief and discomfort, like a child that has just undergone a horrid dental experience and finally risen from the seat. "I don't think I want to speak any further on this."

"That's completely okay," Christie stated quickly. She flashed him a bright smile. "I'm really proud of you, Jed. I know how difficult it must have been to talk about such a thing. You showed remarkable courage and strength." Then, on sheer impulse, she grabbed Jed's hand in her own, squeezing it gently. "Thank you for trusting me enough to share this with me."

Something passed between them right then, something unspoken and undefined, which caused Jed's lips to part slightly in pleasant surprise—which then made Christie drop his hand swiftly and look down, her face flushing red.

God, I shouldn't have done that. Christie thought, feeling mortified. *He probably thought I was making a move on him in one of his weak moments.* She looked up at Jed and found him smirking at her.

"What's that look about?" she asked, the remorse turning into a prick of irritating embarrassment.

Jed stared at her for a moment, his eyes twinkling. "Nothing. Nothing at all," he finally answered, the smirk only widening on his face before he turned around to head back the way they had come.

Christie quickly trotted to catch up with him, her pulse zipping in her veins. "*What?* Tell me!"

Jed simply shrugged. "It's really nothing. I was just amused about what you did there. Dropping my hand so suddenly, as if it were on fire."

"I—" Christie tried in vain to produce a smooth explanation, but her tongue was a knotted mess. In the end, she only looked more flustered, and that seemed to add to Jed's amusement.

He led her to a nearby taxi stand before turning around and regarding her with those mysteriously shining eyes. "I'll see you around, Detective. Today was fun. Let's do it again, but minus the *spilling my whole childhood pains* part."

"Deal." Christie shook his hand with a smile. "And minus the whole *silently laughing at Christie over the joke I won't share with her* part, too."

Jed grinned, his pearl-white teeth glimmering in the sun. "I'll share that joke with you, one day. But that day isn't today."

Christie made a mock expression of being angry before bidding him farewell and stepping inside a taxi. Jed watched as the engine revved to a start and the car began traveling down the road. He kept eyes on its bright yellow exterior, watching it move until it had finally turned a corner and disappeared from view. Then, he turned and began his own long walk back to his office.

Jed hummed lightly while he walked. His mind was calm, as calm as a surface of a pond without a single ripple in it. He felt lighter while he walked, too, like someone had removed some invisible baggage from within him. For the first time, Jed's hands weren't stuffed inside his pockets. They hung by his sides, loose and open. It was a small thing, but to him, it mattered a lot. His posture was already changing, turning from protective to carefree and easy. It hadn't happened completely yet, not by any stretch, but it was still a start.

Jed had reached the elevator to his office when he realized he had never bothered to take his phone with him; it must still be lying on his desk.

Damn, Christie's company is already showing its effects. He whistled softly in surprise; Jed always took his phone with him wherever he went. It had become an almost unavoidable habit.

The elevator doors hissed softly while opening, and Jed crossed the threshold to approach his office. He didn't know his second surprise of the day was awaiting him there.

The office was filled with a crisp coolness like always, the air conditioner working perfectly. Jed shut the door behind him and glimpsed the grey edge of his cellphone peeking through a stack of papers.

I hope there were no work emergencies while I was away, Jed thought as he went toward the table and fished out his phone from beneath the pile of papers. The merriness disappeared from his face promptly, then, when he saw the phone's screen. It was not a work emergency. It was something else entirely.

There was a missed call there from his father. His name was blinking before Jed in pale white letters, the name Richard

Gray so foreign that it took Jed a whole moment to realize who it belonged to. He took a few heavy breaths and continued to stare at the name, perhaps hoping that if he stared long enough, the name would either disappear or he would find the strength to call back. There was no voicemail, just the missed call.

The first of those two things didn't happen, obviously. Eventually, Jed had to muster up the strength to hit the call back option. He waited with the phone on speaker then, his cellphone cradled in a single, lightly shaking palm. He did not have to wait long.

"Hello?"

That voice. It was strange that, after all these years, it still sounded the same to Jed. It still sounded exactly like his father, who had abandoned him without a second thought when he had just been a child.

"Hello," Jed spoke evenly into the phone. His mouth was dry.

"Jed?"

Who else would it be? Or have you forgotten the sound of your own son's voice? But Jed didn't voice that acidic retort. He had that much control over himself. He had developed it slowly over the years, learning how to deal with all the corrosive parts of his past. Being an addict had somewhat helped, ironically. After all, recovering from addiction was all about staring your inner ugliness right in the face and not cringing away from it. It was all about acceptance—acceptance even of that which had caused untold misery.

"Yes, it's me," Jed answered calmly, like he was conversing with a colleague or acquaintance.

There was silence on the other end. Jed stood patiently, not moving an inch, waiting for his father to say whatever he had called to say. Finally, the voice spoke again.

"*The memorial service for Alex will be held the day after tomorrow, at Rosemary Cemetery, at 3 PM. Since they're not releasing his body from the morgue yet, this is the best we can do, to give Cindi some closure. Andy wanted me to tell you.*" A pause, then, as if the voice was considering something. "*Don't feel any pressure to attend.*"

The line clicked, and the call disconnected. Jed stood where he was, listening to the silence reestablishing its foothold in the office—a silence so palpable he could have reached out with one hand and felt its syrupy texture.

Jed went and sat down slowly in his seat, placing his phone beside him. His mind was carefully observing what he was feeling in that moment. Jed's years of providing therapy had taught him the importance of emotions in critical situations. They played a key role in revealing a person's personality and even the hidden demons some people silently struggled with inside themselves.

Jed, however, was pleased to find that the call hadn't rattled him as much as he had expected it to. His heart rate was steady, his palms weren't sweaty, and his mind was also relatively stable. Of course, there was a dim unease coursing through his thoughts still, but that much was to be expected. It would take a little more time to get rid of that feeling, or it might not even go away at all. It didn't really matter. What mattered was that all the painstaking work he had done on himself in his journey of recovery had still worked. His father's stern voice and jagged words hadn't cut into his heart like they used to when he was a child.

The sun was dipping further in the sky now, well on its way toward dusk. Jed looked at the oblong shadows that had appeared at the furthest edge of his office wall. His gaze strayed down to the stack of papers lying on his desk, yet to be studied. Most of them were client profiles, which Jed had made a vow to complete by the end of the day.

Letting out a weary but contented sigh, Jed settled snugly into his seat and picked up the first paper, beginning to read through it.

CHAPTER 7

THE ROOM WAS A small and cozy one, with a quaint little window on its left wall overlooking the alley. There was a bookshelf crowding one of the room's corners, its top three shelves stacked with old, yellowing novels, and the lowest shelf piled to the top with magazines. A seedy sofa sat on one end, facing the bed. On the other end was a cupboard with its wood splintered and peeling from the edges, its rightmost doorknob hanging loosely off its handle.

There was a bed in the middle of the room. It was the only thing in the entire space that appeared new and fresh. There were a pair of clean, fluffy white pillows arranged at the headrest, and a warm woolen duvet the color of hay stretching up to the pillow's corners. There was another blanket lying on the top of the duvet, a gray colored one, which Jed was now folding.

He grabbed the edges of the blanket and brought them together, gathering them up into a neat little square. Then he picked up the light blanket and placed it on the sofa before walking back to the center of the room and surveying it, his hands on his hips.

Jed nodded absently to himself. It would do. The room looked much better now, after he had tidied it up a bit and brought a fresh set of sheets and new pillows for the night.

A dull knock on the door switched his attention that way.

"Come in," Jed called out, his gaze still traveling across the room's tiny, enclosed quarters.

The door opened. His mother stepped in, dressed in a pair of loose pajama pants and a sweater.

"My, my…" Laurie stated, one hand going to her cheek with surprise as she looked at the room. "You've done quite an impressive job cleaning up."

Jed thought it would be a good idea to spend the night with his mom, so she wouldn't be alone after they got the news about Alex. Laurie hadn't really known Alex at all—they'd met only once as far as Jed knew, and only briefly. But anything that had to do with Richard Gray was a terribly sore spot for Jed's mother. It always wound her up emotionally and put her on edge. In times like these, a supportive shoulder and a sympathetic ear proved very useful. Who better to know these things than a therapist?

Jed shrugged. "Not really. I just removed all the junk that was stored here. The room was pretty clean to begin with." He allowed himself a small, nostalgic smile. "It actually reminds me a little of the room I had when I was a kid."

His mother frowned, putting a hand against the frame of the doorway. "Really? I don't see anything similar apart from that bookshelf."

"The view, too." Jed told her. He gestured toward the window. "It looks down on an alleyway, like my room did." He smiled again, then, but this time it was one that brimmed with bittersweet humor. "Maybe that's why I did what I did, when I was young. If you have a room that only gives you a dirty little alley to look down at, then it's inevitable that, one day, you'll find yourself in such an alley, doing things you shouldn't be doing."

Jed's mother regarded him from the doorway. Her eyes were kind and sorrowful. "You and I both know that whatever stupid stuff you did as a child wasn't because of any window," Laurie said softly. "There was a *lot more* to it than that."

Jed nodded then, running a tired hand through his hair to push it back from his forehead. "Yeah, I guess there was," he answered in a distracted, introspective voice. His mother looked at him with concern.

"Jed," Laurie began tentatively. "Are you sure staying in this room is a good idea? You said you came here because you wanted a break from work and to get your mind off that phone call with your father. But if this room is reminding you of your childhood, then…" She let her voice trail off.

"Oh, don't worry, Mom. I'm perfectly fine." Jed glanced up at her again, and suddenly, like a switch being flicked, the distant look was gone from his eyes again. Now, he looked exactly like the old Jed, stoic and calm, with sharp, intelligent eyes and a kind face.

But that distant look is not gone, Laurie thought to herself. *He's just pushed it within him, like he always does with anything that bothers him.*

"I think this room will turn really pretty once the moon comes out," Jed murmured, casually sauntering over to the window and peeking out. "The moonlight is going to come in from here and color everything a nice, magical silver."

"You're right about that," his mother agreed. "Sometimes, I even leave my room at midnight and sit here when I want to read a book or something. It feels nice and relaxing, watching all that silvery light glowing around you." Then she added, her eyes gleaming mischievously, "I bet even Christie doesn't have a room in her house that is like that."

It was only years of training as a therapist that allowed Jed to retain remarkable control over his expressions when his mother made that comment. He forced his lips to remain pressed in a straight, sober line, and he stuffed down the heat that was beginning to rise in his cheeks.

"Pardon? What was that?" he asked innocently, turning toward her with a vacant expression.

His mother stared at him for a moment, silently urging his self-control to break, and upon realizing it wouldn't, she sighed and gave him a half-irritated, half-joking glare.

"You're no fun," Laurie said, looking at him pointedly. "All those therapy sessions with clients have turned you into a bore. I can't even poke a reaction out of you with my jokes. Well, goodnight anyways."

"Goodnight, Mom. Sweet dreams!" Jed called out, letting his lips part into a wide grin once his mother had shut the door and left. He wasn't going to give her the satisfaction of reacting to her Christie jokes. He knew his mother; if he did that, then those jokes would turn into a part of every conversation.

After a long and scalding shower, during which he rinsed both his body and mind of all the grit that had been clinging to them since the morning, Jed changed into pajama pants and t-shirt before heading to bed. The velvety softness of the sheets beneath him was a pleasant surprise, and he sighed with pleasure, pulling the blanket up to his chin and closing his eyes against the day's exhaustion. In less than ten seconds, his mind had drifted into a deep, dreamless sleep.

He awoke the next morning, feeling deeply refreshed and rejuvenated by his nightlong slumber. Even his head felt clearer and lighter, as if someone had come with a broomstick while he was asleep and brushed all the cobwebs of the past away. Suddenly, Jed felt more than ready to deal with the tragedy of his stepbrother's death. He actually looked forward to getting past it all. Picking up his phone from the night-stand, he saw two missed calls from Christie awaiting him.

He had accidentally turned the ringer off sometime last night. Jed promptly redialed her number.

"Hello?" Christie's busy, alert voice roused Jed further from his sleep. He sat up straighter on his bed.

"You called, Christie?"

"Oh, yes—I did because I have good news for you." Christie sounded extremely pleased with herself.

"You do? What is it?" Jed stared out the room's window in anticipation, awaiting the answer he had already guessed.

"I spoke to the superintendent, Mallory, today. Told him you wanted to consult on the case regarding your stepbrother. I made a long, impassioned speech about your merits and abilities, but it turned out the speech wasn't needed at all. Mallory already knew about you and how you had solved the Janet murder single-handedly. He was thoroughly impressed. Agreed quite easily to my request."

"So, that's it, then? I can work with you again, on this case?" Jed was already off the bed, his eyes searching the room for the clothes he had ironed and folded last night to wear to the office.

"Yes, you can—as a consultant." Christie's excited voice danced in his ears. "I'll see you in the office in an hour sharp, partner."

Jed actually made it to Christie's workplace in forty-five minutes, after quickly showering and changing, then grabbing two homemade cinnamon buns, fresh out of his mother's oven. His mother used his aunt's recipe, which she knew was Jed's favorite. He was looking forward to understanding the circumstances surrounding his stepbrother's death much more than he had expected.

Christie was waiting for him in a conference hall, one almost identical to the last one he had visited. The monitor was already set up this time, and she was sitting on the desk, filing through a thin stack of papers.

"Howdy, partner," she said as she looked up from the papers on the table. A large smile lit up her face when she saw the cinnamon bun Jed presented to her. He loved to see her smile. Jed watched her press a few buttons, and then a paused video appeared on the screen before him. It appeared to be the CCTV footage of a sidewalk somewhere.

Christie cleared her throat. "Jed, this is the footage of your brother's... incident." She was watching him closely, her voice careful. "Are you sure you'll be okay with seeing this?"

Jed nodded.

"Okay. I'll give you a brief overview first. The incident happened on 21st Boulevard Lane," Christie began. "At exactly 10:37 AM, the victim went into a coffee shop. He exited 13 minutes later, having bought a coffee, holding the cup in his hands. Then, he stood on the sidewalk for a moment, taking a small sip. As soon as he took the sip, *something* happened. We don't know what that something is yet—whether it was a cardiac arrest or something in the coffee he was given. What we do know is promptly after taking a sip, the victim, Alex Gray clutched his chest with a grimace, rocked once on his feet, and then fell backwards on a rake lying on display in a farming store right next to the coffee shop. The rake's prongs pierced through his heart, and as far as our current intel suggests, that is what caused his death."

Jed sat, the information he had just received brewing in his mind like a potent mixture.

"Now would be a good time to view the footage," Christie suggested gently, "but only if you're up for it. There's no pressure at all."

Jed gave her the go ahead and turned to face the screen. Christie pressed the play button, and the grainy picture sprang into motion. Jed saw Alex walking into a coffee shop.

Then, she fast-forwarded to thirteen minutes later when he reemerged, holding a large Styrofoam cup in his hand. He walked toward the edge of the curb, opening the cup's lid with two fingers.

Jed continued watching… and he felt his heart coiling in his chest, gathering energy like a windup toy, readying itself to leap out of his flesh. He felt the dim, throbbing beat of his pulse in his temples and a light, tingly aching in his palms. This was it. He was now going to watch his own stepbrother live the last moments of his life.

It had been so many years since they saw one another. He was unsure if either of them would recognize the other if they passed on the street. But as he watched the video, he could definitely pick out the similarities that let Jed know it really was Alex.

The video continued, and Alex raised the cup to his lips, beginning to take a sip. Jed almost wanted to cry out: *No, don't do it! You'll die if you do!* But he kept ahold of himself, and the video played on. Alex took the sip, walked back a little, and then an instant later, he was clutching his chest, his face contorting into a look of what was surely pain and surprise. Then Jed's stepbrother rocked on his feet, making as if to topple backward. He steadied himself on his first try, and then a moment later simply fell right onto the rake behind him.

Jed winced as he saw Alex's back descend right onto those sharp, protruding prongs. His left hand curled into a fist as he saw the prong pierce Alex's back and then poke out from the front of his chest. Alex's body convulsed horrifically, spewing blood in a gushing fountain all around him. Again and again, Alex spasmed, as if giant, invisible hands were wringing him like a washcloth.

Then, he went still.

It took only a few seconds before people started gathering around him, and although the video was a soundless one, Jed could imagine very well the horrified screams that must have filled the sidewalk. He let out a short breath, watching the video end.

Christie turned to him.

"Are you okay?" she asked gently.

Jed nodded. He wasn't, exactly… but he would be. Soon.

"Is that all?" he asked.

"Yes. Do you have any thoughts so far?"

Jed considered. "What did the toxicology report in his autopsy state?'

Christie looked like she had been expecting that question. "There were no toxins in his blood—at least none that remained by the time the autopsy was conducted. I did ask them to check for any evidence of the VX toxin, since that is on our radar now."

Jed understood the implied meaning behind her statement. He had thought of it himself. There were certain, fast-acting toxins which disappeared immediately after doing their damage, making them almost untraceable and undetectable.

"Hmmm." Jed stared at the paused video, which showed a horde of people gathered around Alex. His stepbrother was no longer visible amidst the crowd.

"It's a tough case, huh?" Christie asked softly.

Jed nodded. "It is. I'm going to need some time to gather my thoughts about what I just saw."

CHAPTER 8

THE CORONER'S OFFICE WAS as silent and dark as the morgue it was in. Perhaps the man working there was afraid about causing too much disturbance, lest one day a corpse-like hand come knocking at his door.

The office in question was a room, slightly more than five feet in length and width, the floor covered with a dull gray carpet that muffled any and all noise. There were no lights in the room except for a single bulb situated in the middle of the ceiling, trying to cast its wan amber radiance as far as possible.

The coroner himself, Desmond Caine, was an old man—old enough that you would not be very surprised if you one day heard the news that he had joined the ranks of those he worked with. The man had a large, fleshy face, specked with liver spots around his nose and chin, and especially around his drooping jowls. His brows were thick and bushy, almost covering the topmost part of his eyes with their white, wiry coils. His mouth was nothing more than a thin, dark line journeying across the pallid, wrinkled landscape of his face. On the bald dome of his head, the only thing visible was the bulb's reflected glow, glaring brightly as if someone had lit a torch from within.

Yet, despite his age, Desmond was not a man to be trifled with. If you sat with him for even as little as two minutes, and if you were a perceptive individual, you would come to this realization immediately. His hands, which were just as wrinkled as his face, moved on his desk with a dexterity that even a teenager would find hard to match. Sometimes they typed furiously on the laptop that lay before him, sometimes they scribbled just as fast with the pen that lay to his side, and sometimes they rifled with expert nimbleness through the stack of files that lay all around his desk. Desmond had only two hands, and yet he seemed to be doing three things at once—all of them with perfection.

Jed and Christie sat on the two chairs opposite the man's desk and watched him work. Neither of them said a word. One, because they knew Desmond would speak to them when the time was right, and two, because they too were entranced by the man's inhuman ability to multitask, especially given his age.

This was the man who had conducted the autopsy on Alex, Jed knew. Initially, he had found it hard to believe that someone so old could be designated with a task as delicate as opening up a body. But now, sitting here watching Desmond work, Jed could understand why.

After what seemed like an eternity, Desmond finally took a pause from his trio of tasks and glanced up at them. His eyes

were nothing more than pale slivers at this age, trying to hold
their own against a sea of wrinkles slowly inching forward.
And yet, Jed could see the intelligence gleaming behind those
watery gray pupils glimmering brighter than the light in the
room.

"Right. You two are here for the recent autopsy, the boy
that came in yesterday?" Desmond spoke in a voice which
was strained but still clear.

Jed nodded.

"We're here to get some information about Alex Gray,"
Christie confirmed.

"Alex Gray…" Desmond muttered, staring into the distance with a frown. Jed could almost imagine the man going
through his vault of infinite files that he had gathered over a
lifetime of work. A few seconds later, Desmond's expression
cleared up as he seemed to find the right one, and he looked
back at the duo.

"Yes, of course. The boy that fell on the rake and died." He
made a low clicking sound of regret with his tongue. "Truly
a tragic affair."

"Indeed," Christie murmured softly. "Could you give us a
rehashing of your findings from the autopsy? My partner is
new to the case, and he needs to hear it all. Plus, he might
have some questions for you later."

"Absolutely. Just give me one second." Without a single
grunt or sigh, Desmond rose from his chair and ambled over
to the row of steel cabinets situated on the leftmost side of

his office. Strange markings had been made on each cabinet with a red marker. There were numbers and letters and dashes which didn't mean anything to Jed but probably signified a categorizing system.

Desmond went over to a cabinet in the middle and bent down on his knees a little, pulling it open. Jed winced internally as he saw the man kneel, his mind half-expecting to hear a loud popping sound as the coroner's ancient joints cracked from the pressure. But no such sounds came, nothing except for the dry rustle of paper as Desmond thumbed through a stack of files, finally locating the one he wanted, withdrawing it from the rest, and then standing up with a contented sound. He closed the cabinet and returned to his seat, placing the opened file on his desk.

"Alex Gray… Hmmm…" He began to nod slowly. "So, you want me to repeat the overview of what I found in the autopsy?"

Both Jed and Christie nodded.

Desmond frowned a little, studying them closely. "Is there any actual need for this? I wrote my findings in the report. Everything is there already, if yo—"

"We know," Christie cut in, and then added hastily, "it was a very comprehensive report. But we want you to *tell us* what you found, in your own words. My partner here has a knack for picking out things that are usually overlooked. As you begin your verbal account of the autopsy, he might have a few questions for you."

"Right," Desmond grunted, his eyes back on the file as he skimmed through it. "So, here is my recollection of the autopsy and what stuck out to me."

Jed leaned forward an inch.

"The victim died because a rake punctured his heart," Desmond began, his hands placed calmly on his desk. "That's the conclusion any medical examiner would arrive at immediately because it makes the most sense—and the body's condition indicates that, too. Three puncture wounds in the heart caused the victim to bleed out quickly. The rake made a surprising amount of damage to his heart, which was the result of his body thrashing around after he fell on the rake. However…" Desmond looked at Jed and Christie, his gaze flitting between them with an unnervingly penetrating look. "… both of you seem to think that he was poisoned." He regarded them both with arched eyebrows.

"It's a possibility we're considering," Jed admitted reluctantly.

Desmond shook his head. "Two problems with that possibility." He wagged his index finger in the air. "First, I found no trace of any poison—or even a paralytic agent—in the boy's blood. In fact, with most poisons that are commonly used, one of their obvious side-effects is that they cause the blood to congeal. As you might have already guessed, I found no traces of that, either. As far as the tell-tale physical symptoms are concerned, such as blue lips, bleeding orifices, skin rashes, or excessive saliva production, I found none of those either."

Desmond raised his middle finger now alongside his index finger and flashed them both at his guests. "Second point. I know you're going to ask me about those fast-acting toxins which disappear immediately from the bloodstream after doing their damage. You want to know whether there's any way of detecting those."

Silence filled the office for a moment.

"Is there?" Christie asked eventually.

Desmond sighed. He bowed his head for a fleeting second, and Jed had to avert his gaze from the bright glow reflecting on his skull like a searchlight.

"Yes... and no," he answered, interlocking the fingers of both his hands. "No, in the sense that there's no test I can conduct to find out whether such a poison was used. But yes, in the sense that if you give me a list of potential poisons that might have been used, I can try to rule some of them out or tell you which ones were the most likely. I did run the test for the VX toxin you requested, and it was negative."

"A list?" Jed repeated doubtfully. "There are thousands upon thousands of toxins available in the world, and more being manufactured every day. How would we be able to tell you which one out of all those was used?"

Desmond smiled grimly. "That would be where your job comes in, I suppose." He shrugged. "Other than that, there's no way to really know what happened to the boy."

"What about the moments right before he died?" Christie pressed. "Can you tell us whether the victim suffered from a cardiac arrest instead of being poisoned? I know it's an unlikely possibility, given his age, but unlikely doesn't rule something out entirely."

"Indeed." Desmond nodded. "I agree that cardiac arrests are extremely rare amongst young people, whilst not being entirely impossible." He spread his hands before them. "Unfortunately, the autopsy ruled out any such occurrence. A mural or totally occlusive thrombotic mass is the easiest way to confirm a heart attack. I found no such evidence in the boy's body. Other than the punctures, his heart was otherwise healthy. I can tell you with a fair bit of confidence that the boy appeared to have died from a puncture in his heart, causing severe blood loss which led to his immediate death."

The silence returned, thicker than ever, weighing down on Jed and Christie along with their disappointment.

Desmond seemed to guess his two guest's feelings. He shrugged apologetically. "I'm sorry, but there's really nothing more I can say to you with certainty." His shriveled lips curled upward in the beginnings of a bitter smile. "Death is a deceptive thing. It doesn't always reveal its secrets."

Jed nodded. He could feel the sharp edge of disappointment piercing into him, too. They had come here mentally prepared to find nothing of importance, but that still didn't stop the realization from hurting.

"Thank you, Desmond," Christie spoke dully, rising from her seat and extending her hand to the man sitting before her. He reached forward and shook it. Christie felt the sandpapery touch of his skin over hers and wondered, yet again, how such decrepit fingers could still hold the vitality to perform an autopsy. *Some people just don't age the same way*, she guessed.

After Jed too had shaken the man's hands and thanked him for his time, they left his office. Exiting the morgue, they stepped out into bright, unfiltered daylight. Jed looked up at a sky painted with generous golden strokes and sucked in a grateful breath.

"Thank God I don't work inside a morgue," he muttered to Christie. "I could feel myself slowly mummifying there."

Christie shuddered. "Yeah, no joke." Together, the pair made their way to a bench on the sidewalk, deciding to savor the fresh air a bit before going back to the black Ford Explorer waiting for them a dozen feet away.

"What are we going to do now?" Christie seemed to fling the question into the air, not asking anyone in particular. Nevertheless, it was Jed who answered her. The reluctant firmness in his voice caused her to turn sideways toward him.

"There's only one thing left to do now."

"What?" Christie inquired.

Jed let out a pent-up breath. "We'll have to find out if this was just a freak accident. A gut feeling is telling me it was not, that there's something more going on behind the scenes." He shot Christie a worried look. "You remember that poisoned dart that killed Joel and the forensic analyst who was handling it?"

Christie's eyebrows rose. "You think the same person is behind this? Jed... we have no way of proving that."

"No," Jed admitted grimly. "But the only way for us to prove it is if we consider it as a possibility first."

"Consider what possibility? That Alex was murdered?"

Jed nodded. "Yes. What if we base our investigation on this premise from now on? Worst case scenario, we run into a dead-end and the case is closed. Best case scenario..." His voice trailed off.

"We find the person responsible for Alex's death," Christie whispered.

"Exactly. So, let's assume for the moment that Alex was killed. That's the only way we can even come close to discovering the kind of poison that might have been used on him. We have to do it fast—I'm sure whatever traces of the toxin that are still left in him will disappear or break down in a couple of weeks at most."

Christie couldn't help it. She chuckled incredulously. "Find out who killed him? *How?*" She snorted with frustration. "We don't have anything more to go on. We have no further leads. What can we even do now?"

"Can you have one of the team members start researching toxins and poisons that are easily obtainable and can mimic a heart attack? They can provide Desmond with a list, like he said." Jed felt like he was grasping at straws.

"I will have Graham start on that now," she mumbled as she texted Graham at the station.

Jed turned toward her. Christie saw that a shadow had fallen over her partner's face, obscuring the brightness that usually gleamed through his curious eyes. She realized that Jed had already reached this conclusion long before, and it was not one he particularly liked.

"What?" she pressed. "What are you thinking, Jed?"

Jed paused a moment, the shadows deepening on his face, morphing into strange shapes that seemed to be warring with each other, as if he were going through a tremendous internal conflict. Finally, he answered her question in a heavy voice, and Christie understood why he was looking this way.

"We have to question Alex's family."

CHAPTER 9

JED SAT IN HIS office, before a desk that was piled an inch high with books, papers and files. His computer perched precariously on this stack in front of him, the whitish glow emanating from its screen and hurting his eyes. Client profiles were open on the monitor, each one detailing a different client's background and clinical history. It was this list that Jed was scouring through now, giving each profile an in-depth review before deciding whether he had the time and capability to consult them as a therapist.

This was all a play, of course. All of it was constructed so Jed could avoid doing what he should have done two days ago. Even as his eyes scanned the paragraphs of information pertaining to his potential clients, a part of him continued to studiously ignore the books and papers that haphazardly littered his desk. There were encyclopedias on different kinds of toxins and where they originated from, as well as historical excerpts detailing the various kinds of assassinations that had been conducted via poisoning. On top of these meaty volumes of knowledge also lay slim textbooks which discussed human anatomy—more specifically, the human heart and the different ways in which it was prone to shut down.

Jed had been repeatedly raiding this treasure trove of information over the past 48 hours. He had spent most of this time close to his desk, methodically skimming over each book, file, or paper turn-by-turn, stopping only to eat, drink, and relieve himself. It was extremely difficult for him, being a creature of routine, but they had little choice and even less time. Every moment that passed resulted in the trail getting colder. There was no reason for them to pursue this investigation further, considering zero evidence pointed toward anything suspicious having taken place. The police chief had already told Christie to wrap things up, but she had personally requested an extension, which she had been granted. The chief was aware of the help Jed had provided to the police department in prior cases and knew the value of his gut feelings.

But still, even personal favors had a limit. There was only so much extra time they could be given, and Jed knew he had to utilize every bit of it. As a result, even sleep had been put aside. He only closed his eyes and rested when he absolutely couldn't stay awake for a second more. During the last two days, he had spent a little over five hours napping in his office, curling up on the sofa with its rough, itchy cushion being used as a makeshift pillow. The time he didn't spend sleeping or indulging in his basic biological needs, he utilized in devouring the volumes of information he had gathered on his desk. His only sustenance was coffee and quick escapes to

Jamie's hot dog stand. The quick walk outside was enough to give him the renewed vigor to continue.

All of it, to no avail.

Deep, deep inside Jed, a tiny part of him knew he was just wasting time. All this tireless work, burning the midnight oil and drinking a dozen cups of caffeine a day, was just so he could avoid doing what actually needed to be done. That was going to his family to ask them questions pertaining to the case. Jed knew very well he was a therapist, not a detective. His job wasn't to become an expert on fast-acting toxins or cardiovascular problems; his job was to ask people pertinent, revealing questions which brought the truth into light. Instead of doing that, a role he had spent years training for, here he was: procrastinating.

Well, the show was almost over now. Hovering just beyond his facade of busyness, Jed could sense the vast, bone-deep exhaustion waiting to take hold of him. He had burnt himself out completely in the last two nights, and today was all that he had left. Jed guessed that if he didn't stop this madness and take a proper rest within a couple of hours, his body would collapse completely.

"Two days of grueling work," he muttered resentfully to himself, "and all I've achieved is a big, fat nothing." This fact wasn't made any more digestible by the realization that if he had simply gone to his father's house to ask him the questions that needed answering, these last two days wouldn't have gone to waste. It was too late for regrets now. The past was the past. It couldn't be changed. As a therapist, Jed knew that better than most; he had spent a good portion of his life telling his clients the same thing. His youth had been spent learning to deal with difficult memories. Now, even though he knew he was equipped to handle them, some part inside him continued to come up with excuses to delay that inevitable meeting.

Jed was surprised with himself. He thought he had done all the work and had already processed his past. He started nodding as he reminded himself that traumas have a way of resurfacing at any time, anywhere. They demand you to acknowledge them and work through them, or else you risk pushing them away with whatever vice you can.

Jed buried his face in his hands and groaned softly, feeling his head pounding in the throes of a terrible headache. He needed to sleep, and he needed to sleep *now*. His mind was in wild disarray, and his body felt like it was an embalmed mummy recently excavated from its tomb.

Standing up from his desk, Jed pushed back his chair and shuffled over to where the light switch was. He shut off every single light in the office, including the pale fluorescent one in the bathroom that could always be seen peeking through the bottom of the door. Shadows enveloped his working space instantly, brightened only by the city's glare streaming in from the large, floor-to-ceiling window. Jed went there next, ambling over to its corner like a zombie, and pulled down the blinds with a single, swift motion.

Now, there was perfect, pitch-black darkness, exactly the kind he wanted. With a grateful sigh, Jed flopped down on the sofa, throwing that horrid, prickly cushion to the floor and nestled his folded jacket under his head. He stretched out his legs, sinking his face gratefully into the soft, velvety folds of his improvised pillow.

Sleep hit Jed before he even had time to realize what had happened. A few seconds after lying down on the couch, he was out like a tranquilized lion, his mouth parted softly, the quiet office filled with his light breathing.

Jed awoke later to the sound of his ringing phone. When he opened his eyes, expecting to see his office's interior, nothing greeted him except for darkness. It took a few moments before he realized where he was. He rose up from the sofa and groped in the blackness for the blinds' cord. As his fingers wrapped around it, he pulled, and the office came into view again.

It was still night, and the moon was a blazing crescent in the sky. Jed looked blearily at the clock and saw that it showed 3:24 AM. He had slept for around six-seven hours—not enough at all considering what he had put himself through, but it would have to do for now.

The phone was still ringing, vibrating insistently on his desk. Slowly, with a much clearer head, Jed walked over to it and began searching within the unending, silt-like layers of papers covering the surface. He eventually managed to locate the phone and fished it out from beneath two encyclopedias and a stack of textbooks.

Jed frowned as he saw the screen. It was his mom calling. His stomach felt like it fell and hit the ground. A call at this hour was never good. An ice-like dread expanded in his veins while he answered the call and put the cold metal against his ear.

"Hello?"

"… Jed?" Yes, something was *wrong*. He sensed it immediately in his mom's raw voice. Steeling himself for the worst, Jed spoke in a calm, unwavering tone.

"Yes, it's me. What is it, Mom?"

"Jed… I just received some news."

The human mind was truly a miraculous machine. In that split-second, a trillion different scenarios, each more horrible than the next, played in Jed's mind with lifelike vividness.

"What news, Mom?" He asked in that same, even tone.

"Jed, it's… it's y—your stepmom, Cindi."

"What about her?" Jed fought to keep the impatience out of his voice.

"She's…" His mom's voice faltered. She gathered her strength and finally squeaked out the feeble words, "S—she's dead."

What? Jed felt himself reeling from the shock. He swallowed and loosened his grip on the phone, realizing he had been squeezing it with bone-white knuckles.

"She's dead?" he asked, wondering if he had misheard.

"Yes. I was just told." His mom paused, and Jed could practically sense her holding back tears. "Richard called and told me."

If the previous news had been a sledgehammer of shock pummeled into his stomach, this was an entire wrecking ball that came crashing down on him with a deafening screech. Jed stood in his office with his mouth opening and closing repeatedly, unable to form the right words for the first time in his life.

"Why did Dad call you?"

His mom sniffled. "He was furious at me, Jed. Was practically shouting at me during the entire phone call, saying I was responsible for ripping his family apart."

"*You?*" Jed echoed. "Why would he say that? How did Cindi even die?"

"She just passed away from a heart attack in the bathroom. Richard said that the news of Alex's death… it was too much for her—far too much."

"But Alex's death wasn't your fault," Jed interjected sharply. "He had no right to call you and berate you, especially not at this ungodly hour."

"It's fine… you don't have to worry." His mom sniffed again, and when she spoke, she sounded more composed.

"Now that I think about it, I'm sorry for calling you so late. This news could have waited until the morning. It's just that when I heard about it, I—I panicked... and to hear from your father..."

"It's okay, Mom. It's completely fine." Jed found his regular, soothing therapist voice returning, acting as a balm to his mom's frenzied mind. "You don't have to worry. Everything will be okay. You did a good thing by calling me right now; I needed to hear this immediately."

"Really?" His mom sounded hopeful. "Didn't I disturb your sleep? I was in such a panic that I called without even checking the time."

"You didn't ruin my sleep," Jed told her softly. "I'm a light sleeper, as you know, and I was about to wake up anyways. You did me a favor, actually, if you think about it, because you acted like my alarm clock."

His mom laughed softly, her nerves calmed. "You always know the right things to say, Jed," she murmured, then chuckled briefly again. "I guess that's why you're such a brilliant therapist. Anyways, I'm going to try and get some sleep now. Hearing your voice always calms me down, you know? Hopefully, I'll be able to think about this entire catastrophe much more rationally in the morning."

"You do that," Jed told her. "I'll call you after the sun comes up."

He had cut the call and was only beginning to put the phone in his pocket when it vibrated again. This time, it was a message from Christie:

Call me as soon as you see this.

Jed obliged, and a moment later, Christie's startled voice spoke into his ear.

"You're awake? I thought you'd be asleep."

Jed rubbed his eyes with one hand. "I'm trying to, but this case isn't letting me."

"Same." Christie sounded weary herself. "Unfortunately, I have some further bad news for you."

"Yeah, I know. Cindi Gray is dead," Jed uttered with exhaustion.

"Wait, how did you know?" Then a moment later. "Oh, never mind. It is sort of your family, after all. That's not the only bad news, though. Remember all those toxins we asked Graham to check for? Well, the results came back, and they're all negative."

"It's not my family," Jed retorted instantly, forgetting the other news, and then grimaced at the unintended sharpness in his tone. He spoke again more gently. "Christie, it's time that we go together and question these people. We've already lost one of our possible sources of information on Alex. We can't wait any longer."

"I agree." Christie's voice came through. "We'll give them a day at max to get their affairs in order, and then we have to question them, no matter how much our questions hurt them. We have a possible murder to solve here."

"I agree," Jed answered grimly. "The more I think about this whole business, the more I get the nasty feeling that Alex's death wasn't an accident. We must get to the heart of this mystery, Christie. And fast."

Chapter 10

It was a drab, cloudy day. Not even the faintest ray of sunlight could be seen streaming through the clouds. Everything stood tired and listless, including the grass, the trees, and the guests milling around the cemetery grounds.

There was an equal mixture of men and women present at the funeral, the former dressed in somber black suits and the latter wearing all-black cardigans. Some of them were talking, whispering secretively amongst themselves, and the rest just stood there with a melancholic stillness, staring off into nothing.

It was Cindi's funeral.

Jed stood near the back of the crowd, his eyes casually surveying everyone. He was the only one in this entire army of grievers who didn't fit in, and he seemed to stand out like a sore thumb. He felt anyone looking at him would know instantly that he knew almost no one here and had no reason to come.

But still, Jed had arrived. He had forced himself to get into the taxi and tell the driver to drop him there. He had gritted his teeth and put on his charcoal suit, while every fiber of his being screamed at him not to go.

Some things just had to be done. Jed's inability to face his family was hindering the investigation. It had even caused him to continue delaying things until Cindi had passed away, and now they no longer had one of their most important sources of information regarding Alex. Jed's past, which he had always believed was tucked away for good in some forgotten crevice of his mind, was finally coming back to haunt him, and it was high time he faced it head-on.

Thus, the decision to attend the funeral had been made. What better way was there to face his father than with a crowd of other people acting as a buffer to soften the one-on-one encounter? It would also help prepare him for the eventual visit he would have to pay the family with Christie. There was no way around that. He didn't want Christie to witness their full family dysfunction. Hopefully, this would make their next meeting less of a shock.

Then, there was the third reason, an equally important one, which had actually been what propelled Jed off his couch and made him get ready. There would be a great many friends and relatives of the family present at the occasion, people who had known both Alex and Cindi well. What better opportunity to finally obtain some information regarding his deceased stepbrother? It had been over twenty years since he saw this side of his family. He was able to recognize some of the faces, but he didn't think anyone could recognize him since he was a young boy when they had last saw him.

Jed had already decided who he would converse with. There was a rotund, middle-aged man in a bulging suit, with graying hair and a reddish nose, he had seen talking to the family multiple times. From Jed's analysis of the man's gait and the way he talked, it was not a far-fetched guess that he was a close friend or relative of the family.

Jed watched the man now from the corner of his eye, talking to his father and stepbrother. He waited patiently at the crowd's edge, letting the man's conversation finish so he could step up to him. He had to do it in such a way that his stepfamily didn't notice. It was clear that he wasn't welcome here. From the moment Jed had entered the cemetery grounds, not a single person had come to greet him. His father had shot him a stern, harrowing look when his eyes had first fallen upon Jed, but that was all the attention Jed had received today. Even his other stepbrother, Andy, who was the same age as Jed, two years older than Alex, was continuing to pretend he simply wasn't there.

The man's conversation with Jed's family ended right when the coffin was brought out and the priest rose up to the head of the grave, preparing his sermon. A murmur went through the throng of mourners, and they all inched forward slowly, peering straight ahead. Jed did not do the same. He snaked his way deftly sideways through the sea of people, acting casual enough not to attract any attention. At the same time, his gaze was on the heavyset man who had left Jed's family and was now shuffling toward the crowd's center.

Their meeting happened like a perfect coincidence, exactly as Jed had intended. He slid his way through to the front of the crowd just as the man took his place there. Now, they were both standing shoulder-to-shoulder, with no one the wiser. Jed risked a glance his stepfamily's way and found that no one was looking at him. His father and stepbrother were both staring at the priest, their haggard faces listening to him utter Cindi's final rites.

The priest cleared his throat once, his rheumy eyes regarding the crowd, and then he began to speak. Jed let his attention drift after the first sentence. He still heard bits and pieces of what the man was saying, most of it related to Christ, the eternal kingdom, and not fearing the shadow of the valley of death. But the majority of his focus was on the gentleman standing beside him, the sound of his heavy breathing audible.

Jed acted. It was easy enough for him because this was what he had been doing for years. It was his entire profession, making conversation with people and getting them to open up. Once you mastered the task, you could do it anywhere, with anyone.

The man standing beside Jed heard him sigh. It was a deep and ragged sigh, punctured with the pain of inexpressible loss. As the sigh ended, he heard Jed mutter morosely under his breath:

"First the boy, and now this. May God give these people strength during such a terrible trial."

The man had been bored, half-listening to the priest's dry, unmoving speech. When Jed spoke, he heard himself answering, almost automatically.

"Indeed. Imagine what it's like for the other son. Losing your mom and brother in the same week."

Jed nodded and made a murmur of agreement at the man's words.

"Especially considering how young Alex was. I'd heard so much about him from others."

"Yeah, that kid certainly had a will of his own," the man grunted, and then shook his head ruefully. "I always remember Richard fighting with him about everything—the friends he kept, the places he used to go…" The man shook his head some more, his eyes on the ground. "Guess Richard will have no more complaints about his boy from now on—nor will Cindi."

The priest finished his short and uninspiring speech right then, and a meagre handful of people in the crowd muttered an *amen* loud enough for it to be heard. The man joined in too, his voice louder than the others, as if he were making up for his lack of attention by participating with more enthusiasm. He turned toward Jed, a question half-formed on his lips which he had been meaning to ask earlier.

"By the way, how do you know th—"

The question died on the man's lips as he turned fully to the side. Jed was no longer there. An empty patch of ground stood where he had been seconds ago, and beyond it was a woman in a grey dress dabbing at her moist eyes with a handkerchief.

The man blinked, looking at the crowd. He could not see the stranger he had made conversation with anywhere, even though he had been standing by his side just a moment ago.

Did I just talk to a ghost? he wondered, shivering involuntarily. Such things were not unheard of. There were many stories of people narrating their conversation with a stranger at a funeral, a stranger who vanished a split-second after their talk ended and was never seen again.

The man shivered lightly again, his eyes searching the crowd, but he could not spot the mysterious man he had spoken with anywhere; he seemed to have disappeared like fog on a bright, sunny morning.

Pushing his hands into the pockets of his coat and pulling it over his chest, the man sucked in a breath and began to walk toward a friend of his on the other side of the crowd, suddenly not wanting to be alone.

Back in the cab, Jed stared out the window, watching the blurred grayness of the world zip past him. Much to his surprise, he felt normal—much more normal than he had expected after going within such close proximity of his father. Furthermore, he had gotten some useful intel to act upon from the stranger.

So, Alex had been mingling with bad company prior to his death, or at least that's what his father had thought. It was interesting. But more importantly, it would finally give Jed and Christie a way forward in their investigation. It would also lay the groundwork for the questions they would ask the family upon their later visit.

The taxi traveled past an intersection onto an empty road, and the driver gunned the accelerator, pushing the car forward. Jed kept his gaze on the world outside, watching it morph from a gray blur into a gray streak, as if he were on a jetliner roaring through a canopy of clouds. He reclined against the seat and closed his eyes, satisfied for the time being with where he was and what he was going to do.

When his phone vibrated in the pocket of his suit a few minutes later, Jed wasn't startled. Not really. A tiny part of his subconscious mind had already been waiting for it to happen. He took the phone out and stared at his father's name blinking on the screen. Of course. There were no actions without consequences. Jed put the phone to his ear.

"Hello?"

"What was the point of today's stunt?" His father's voice was cold, utterly cold.

Jed paused. "What do you mean?"

"You know exactly what I mean. What game were you playing, coming to Cindi's funeral?'

Jed swallowed. He felt a chasm opening up inside him, a black hole that was sucking all his words into its hungry depths. This always happened. Whenever he spoke with his father, Jed found himself struggling to say something coherent.

"... I came to pay my respects," he finally managed.

"Listen to me," his father demanded with such viciousness that Jed recoiled in his seat, looking like a schizophrenic patient fighting invisible phantoms. "Your mom has already caused us enough pain. I don't want you adding to it with your stupid theatrics. Whatever you did today, I don't want it happening again. Ever." His father spit that last word out with such venom, his voice was practically a hiss.

Jed frowned. "Mom? What did she do to you?" He found anger rising within him, carrying with it a newfound clarity. "Don't involve her in this. She has nothi—"

The line was cut then, before he could say anything more, and the dial tone beeped in Jed's ear. He let out a shaky breath and put the phone down, glancing upward to find the taxi driver giving him a curious look.

Jed cracked a thin smile. "Family issues," he muttered, returning his gaze to the world outside the car, which had slowed down again to a gray blur.

The taxi dropped him off at his apartment's entrance fifteen minutes later. Jed trudged up the stairs, opening the door to his place and heading straight for the bathroom, where he dropped all his clothes on the floor and stood in the hot shower to scald the cemetery and the memories of the day away. After he was sure he was squeaky clean, he got out of the shower and headed into his bedroom where he slumped down on the mattress with a grateful sigh. He felt muscles in his body relaxing. Jed had been tense the entire morning, ever since he had stepped foot inside that cemetery. At least that challenge was over now, thankfully.

Jed finally drifted off to sleep that way, with the mattress tickling his bare skin.

CHAPTER 11

THE COFFEE SHOP WAS nearly filled. A long queue stretched from the door to the counter, comprised mostly of busy professionals needing an extra energy spike in the afternoon. The seating area was bustling with younger folk, predominantly college students with their friends or partners. Waiters navigated the teeming nest of humans like rats scurrying through a maze, their upturned palms holding trays stacked with beverages and confectionary goods.

In the middle of this unending chaos, the door to the coffee shop opened for the hundredth time that day, and Jed and Christie stepped in. Christie was wearing a dark gray sweater along with matching charcoal pants, her badge clearly pinned on the side of her belt, and Jed was dressed in a navy-blue mock neck and black chinos to go with it. The pair walked to the counter together, their stride purposeful, their eyes scanning the shop's interior.

Lizzie, who was manning the counter that day, saw the two officials approaching and leveled her gaze with them. She nodded once in acknowledgement, then gestured with her hand for them to wait five minutes.

Jed and Christie obliged. They stepped to the side and mutely observed the people inside the shop, the constant din pouring into their ears.

"Doesn't look much like a lair for murder, does it?" Christie called out, bringing her head close to Jed's.

Jed shook his head, smelling her shampooed, strawberry-scented hair and losing all focus for a fleeting second. "Hard to sneak a poisoned coffee in here," he answered, his eyes briefly resting on a young man and woman who seemed to be nervously enjoying a first date. He blinked at Christie for a fleeting second, as if seeing her in a different light. "Judging by the chaos in this place, I'd reckon it'd be hard enough to get a normal coffee to its intended recipient, let alone a poisoned one."

Christie began to nod before stopping, abruptly, midway. "You wouldn't necessarily have to sneak it in," she stated.

Jed frowned at her.

Christie gestured with her eyes toward a waiter who hurried past them, a plate of coffee cake balanced in his hand. "Most of the people working here are young, trying to chase their dreams while doing odd jobs to make a living." Her face turned thoughtful. "It wouldn't take much to bribe them into delivering the wrong coffee to someone."

Jed's eyes narrowed at the idea. He looked over the coffee shop again, this time with an entirely new gaze, one that cast everyone in a suspicious light. Was what Christie said possible? Could their murderer be walking these polished floors right now, passing within a hair's breadth of them, without either of them realizing? Or had the killer resigned the moment their duty had been fulfilled, fleeing somewhere they would never be found?

Jed looked at the thronging mass of bodies around him, assessing which one it could be, if he had to choose. Perhaps it was the barista at the far end, the man in his early thirties with the buzz cut and a single gleaming earring, skillfully juggling multiple cups at once as if they were nothing but tennis balls. Or was it the waitress to his right, the young, Sudanese girl with a scrunched ponytail who was serving coffee to a group of college students? Or maybe it was the man at the other counter, the one with the tawny blonde hair and effeminate gestures, the one receiving all the dine-in orders. Or could it b—

Christie nudged Jed with an elbow, breaking him out of his reverie. He turned and found the girl who had initially signaled to them walking in their direction.

"Hello," the girl said, staring at them seriously.

"Hello," Christie answered with a small, disarming smile.

"Hey," Jed added in a polite tone, noticing the girl's unsmiling face and tense shoulders.

Is she nervous because we're police officials or because she's the killer? he wondered, then pushed aside his suspicion.

"Follow me, please," the girl, Lizzie, told them both, turning on her heels and walking promptly to the shop's backside. Jed and Christie followed. Lizzie led them through a door which read *Shop Personnel Only*, and then they were passing a corridor lined with three doors. There was a room serving as a broom closet, littered with mops and buckets of dish soap. Past it was a storage space where Jed saw a further three coffee machines standing as spares, wrapped in plastic. There were also scattered cardboard boxes lined with surplus ingredients. Lizzie led them to the third room, turning the knob briskly and motioning for them to enter.

Jed and Christie stepped inside the warm, cramped confines of the shop's surveillance room. A single monitor took up most of the space on an old, wooden desk, and a faded rotating chair was placed before it. The room belonged to the place's only security guard, Jeremy, who was standing in the corner, his arms folded behind him.

"How do you do?" Jeremy asked each of them politely, extending his hand from his back to greet each of them, turn-by-turn. The man was young, with fair skin and easygoing, honest eyes.

"I've asked Jeremy to take out the recordings for the date and time you requested," Lizzie told them both, her left foot fidgeting as if she were eager to leave. "If you need anything else, let me know." Then she was gone, shutting the door behind her, leaving Jed, Christie, and Jeremy in this suffocating cubicle which could barely fit one human, let alone three.

"Right, if you'll just give me some space..." Jeremy squeezed past them and wedged himself into the tiny seat, his fingers going to work on the keyboard. "This is the recording of the day the boy died, from the moment he entered the shop to the moment he left it."

Jed leaned over the man's left shoulder, peering at the screen as Jeremy pressed the play button. The grainy footage sprang to life, and Jed watched for the second time as his stepbrother lived his final moments.

The coffee shop was almost as busy as it was today when Alex entered it, Jed noticed. There was a queue still ending at the door, and the sprawling sofas and chairs were fully occupied. With bated breath, Jed watched the door swing open, and his stepbrother's lean figure stepped through it. From the angle inside the shop, he could see Alex's face and expressions much better. The boy had an impatient look on his face, the way most other people who venture inside a coffee shop do. His straight, dark hair was hanging over his forehead, almost obscuring his eyebrows. One of Alex's hands was stuffed into his jeans, and the other was holding his phone, his thumb rapidly tapping and swiping the screen.

Jed watched with quiet focus as his stepbrother took his place at the very end of the line. From here, he knew it would be approximately twelve to thirteen minutes before Alex received his order and stepped outside to enjoy his final moments in the world of the living. That was all Jed had, too—just thirteen minutes to find out what had happened. Taking a deep breath, removing all other thoughts from his mind, Jed stared at the screen with an almost entranced attention, his eyes fixed on his Alex's figure.

Jed observed him patiently and carefully, looking for any signs of abnormal behavior which could indicate that something was amiss. Standing at the very end of the line, Alex's head was bowed down, looking at his phone. His other hand was still in his pocket. Every once in a while, he would crane his neck up and lazily glance at the people around him. Then, he would return his attention back to his phone.

This went on for almost five minutes, until Alex was nearly at the counter. Jed heard Christie let out an exasperated breath, one which echoed his own feelings. There was nothing so far in his stepbrother's behavior which indicated that he was in danger, or at least wary of his surroundings. As far as Jed was concerned, Alex was the typical city patron, bothered only with himself and not a single other else.

The video continued. Alex gave his order and paid. Jed stared hard at the clerk's expressions when he took his order, then handed him a receipt a moment later. Alex jammed the receipt into one of his pockets and shuffled over to an empty corner in the shop, waiting while he fiddled with his phone.

Now, this was the critical part, the part when his stepbrother's drink was made. Unfortunately, the cameras were all front facing, and they showed nothing beyond the clerk and his cash register. Jed had no way of knowing what was being done in this interval, what unholy ingredients were possibly being poured into Alex's coffee.

The remainder of the time passed. Alex spent all of it as unbothered as one could be, swaying idly in one place, scratching the back of his head, chewing his upper lip, doing everything that people who were not worried about losing their lives did. Finally, once his name was called out, he stepped toward the counter and took his drink from the clerk. Jed watched his stepbrother mouth a brief *thank you*, the last words he would ever say to anyone, and then he was gone, the shop's doors swinging shut behind him.

Jed looked at Christie. Christie looked back at Jed. Both saw disappointment flickering in each other's eyes, the realization that every lane they were investigating was turning into a dead end. Pressing his lips in frustration, Jed turned back to Jeremy.

"Play the clip again, please," he instructed.

Jeremy did. The same video began from the start, and Jed watched it again with equal concentration, this time shifting his focus to *everything except for Alex*. This was their last hope—a slim chance, but one that existed, nevertheless. It was possible that the killer was in the coffee shop when Alex entered it, and if that was true, then it was also possible that Jed could deduce who it was through their behavior. This was what he did now, closely analyzing the facial expressions and gestures of everyone who was in the shop when Alex entered it.

Four of the seven tables were occupied by college students, and Jed found it hard to direct his suspicion at any of them. They were all engrossed in their own conversations, chattering away about everything and nothing, barely paying attention to the young man who had just entered. That left the remaining three tables, and one of those three was occupied by a couple so elderly Jed surmised they would have trouble enough taking their arthritis medicine on time, let alone concocting a plan to murder somebody. That left two further tables, and the people sitting at these also didn't fill Jed with much hope. One table was occupied by a couple on a date, and judging by the way they were making doe-eyes at each other, Jed guessed they had other things on their mind. The final table was also taken by a man and a woman, but Jed did not see them give Alex so much as a glance when he entered. As far as the evidence showed, the customers clearly weren't involved.

Now, there was the queue itself to check. Once again, almost all the people comprising it were young, college-going folk, not exactly the murderous thugs Jed had envisioned. Then, finally, there were the waiters in the shop, who were darting on and off-camera so fast that Jed barely had any time to properly glimpse their faces.

The video ran its second round and ended once more with Alex stepping out the shop's doors. Jed straightened his back with a muffled sigh and ran a hand through his hair. He turned toward Christie, who appeared equally forlorn.

"Could you check one more thing for us, please?" Jed asked Jeremy. "Could you speed through the footage for the previous month and see how frequently Alex visited this place?"

Jeremy obeyed, his fingers flying over the keyboard and scrolling quickly through a large database of files. He began pulling up videos and fast-forwarding them to the time Alex had visited the shop on his last day. As the videos played, Jed observed with interest that Alex had been a semiregular visitor, frequenting this place once or twice every week.

"Thank you for your help, Jeremy," Christie told the guard once he had shown them all the footage, and then left the room with Jed.

"What now?" she asked him, as they made their way toward the shop's entrance.

"I guess we just need to check the place where the coffees are made," Jed answered with a grunt, his eyes on the floor. "We can interview the baristas to see what they know. If all that turns out useless as well, then there's nothing left except for questioning Alex's family."

CHAPTER 12

LIZZIE SAW THEM APPROACHING from the back, noticed their grim expressions, and came up tentatively to meet them.

"Is there any problem?" she inquired with that same stiff voice, her eyes flitting from Jed to Christie, then back to Jed again.

"No, no problem." Christie smiled thinly again. "We need to conduct a survey of your kitchen, where the coffees are made."

Lizzie brightened. "Oh, sure! But there's no kitchen. Whatever happens, happens behind the counter. Come, I'll take you inside the hallowed grounds." Jed and Christie both followed the young girl as she opened a swinging slot next to the counter and ushered them both inside. Jed could see a stretch of empty space spread before them, where the baristas were hastily working. Espresso machines and other kinds of fancy equipment lined the walls on the rightmost side, and on their left, the backs of the cashiers and clerks taking the orders could be seen. It was the same coffee shop, the same people, but with an entirely different perspective. They were no longer the customers now, but the servers.

"Is there anything else you… need?" Lizzie stared at them both inquisitively, swinging her shoulders where she stood.

"Not at the moment. You can go, Lizzie," Christie stated gently, releasing her from her position. Lizzie gave a curt nod before turning around and walking back to her spot at the counter, where her own back joined the row of others. Christie turned toward Jed.

"I have a gut feeling that we won't find anything here either," she muttered.

Jed's eyes were scanning the kitchen area. There were three baristas working today's shift, he noticed, and there were two espresso machines in total.

"Come on," Jed said, beginning to go forward, urging Christie with one hand to come with him. "We'll never know until we take a closer look."

Unfortunately, unlike the surveillance footage they had just seen, there was even less to inspect here. All Jed and Christie really could do was stand to the sides and watch the baristas doing their job, slipping paper cups in and out of their fingers with captivating smoothness. Every so often, a barista would scurry over to one of the machines, then return back to their workstation, their hands never pausing. Jed observed these acts unfold over and over, ruminating on the single thought that was filling his mind.

Is it possible that, while making a coffee, one of these baristas could secretly slip in a poison without anyone noticing? The answer was a resounding yes. In fact, the workers moved so swiftly that it was also possible for them to poison a drink while someone *was* watching. But possible didn't mean probable, and Jed knew that the mere existence of something's possibility would not lead them anywhere. They needed something more—something concrete.

"Any inspiring thoughts or insights yet?" Christie asked, leaning her head to the left.

Jed shook his head, grunted. "None, I'm afraid."

"Same. If this really was a murder, then we might just be dealing with a mastermind criminal."

"Or maybe the criminal was nothing more than an average joe, and we're simply unable to see how he made his move." Jed bit his lip with suppressed agitation. This wasn't working. Nothing was working. They needed a lead in this investigation, and they needed it fast. Alex's family would not allow his body to remain in the morgue for much longer.

"Hey." He felt Christie's soft hand brush his own. "It's okay. We'll find something. This is not the end."

"Of course." Jed looked at Christie, his face once again a mask of calm. "I just hope we find it before Alex has been put in the ground."

"We will," Christie answered firmly. "After this, there's only one thing left for us to do, right?"

Jed sighed. "Question Alex's family. Yes, I know. I haven't forgotten."

"Would you be available for that tomorrow? I can call them today and set up a meeting."

Jed did not answer immediately. His eyes were on Lizzie, who was rushing past them, probably on another errand.

"Hey," he called out, grabbing her attention. Lizzie turned toward him, stopping midway in her dash to the door. Her brows rose quizzically.

"Yes?'

Jed took a step toward her so he wouldn't have to shout over the noise. "Has the worker roster here changed over the last two weeks?"

"Pardon?" Lizzie leaned closer to him, frowning.

"I said, has the working roster here changed over the past two weeks? Have any workers joined or left during that time?"

She put a single finger to her lip thoughtfully, her eyes cloudy. A few seconds later, her head began to shake. "No, no new additions or losses in that time."

Jed muttered an internal curse. "Are you sure?" he asked Lizzie again, staring at her intently.

"Positively sure," Lizzie replied, her voice filled with certainty now.

"What about slightly more than two weeks?" Christie added from beside Jed. "Have any new workers joined in the past, say month or something?"

Lizzie paused again, and her finger returned to the corner of her lip. "Well, we have Gary who joined two months ago," she said, "but that's it." Her face was suddenly wary. "Would you like to speak to him?"

Christie sighed and shook her head. "Could you just point him out to us right now, if he's here?" She added with a wry smile, "and do it without being noticed, please. I think we've caused enough disruption as it is."

Lizzie swiveled around where she stood and began scanning the workers behind her. A moment later, she turned back around to face Jed and Christie, and pointed a single finger furtively over her shoulder.

"The guy right behind me," she murmured in a low tone. "The one with the black apron."

Jed stared at who she was pointing at, and his heart sank. Their hopes had been low to begin with, dismally low, but after seeing Gary, he felt them being snuffed out completely. The boy Lizzie was pointing toward couldn't have been older than his late teens and was the most innocuous-looking fellow Jed had ever seen in his life—pale and gangly, with bright blue eyes and a boyish face that appeared to be permanently laughing at something, Jed could not imagine that this was their killer. Plus, like Lizzie had said, the boy had joined two months ago. If they began casting their suspicion on him, they would truly be grasping at straws.

'Thank you, Lizzie," Jed sighed, his shoulders sagging. "We'll be leaving now. We appreciate your help."

Lizzie tried to hide the relief that washed over her features but was unable to do so. Jed didn't mind. Everybody here had their own lives, their own problems to deal with. He knew it was stressful speaking to the police.

The doors swung open, and the two of them walked out into the open, windy air. For a while, they simply walked in silence, their eyes trained on the pavement below them. Finally, it was Jed who slowed to a halt and looked up at his partner.

"Pretty sodden day, huh?" He grinned ruefully.

Christie shrugged. "Not my first. Won't be the last. Comes with the job, you know."

"Uh-huh." Jed couldn't imagine having a profession where days like these were a normal thing. Once again, he felt a deep admiration for Christie's patient endurance. "What do you usually do when you have a day like this? To unwind, I mean."

Christie crinkled her eyes, pondered the question, and then opened them a moment later, regarding Jed brightly. "I have ice cream!" she exclaimed.

Jed paused. "Would you like to have some now?" he asked a bit too eagerly.

A smile made its way onto Christie's lips, spreading to the rest of her face. That was how she always smiled, Jed had noticed—first with her lips, and then with the rest of her face.

"I would love some," Christie answered, beaming.

They strolled their way to an ice cream cart that was three streets down from the coffee shop. Christie led the way, her excitement visible in each springy step. Five minutes later, they were at the cart, and Christie was giving the order for them both. Jed stood at the side, staring quietly at the city, his pensive mood returned.

What am I not seeing about this investigation? he wondered, his eyes falling on the ceaseless waves of people before him. *What key detail are Christie and I missing?*

But the answer would not come. Luckily, however, the ice cream did, five minutes later, and Jed's mood improved considerably when he looked down at it. Christie was holding two waffle bowls in her hand. Each bowl held a generous dollop of the richest, most decadent Belgian chocolate Jed had ever seen. It dripped and oozed before him in rich brown shades, and Jed had to hold himself back from chomping down on it directly. Instead, he plunged his plastic spoon into the dessert's soft depths and tore off a large portion of dreamily thick chocolate and crunchy biscuit. Jed placed the morsel into his mouth, began to chew, and for the next two minutes, he was in heaven. All thoughts about the murder and his stepfamily disappeared, and the only thing that mattered was the luscious flavor exploding in his mouth like fireworks.

"Grrhmmmm." Jed closed his eyes, sighing with pleasure.

"Mrrhmmm," Christie responded, equally zonked out.

Both of them opened their eyes then, looked at each other, and burst out laughing. Jed held a hand over his mouth while he chuckled softly, feeling lighter than he had this entire week. He looked at Christie, who was giggling softly, too, her lips coated with brown.

"You," Jed leaned forward impulsively to wipe the ice-cream from her lips and caught himself just in the nick of time. He drew back quickly, his eyes flashing with embarrassment. "You have something on your lips," he told her, gesturing with his hand.

Christie took a folded tissue from her pocket and wiped her lips clean. She looked at Jed, her eyes twinkling.

"Is that better?" she asked softly.

Jed nodded, feeling a rush of heat reddening the side of his neck, He cleared his throat, busied himself finishing the remainder of his ice cream, and then flung the cardboard slat away into a nearby bin.

"That was…" He stopped, searching for the right words.

"Amazing?" Christie suggested.

"Life-changing," Jed grunted with satisfaction. He gazed at his partner with admiring eyes. "It was so good, you just made me forget that we made absolutely zero progress on our investigation today."

Christie waved a dismissive hand. "Don't worry about today so much. These things happen during investigations; the trick is to not fret over them unnecessarily." Her eyes turned suddenly serious. "But we do have to question Alex's family now. I'm thinking it shouldn't be delayed beyond tomorrow."

Jed nodded in agreement. It was time. "Me, too. Call them today and set up an appointment for tomorrow. I'll join you."

"Done." Christie jammed a hand into her pocket and tucked a stray strand of her windblown hair behind her ear with the other. She looked around at the milling crowd. "I guess we part ways for now, then. See you tomorrow, partner."

Jed smiled. "See you, Detective." He took a moment to glance back and watch Christie gliding down the street in the opposite direction. Then, he turned around and went his separate way, searching for a taxi that would take him back to his apartment. At the last moment, he decided he would walk home instead. His mind was still swimming with the case, and there were many ideas filling his head which needed untangling. Perhaps some time in the open air would help.

Turning around from the taxi stand, Jed joined the flowing crowd of people and was soon lost in a sea of voices and colors.

CHAPTER 13

THE DAY HE WAS dreading arrived.

Jed's eyes opened on his bed, and he stared at the window opposite him. His chest rose and fell slowly in deep, heavy breaths. His hand clenched and unclenched on the pillow beside him. In a last, half-hearted attempt, he turned to the other side and closed his eyes once more, trying to see if sleep would catch him again and drag him away to the land of peaceful oblivion. But of course, that didn't happen. He was more awake now than he had been in a long, long while. His heart was a pounding bass drum, and his blood fizzed through his veins. Despite his best efforts, Jed was totally and irreversibly awake, which meant that he had no choice but to face the day.

His legs swung off the bed and landed on the soft, plush carpet. Jed rose to his feet, watching as the comforter slipped from his shirtless body and the sunlight gilded him with its radiance. He shuffled over to his cupboard mirror and stared at himself.

His hair was tousled, puffed up on one end in a long wave of brown. His stomach was taut, his chest still showing that pale whitish scar he had gotten from a skateboarding accident in his youth.

What scars will I receive today? Jed wondered, one finger absently tracing the scar's bumpy, crusted surface. *What new wounds will my father gift me with on this auspicious afternoon? Wounds that I'll bury somewhere inside me, only for them to spring up ten years later like weeds, spreading their poison everywhere.*

In the room's lulling silence, no answer came. Jed continued to stand in front of the mirror, his gaze locked on his own stolid figure. In that moment, he looked like a man who had just been woken from a pleasant dream and wanted nothing more than to return to it. His gaze drifted to the bathroom door, eyeing it with contempt. Suddenly, the process of showering and changing seemed like the most exhausting activity he could imagine. Even the mere thought of taking that first step toward the door filled him with a bone-weary fatigue.

"Get a grip on yourself," Jed muttered. "You know why this is happening. You know why you're feeling this way. The quicker you get today's business over with, the sooner you'll return to normal."

The thought seemed to calm his racing mind a little. It also gave his lethargic limbs some energy, and he was gradually able to drag himself to the bathroom. Once there, Jed turned on the shower at full burst and stood beneath the ice-cold spray, letting it rinse all the hesitation and reluctance out of him. His skin contracted, and his muscles shivered at the chilly liquid's touch, yet he continued to remain there, refusing to move until the cold cleared his mind completely.

It took a whole ten minutes. Once done, he finally began to feel like his old self again, his fingers moving briskly as he put on a tan shirt alongside black trousers. His phone rang while he was halfway through combing his short, chestnut strands. Putting the brush aside, Jed picked up the cell and answered.

"I'm getting ready."

"Whoa, you're already up?" Christie sounded surprised. "Even by your standards, this is early."

Jed stared at his severe, hardened expression in the mirror. "I know. I could barely sleep at all, so I thought I might as well start the day."

"Oh." A pause then, from the other end. "You sure you're okay?"

"I'm perfectly fine," Jed answered, keeping the trepidation out of his voice. "I'll see you at the station in 30 minutes."

"Perfect. I'll be waiting for you. Bye."

He hung up the phone and resumed combing his hair, methodically slicking back every damp strand until he had achieved the perfectly-groomed therapist look he wanted. Then, Jed exited his bathroom and left his apartment, grabbing his wallet and keys on the way.

It really was a nice day, much nicer than it had right to be. The wind was blowing in cool, refreshing gusts, and the sun shone through a gauzy curtain of clouds, spilling its bright, golden hue everywhere. Jed stood on the sidewalk in front of his apartment, waiting for one of the taxis that frequented this area to pass by him. He sucked in a deep lungful of the late fall air while he waited, and the fresh scent of pine and rich, loamy soil filled his nostrils. Damn, today's weather really was perfect. Almost as if the universe were taunting him, daring him to enjoy even a single thing.

I will soon, he thought to himself, *once this day is over.*

A taxi passed by him soon after, and Jed raised a solitary hand to call it. He told the driver the address and slid in the back seat, feeling the car's artificial chill replace the weather.

It was during the drive that he felt his nerves beginning to jangle again. Jed's palms began to ache with a tingling current, something they always did when he got nervous. His throat dried up a bit later, and Jed took a swig from the small plastic bottle he had brought with him. He swallowed deeply, then turned his gaze out the window, watching the city's landscape whizz by him. It was a basic anchoring technique, focusing your mind on moving objects to steady the anxiety inside you. The brain generally hated multitasking, and one way to stop it from worrying was to distract it. This was what Jed did now, keeping his gaze firmly fixed on the city's greyish blur filling the window.

It was approximately a 25-minute drive to Christie's office. For the first ten minutes, no matter what he did, Jed felt his apprehension continuing to ascend, expanding inside him like a balloon filled with acid, threatening to pop any minute and shower his insides with its corrosive contents. He swallowed again and felt bile rising in his throat. The driver swerved sharply to the left, and Jed's stomach did a little somersault. He placed one hand on the door's handle, ready to hurl it open should last night's dinner come rising back up. It didn't, but the feeling of impending doom also did not subside. It only grew in size and weight, an ominous cloud casting its gloomy shadow over his entire mind's expanse. Jed closed his eyes and leaned back against the headrest, hoping the ride would pass soon.

It was then that the idea came to him. Of course, there was one thing that would help, one thing which had always helped—focusing on other people's problems instead of his own. It was why he had become a therapist in the first place, apart from his deep-rooted desire to help other addicts. Although that had been the main driving factor pushing him onto this professional path, Jed had discovered later that therapy offered plenty of benefits, even to the person who was providing it rather than receiving it. One such benefit was that it allowed you to approach your own problems with a newfound freshness. By focusing your attention on other people's worries and trying to solve them, you became better equipped to get your own life in order.

Jed fetched his phone from his left pocket and quickly dialed his mom's number. She had messaged him late the previous night, telling him to call in the morning whenever he got time. Jed had seen her message upon waking but had been so distracted by his own approaching appointment that he had forgotten all about it. Now, the memory returned to him, and he put the phone against his ear.

"Hello?"

"Hi, Mom," Jed greeted her cheerfully, his tone devoid of all that he had been feeling a moment ago. "How are you?"

"I'm doing okay, Jed." His mom, like Christie, sounded surprised, too. "Just a bit taken aback that you're calling me at this hour. We usually don't talk until noon at the earliest, once you're done with all your exercising and journaling."

Jed forced a chuckle from his mouth. "Well, you know how life is. The early bird catches the worm, as they all say."

"Is that so?" His mom's voice was a tad skeptical. "I didn't realize you had developed a fondness for worms, son."

"I haven't, but you know what I mean." Then, before the conversation could meander any further toward his own life, Jed added, "I called regarding the message you sent last night, Mom. Is everything okay?"

"Well..." his mom paused, and Jed knew instantly that there was something she wanted to share with him but couldn't because she didn't want to upset him.

"What is it?" Jed probed gently. "You can tell me."

"Well, yeah, I can." His mom hesitated. "But it's not a big deal or anything. I don't want you to start worrying."

"I won't," Jed assured. "But first tell me what it is."

"So... I received a call last night at around 10:30."

"A call? From whom?"

"From an anonymous number."

"What?" Jed frowned. "What did the person say?"

There was silence on the other end, and Jed could picture his mom pressing her lips together into a thin line, something she always did when discussing nasty business.

"Nothing much… except telling me to beware."

Jed's hand tightened on the cellphone. "Beware of what?"

"I don't know; that was all he said. Then the call got disconnected before I could speak further."

"Did you recognize the voice?"

"No, I cou—I think the guy was using some sort of a voice distorter. He sounded very robotic, artificial."

A voice distorter? Jed was immediately in protective mode. A voice distorter changed things significantly. It meant that the caller was serious and had gone to great lengths to hide their identity. Not simply a nutcase, making a prank call then. In fact, Jed reached the opposite conclusion: a very clear-headed and smart individual, someone intent upon not getting caught. This was not good.

"You probably have no need to worry," Jed lied, keeping his voice calm. 'Can you send me the number, though? I'll ask Christie to do a check, see if anything turns up."

"Oh, no, that won't be necessary." Laurie sounded apologetic. "I don't want your girlfriend inconvenienced on my behalf."

"She won't be inconvenienced, Mom," Jed groaned. "It's literally her job." A small smile touched his lips. "And stop calling her my girlfriend. She i—"

"—Well, you spend almost all your time with her," his mom interrupted, "so pardon me for jumping to the most reasonable conclusion. Anyways, I've got to run now. I have a small meeting with a publishing agent in an hour. Have to get ready for that. First impressions count, you know."

Jed grinned in the back of the car. "Good luck, Mom. I will talk to you later. Bye." He hung up the phone and spent the meagre rest of the journey gazing outside, his worries about today's meeting temporarily suppressed.

Christie was waiting for Jed outside her office when he arrived. She was dressed in a navy-blue shirt and khaki pants, with her hair tied behind her in a neat bun.

"Good afternoon, Detective." Jed stepped forward to greet her. Her faint, sandalwood perfume invaded his nostrils, and he felt his worries decreasing further—but not enough to make him forget the phone call his mother had received. "I need to talk to you."

Christie blinked, sensing the seriousness in his tone. "Yes?"

Jed told her everything. The call his mother had received, the threats that had been hurled her way, and most important-ly, the voice distorter her mysterious caller had been using. As he had been expecting, Christie's eyes widened when he mentioned this distorter.

"The caller was masking his voice?" Christie's jaw tight-ened. "That's really worrying, Jed. Usually, crank callers don't go to such extreme lengths."

"I was also thinking that," Jed agreed, "which is why I told you."

"You did the right thing." Christie fished her phone out of her pocket. "I'll have a team of two guards at standby outside your mother's door by the end of today—in case this caller decides to pay a personal visit."

"Thank you," Jed uttered with genuine emotion, feeling some of the burden rise from his heart. A moment later, his cell phone beeped, the screen blinking with a text from his mom. As he read the text, his fingers stiffened around the phone, as if he were trying to snap it in half.

"Jed?" Christie spoke with concern, noticing his tense posture. "Are you okay?"

For a few seconds, Jed did not reply. The screen's glow seemed to have him hypnotized, sucking all his attention into its fluorescent depths. When he finally did look up at Christie, his face was hollow and afraid.

"My mom just messaged," Jed said weakly, swallowing. "She said she can't tell me what the caller's number was. The details on her phone only say '*unknown caller*'."

Christie fought the urge to bite her lower lip in worry. She knew that would only make Jed panic even more, and she couldn't have that. He was already looking like he had been given a close-up view of hell. The phone was shaking almost imperceptibly in his hands, its screen threatening to crack under the immense weight of his duress.

"Hey, it'll be okay, Jed." Exerting tremendous self-control, Christie suppressed the urge to walk over to her partner and let him sag in her arms, so that his burdens could be divided between the two of them. Instead, she phoned Carter.

"Hello, Carter? Yes, I need you to do a favor for me." With one hand, she motioned for Jed to hand over his phone to her. Then, she read out Laurie's number to Carter. "Carter, this woman received a threatening phone call. I'm texting you the exact time and day. Can you do a phone trace and check whether we can pinpoint the location of the culprit? Make this task high priority, please." Once done, she texted her colleague the details then turned back to Jed.

"Don't worry—we will get to the bottom of this. Whatever it takes."

Jed nodded heavily, not saying anything. "I hope so."

They went together to Christie's Ford Explorer and began the final leg of their journey toward Alex's house. To his surprise, as the car throttled to a start, Jed realized that he hadn't even known where his father lived until now.

Well, better late than never, he thought to himself, letting the irony of those words ring in his head like a dozen clamoring bells.

Alex's family, Jed's stepfamily, lived on the suburban side of the city, away from the towering skyscrapers and the convoluted mazes of highways and flyovers that dotted the landscape like honeycombs. Their home was situated in an area comprised of neat little streets bordered by modest residences with white picket fences and squarely-trimmed hedges.

Christie parked the car opposite one such house, which appeared not very different from the others surrounding it. She opened the door and stepped out into the street, turning to frown at Jed, who had still not moved.

"Jed?" Christie called. "Are you coming?"

Jed started, like a man broken out of a deep reverie by being pricked with a thorn. He gazed at the area around him, seeing it for the first time, and then stepped out of the car.

Together, they made their way to the front door. Christie walked slightly ahead, and Jed lagged behind her, hauling his feet over the smooth tarmac as if they were being weighed down by cinderblocks. A simple jingling tune could be heard filling the house's interior when Christie's finger pressed the doorbell. The merry tune slowly dwindled away to silence, and the two of them waited, their eyes watching the door.

Jed stared hard at the brass doorknob during this quiet interval, and his mind wandered down many different lanes. Like all others who had suffered a scarring past, he wondered how his life would have been right now if things had gone differently. What if his father hadn't left him and his mom? Or what if he had left but had still kept in touch with his son and ex-wife, staying on good terms with them? Would Jed be visiting this house for a nice lunch with his stepfamily now instead of standing at the door with a police detective?

Would he even have been a therapist if things had gone down differently? He didn't know.

The remainder of his thoughts scattered like startled crows as the doorknob turned and the door swung open. Andy stood at the entrance, wearing a simple t-shirt and jeans, his hair falling broodingly over his forehead. Jed watched his stepbrother's eyes fall upon him, and with a feeling of dismay, he noticed the pupils expanding in shock. Andy's mouth opened wide, and a single, curled finger raised upward.

"What is *he* doing here?" His voice was thick and guttural.

Christie clasped her hands together. "He's consulting with me on the case," she answered in a firm, unyielding voice, her face calm. "Could we come in, please?"

Andy breathed hard, eyes flitting between Jed and Christie, his face strained with anger. "He—I don't think he's welcome here," he finally answered, pointing again at Jed as if he were some shunned leper.

Christie's impassive expressions did not change a bit. "As I said, he's consulting with me on this case." She spoke in the tone of a doctor trying to calm down a terrified toddler about to receive his first shot. "The police department hired him as an investigative therapist some time back, and he's proved himself more than useful since. Now, do you have any more questions, or may we come in?"

Andy scowled at Christie, his lips curling with distaste. He shot another long, harrowing look Jed's way, then reluctantly stepped aside.

And thus, we walk into the lion's den, Jed thought with dark amusement, following Christie as she stepped inside the house.

The place was neat and prettily decorated, Jed noticed. A few of the walls had been painted pastel blue, and chic, cream-colored couches filled the living room. There was also a wine-red bean bag chair thrown in one corner, and two renaissance paintings hung up side-by-side. A small chandelier hung from the ceiling in the middle, brushing the entire place with its warm, buttery glow.

Despite the aesthetic appearance of the interior, Jed could also sense vast and jagged grief lurking just below the surface. It hung over the entire house, coating every surface like a very fine layer of sulfurous powder that could never be seen—only felt once you inhaled its noxious fumes. Jed did feel it, the tremendous sense of grief and loss that had ransacked this entire place. Beneath the order and the inviting colors, disarray and chaos lurked everywhere.

Andy pointed toward one of the couches in the room and motioned for them both to sit. They did. He sagged down on a couch opposite them, twining his fingers together. As the chandelier's yellowing light fell upon his features, Jed saw for the first time how haunted his stepbrother really looked. There were dark circles beneath his eyes, and his face was gaunt and tired. His hair now appeared dry and straw-like in the room's brightness.

"Ask your questions," Andy muttered, staring at the floor with a bowed head.

Christie looked at him for a second, and sympathy flickered in her eyes. "Is your father here?"

Andy nodded. "Yes, but I'd prefer not to call him." His gaze drifted toward Jed in a single, admonishing look. "He's going to throw a fit if he sees *him* here." Again, he spat the word *him* like it was some vile glob of filth stuck in his mouth.

"Andy," Christie continued calmly, unbothered by his attitude. "We need to speak to your father as well. I told you all this on the phone, remember?" A few seconds passed, and when Andy still didn't move, Christie's tone hardened a bit. "You do realize that we're doing all of this to solve your brother's murder, right? If you want, I can leave right now and file this case away as unsolved. Do you want me to do that, or do you want me to catch the person responsible for Alex's death?"

Christie's blunt words fell like blows, each striking Andy square in the chest. He winced and straightened up a bit, his sullen expression showing a tinge of remorse.

"I'll go get Dad," Andy muttered, beginning to rise from the couch. "He won't like this. He won't like this at all, but I'll get him if it means finding Alex's killer."

Christie and Jed waited in the living room, listening to the clock's quiet ticking.

"Are you okay, Jed?" Christie asked softly.

"No." This time, Jed couldn't be bothered with pretending he was fine. He wasn't, and it was okay. Besides, no one else would be either, if they were in his position.

He felt the softness of her hand descending upon his, her fingers squeezing lightly, just enough to wring out his worries. She scooted closer to him until he could feel her comforting warmth, her calming presence. Jed's eyes closed briefly and let out a long breath, resting secure in the fact that his partner was with him. She would be there to help if anything went wrong.

At the other end, Christie was squirming with indecision, despite having given Jed some calm. She wanted to do more—a *lot* more. She wanted to really comfort him, let him settle his body against hers so she could give him the tightest embrace of his life and squeeze every last drop of worry from his soul. But Christie simply couldn't find the courage to do something like that. Her hesitation stopped her, and it was all due to this case. This damn case. It was just too close to home, and any gesture of closeness she made right now could be misread terribly. It would probably be better to wait.

Right at that moment, Jed's father came down from his room. He was a tall, grizzled man with his hair and beard sticking out from his face in wild disarray. His eyes were sharp, hawkish, and he had a face which had once been slim but had now turned gaunt after the passing of his loved ones.

Unfortunately, Andy had grossly underestimated the man's reaction to seeing Jed in the house. Richard did not throw a fit when his eyes landed on Jed—he *exploded.* For a fleeting second, Jed thought the man would literally pop. His face turned beetroot red, and the tip of his nose quivered wildly, his eyes threatening to bulge from their sockets.

"How dare you enter my house after what you did!" Richard shouted, spittle flying from his mouth while his hands curled into fists.

Jed did not respond. He could not respond. Suddenly, he was no longer a grown man. He was a child, a petrified, paralyzed child, staring at his monster of a father with saucer eyes. He felt like that fifteen-year-old boy who never belonged in this family all over again.

"Answer me!" his father cried out, taking a wobbling step forward. The crimson shade on his face deepened, and his entire body seemed to be shivering like a plucked guitar string.

"Sir, calm down this second before I arrest you for obstructing an investigation." Christie did not shout, but her voice rose just as high as Richard's had, cutting through its fury with ice-cold sharpness.

Richard looked at Christie and seemed to see her for the first time. He took a step back, sucked in a shuddering breath, and let some of that awful redness drain from his face.

"What? Y—" His voice faltered, and he took a step backward, gripping the sofa with one arm for support. Andy watched the entire scene unfold from the corner, appearing just as distressed as Jed.

"Sir, sit down," Christie commanded in a voice that allowed absolutely zero disobedience. The unmistakable clarity in her voice finally seemed to make its way inside Richard's head, and his eyes contracted to their normal size, the seething fury within them draining away. He swallowed once, then cast his gaze toward Jed again, staring at him with an unnamed emotion.

"Why are you guys here?" Richard croaked, all his bluster falling away to reveal a tired old man who just wanted to be left alone.

"We're investigating your son's death," Christie responded. "We're here to ask you and your son some questions pertaining to that investigation. Please sit down so we can get this over with."

The mention of Alex was what quenched the final embers of anger burning inside Jed's father. His whole body seemed to droop then, as if it were made of melting taffy, and he shuffled over to the couch where Andy had been sitting a few minutes ago.

The springs in the couch protested feebly when Richard's weight dropped on them. He gestured for Andy to join him, and then motioned for them to sit as well.

Still wary but feeling a bit more secure, Christie cleared her throat, calling for everyone's attention. "Shall we begin?"

Richard nodded, his hollow gaze resting on a vase standing between Jed and Christie. Andy was staring hard at the floor.

"All right. First question." Christie cleared her throat again. "Is there anyone, anyone at all, who you think had reason to harm Alex? Could be a fellow classmate of his, or even an old girlfriend."

Richard shook his head slowly. Jed heard the sound of popping joints as his father's neck swung on its rusted hinges.

"No. Alex never had any enemies," Richard murmured. "He was a golden boy. Everyone liked him, and they had good reason to."

"All right." Christie continued, "Was Alex acting strangely in the days leading up to his death? Did you see his behavior stray from normal at any time?"

A momentary silence, and then both Andy and Richard shook their heads, grumbling.

"No, he was fine, as far as I can remember," Richard answered, and then scratched his chin doubtfully a moment later. "Although I have to admit, I was a bit out of it the week before Alex's death—facing problems in my business and what not." He jerked a thumb in Andy's direction. "I think he might be able to answer your question better."

Christie's eyes flicked towards Andy, inquiring. She watched as he rubbed his eyes, thinking through her question.

"I don't... No, I don't think so." Andy let out a frustrated sigh. "It was hard to tell with Alex. He was always a recluse, you know? You could never guess what he was thinking or feeling. He kept those things close to his chest, away from the prying eyes of everyone—even us.

"Hmmm. I get it," Christie nodded in understanding. "Okay, third question. Was Alex involved in any kind of suspicious activities, as far as you both know?"

"No," both father and son replied in unison, and Jed knew immediately that they were lying. It was clear as day, in the way they had answered the question with forced certainty, whereas for every previous question, they had hesitated. He saw the way their gazes had momentarily met while they were answering, as if following a silent pact.

They're hiding something, Jed thought to himself, glancing Christie's way, who did not seem to have noticed the evasion. Well, she wasn't a therapist, and it wasn't her job to notice such minute details. It was his. That was why he was here.

Why would they lie about something like this? Jed wondered, keeping his silence because he didn't want to disrupt the questioning. If he called the family out for being dishonest right now, it would only ruin things. *Why wouldn't they want to help catch and punish whoever hurt Alex?*

Christie continued her line of questioning, asking Andy and Richard about Alex's habits, his line of work, his hobbies, his temperament, and what he did during his free time. The pair answered each of her questions, and Jed did not find them to be lying in any other matter Christie questioned them about. Alex had never really been a good student at school. Yes, he had hung out with friends Richard wasn't very happy about, but they were your usual marijuana-smoking, girl-ogling variety, not hardened criminals or deviants.

"Alex would spend most of his free time at home," Andy said, answering Christie's final question. His eyes lit up for a moment then, as he recalled a memory, and he chuckled briefly. "In fact, the only time we would get to see him would be when he would leave his room to get his food deliveries from outside."

Christie gave Andy a small, knowing smile. She made to rise from the couch, smoothing her shirt and pants while she did so. "Thank you for your cooperation, both of you. If we find out something, we will be in touch. I may have further questions for you both, depending on what the investigation turns up."

Jed did not bid his family farewell when he left with Christie, and they said nothing to him either. All the words had already been spoken during his father's outburst, and their message was clear: *You're not welcome here.*

Back in the car, he sagged against the seat, breathing a sigh of relief that it was all over. Christie gave Jed a sideways look, saw the weary lines crisscrossing his face, and sighed.

"Come here," she said, and let him fall into her embrace.

For a long while, Jed's head rested in the crook of her shoulder, his heart pressed against hers, beating in a staccato rhythm. She laid a hand over his back and stroked him gently, murmuring reassurances. A minute later, when Jed was somewhat composed again, he withdrew from her embrace. Embarrassment and peace fought for control of his face.

"Sorry about that." He coughed with down-turned eyes.

Christie placed her hand on his lap. "Don't apologize, Jed. You're very brave for doing what you did today. If you ever want to talk about it, I'm always here for you."

"Thank you, Christie." Jed sighed and massaged his temples with both hands. "Maybe some other time. Right now, I really want to go home. I have a feeling I'm going to have the best sleep of my life."

CHAPTER 14

IT WAS A STRANGE dream.

Jed was standing on a curb in blazing daylight, watching the amorphous crowd of bodies twisting and turning around him. He glimpsed a hail of yellow taxis racing down the street, music blaring from their open windows. Behind him, a giant coffee shop loomed, taller than any other building in the area—even the skyscrapers.

This isn't real, he thought, and the world seemed to agree with him. It shimmered momentarily, like a mirage about to disappear. When the ripples disappeared and it returned to normal, all the people surrounding him were gone. The taxis roaring down the street had vanished, too. Jed was standing in an empty graveyard of a city, with no one else around him.

No one other than Alex.

Jed saw his stepbrother standing at the entrance to the coffee shop, a paper cup nestled between both palms.

No! Don't drink it! Jed tried to shout, but his mouth didn't move. His lips were twin ridges of stone, and his tongue a rocky slab in his mouth. No words would come out.

Alex, stop! Jed tried again, but his efforts were in vain. He watched with growing apprehension as his stepbrother strolled, unaware, to the edge of the curb, the cup still in his hands. This was it. This was the moment. Alex was going to take a sip now, then die.

Some part of him knew this was a dream, knew it wasn't real, but that didn't stop the fear from spouting in him like a geyser. Jed tried to move forward, intent on slapping the cup out of his stepbrother's hands, but his legs wouldn't obey him either. He seemed to be a statue that someone had breathed life into on this sidewalk—capable of feeling and thinking, but not of moving. The moment unfolded with the slow inevitability of a boulder trundling off the side of a mountain. Alex looked around one last time with hawkish eyes, unable or unwilling to see Jed at all. Then, he raised the white cup to his lips and took a large gulp. He grimaced momentarily as the bitter, scalding liquid poured down his throat. A second later, his eyes widened. His hand began to flop madly like a dying fish around his chest, groping for something invisible. His mouth opened, and a choked wheeze came out. Jed watched with horror as thin red lines began to spread across his stepbrother's face, crisscrossing rapidly between his nose, cheeks and lips, dividing his features into dozens of tiny boxes. The lines thickened, and blood began to ooze from them, falling in gentle spurts down Alex's brows, his chin, the slope of his nose. And then, finally, Alex seemed to spot Jed for the first time. His feverish eyes locked on Jed's, his bleeding lips parted, and Alex's throat began to convulse, as if he were saying something but the word had gotten stuck in his throat.

Jed waited, but the message never left his stepbrother's mouth. After a few seconds, he tumbled to the ground, the oozing blood turning into streams and drenching his face in a thick, crimson blanket.

Jed woke in a sweat.

In the dimness of his room, he threw his blanket aside and sat straight up in bed, breathing hard. There was barely any light in the room, and everything resembled a tiny, crouching shadow. Using one hand, he swiped his hair away from his forehead and wiped his slicked brows clean. Then, he waited a few more seconds, letting his heart settle a bit, before rising off the bed and to his feet.

Jed fumbled in the dark to locate the switch while fragments of his dream flashed repeatedly in his mind. The most disconcerting of them all was the final moment before Alex had died. Jed shivered involuntarily as he saw, once again, his stepbrother's face staring straight at him, marked by those horrible red lines. He saw Alex's final gesture in the dream appear once more in his mind, as if his stepbrother's spirit was right here with him, trying to whisper something urgent.

But what?

What did it mean? Was it just like any other dream Jed had had, entirely devoid of meaning? Or was Jed's subconscious mind trying to tell him something, perhaps that his stepbrother was disappointed in him for not having solved his murder yet?

"I'm trying," Jed muttered to no one in particular, his finger locating the switch and flicking it on. Light rushed into the dark void of his room instantly, turning the small crouching shadows back into the harmless pieces of furniture they were. In the light, Jed's dream suddenly didn't feel so ominous anymore. In fact, he found himself analyzing it more rationally with every passing second.

What *did* the dream mean? Jed understood the importance of dreams in revealing a person's psyche. He knew the different aspects of a person's personality a dream could represent, from depicting suppressed emotions to buried traumatic memories, unhealed wounds, and even thoughts floating around in the subconscious mind.

Yes, it was probably one of those things for him, too, Jed decided with a contented grunt. The dream was most certainly signifying his own secret and irrational guilt at failing repeatedly to solve his stepbrother's strange death. That was why he had failed in the dream to save Alex's life. That was why Alex had given him that accusatory look toward the very end and tried to say something which was more a transference of blame than anything else.

Jed winced internally as the image flashed in his mind yet again. This time, he noticed details about it that he previously hadn't. Alex's upper lip curling in distaste, for example. The corners of his eyes slitting, like he couldn't even bear looking at his failure of a stepbrother. Then, of course, there had been his stepbrother's entire expression to begin with: that look you give someone when they have been unsuccessful in measuring up to even a single standard you set for them.

"Oh, sue me," Jed murmured with a half-chuckle, rising from the couch. "I'm trying, aren't I? That's the best I can do."

The following morning, Jed found himself in a much better and clearer mood. A good night's rest had removed the remaining sinister traces of the dream from within him. He even felt a bit sheepish, considering the way he had let himself be affected by something as harmless as a dream. Alex's attempt to say something to him did not stir up the same guilt within Jed anymore. Why should it? It wasn't his job to solve every murder, and especially not his stepbrother's, someone Jed had hardly known. Why should he feel guilty about something that had never been his responsibility to begin with?

Stepping into the shower, Jed pulled the lever as far to the left as it would go and stood beneath the steaming jet of liquid, enjoying the way it burned his skin. He let his mind drift toward the case and began to analyze it with a more critical and objective eye.

So, what new insights had they gleaned from their conversation with Richard and Andy? Just one: Alex was clearly involved in something shady. His father and step-brother had unwittingly revealed it, not by their answer to Christie's question but by their reaction to it. Jed had glimpsed the lie evident in their demeanors. Now, the only question that remained was: How were they supposed to find out the truth the family had hidden from them?

Visiting Alex's workplace was one option. He had occupied the dayshift there from early morning to mid-afternoon. Perhaps, the unscrupulous hobbies he had picked up had been from there, although Jed had a hard time imagining what illegal stuff a person could get up to in a steel mill. Nevertheless, they still had to check, to make sure.

What if Alex's workplace turned out to be a dead end? What then? Well, there wasn't much to go on if that option didn't work out... except for one thing. Jed had glimpsed it when he had gone to interview his family, while stepping out of the car.

He had been scanning the area when his eyes had spotted it peeking out of the corner of a lamppost. In the sun's reflected violet glow, the CCTV camera's black-mirrored eye had been unmistakable. It had been pointed at such an angle that it would show footage which included the Grays' house in it. If nothing else, at least Jed and Christie would know how often Alex was at home and how often he left. If they were lucky enough, they might even get to glimpse the friends who came to pick him up. Perhaps the killer was one of them. The possibilities were endless.

Jed stepped out of the shower and began to get dressed. He put on a sandy sweater over a sky-blue shirt, along with a pair of navy pants. Combing his long, wet hair back, he picked up the phone and dialed his partner's number.

"Rise and shine," Jed muttered with a sardonic grin when Christie answered the call.

"Wow, you seem to be in a good mood." Christie sounded pleasantly surprised. "Any new developments in the last twelve hours since we were together?"

Jed found himself grinning unabashedly. "None yet. But the day is young and full of possibilities. What say we start exploring them together?"

He could feel Christie on the other side returning his grin with one of her own. "That sounds like a brilliant idea, partner. Why don't you come to my office, and we can get going?"

"Done. I'll be there in thirty." Jed hung up the phone and trotted out of his room toward his fridge, where he had a light breakfast consisting of a sliced apple, a banana, and a bowl of cereal. He left his house then, his eyes searching the streets for a taxi that would deliver him to his partner's doorstep.

Forty-five minutes later, Jed was sitting in Christie's car, pulling up the steel mill's address on his phone's map.

"How far away is it?" Christie inquired.

Jed made a noncommittal noise, his fingers swiping.

"An hour and ten," he finally stated, staring at the estimated time showing on his screen.

"Oh, wow, that means a road trip." Christie flashed him a smile brimming with childish excitement, and Jed couldn't hold back the laugh that bubbled from within him.

"Indeed. Our first as partners," he murmured, gazing through the windshield at two toddlers that were being escorted by their father into a silver Escalade.

"Let's hope this trip is the first of many in what will be a fruitful professional relationship," Christie raised her coffee cup toward his in mock celebration.

Jed smirked. "Professional relationship?"

"I mean, that is the foundation for whatever exists between us," Christie answered quickly, busying herself sipping her coffee so that Jed wouldn't notice the color rising in her cheeks.

"*Whatever exists between us*," Jed echoed, enjoying himself now. "So strange, the way you say that word. What *does* exist between us, by the way?"

Christie locked eyes with him. "Why don't you tell me, for once?" she asked in a deadpan voice.

Jed's amused expression faltered. For a moment, he seemed on the verge of speaking, actually answering her question rather than deflecting it with another joke, but then the playful glint returned to his eyes.

"All things in due time. Besides, I was only messing with you. Come, let's go."

Were you? Christie thought to herself, turning the ignition and revving the car to a start. *Or did I also see a spark of nervousness in your eyes when I spoke those words?*

The riddle remained unsolved, at least for that moment. Christie's Ford Explorer melded seamlessly into the road's flowing traffic, making its way toward the highway that would lead to the steel mill, where one of their final hopes of solving this murder lay.

CHAPTER 15

"JED, I HAVE TO be brutally honest with you," Christie stated abruptly, her eyes still on the road ahead, her hands clutching the steering wheel.

Jed sat up a bit straighter. "Yes?"

"Your choice of music is terrible." Christie paused a moment after saying that, then burst into helpless giggles.

"Is it, now?" Jed asked numbly, feeling the tension seep from his shoulders. *Damn, she almost had me there.* He didn't think Christie knew it, but the way she had asked him that, he had been expecting something entirely different. His stomach had jumped up to his heart, and his heart had lurched up into his throat.

"I'm sorry, but you have such old-man taste!" Christie exclaimed, continuing unbothered, and entirely unaware of the storm she had stirred up within Jed in that moment. "I mean, who listens to *jazz* on a road trip?" She clamped her lips tightly, trying to hold back the laughter, but it burst forth yet again, filling the car with its staccato high notes.

"It's not old-man taste," Jed retorted playfully, and then sniffed. "It's *refined* taste. I trust you wouldn't know what that word means."

"Oh, you want to bet?" Christie's voice rose, taunting him. She put out her hand. "Hand me my phone from my purse, and disconnect yours. Its time I showed you what real music is like."

Two minutes later, Jed heard Christie's version of *real* music. The beginning instrumental filled his ears, and he instantly recognized the song.

"Taylor Swift?" Jed's voice was marked with dismay. He gave Christie a look which was the very antithesis of a thera-pist's gaze: judgmental.

"Please tell me this is a joke and that you're pulling my leg," Jed uttered with a sigh. "Otherwise, I don't think I can take you seriously after what you just did."

"What?" Christie laughed, delighting in his unease. A sec-ond later, the familiar, swoony voice of the female artist filled the car's interior. "Isn't she just magical?"

"Yes, if you're talking about dark magic," Jed muttered, his comment going unnoticed amidst the song's rapidly ascend-ing tunes. "Can you at least lower the volume a bit, so I'm still sane by the time we reach the steel mill?"

Christie gave him a sidelong look, her mouth parted in a grin, her pearl-white teeth glittering perfectly in the sunlight. Jed's insides turned a little topsy-turvy as he gazed at the sunlit, smiling portrait of Christie. He felt a gush of something hot and buoyant rushing within his veins right then and realized that it was happiness, an emotion he hadn't been on very good terms with for the past few weeks.

Where did I find a partner as mad as her? Jed thought to himself, shaking his head with a small smile.

"What?" Her voice broke his stream of thoughts. He turned toward her and found her attention pinning him.

"What, what?" Jed asked.

"Just then, you were thinking something." Christie shot him another knowing look before returning her attention to the road. "I saw it in your eyes, and in that tiny smile you sometimes give. What were you thinking?"

"I don—it really was nothing," Jed lied.

"Come on, *partner*," Christie pronounced the word so emphatically that it turned comical, causing both of them to crack up. "Aren't you going to share your thoughts with your *partner*?" Once again, she stressed that word to humorous effect, breaking into giggles immediately after. Jed had to fight hard not to join her.

"There's nothing to share." He licked his lips. "I was just thinking about how we're the perfect team."

"Is that so?" Christie's eyebrows arched with surprise. She reached forward a hand and dialed down the music. Taylor Swift's poignantly sad voice quickly faded away to a dim background noise. "Please, tell me why. I'm curious."

"Well," Jed clasped his hands together, rubbed them thoughtfully. "Our personalities, for one. They perfectly complement each other. Like bread and butter. Like morning and night. Like a shower and sleep. Like strawberries and kisses."

Christie smirked to cover up her nervousness at that last bit. "Hmm. Interesting. Care to elaborate?"

"Well, for starters, I'm someone who likes staying in his own shell, and you're the exact opposite of that. Ever since I've met you, you've slowly been prying me out of my cocoon. So, in that sense, we make a good team. You with the loud, easygoing, sociable nature, and me with the brooding, re-served, thoughtful nature. When we come together, we enjoy the different aspects of each other's personalities—things we never found within ourselves."

"Wow." Christie's voice was softly admiring. "That's a deep analysis. Go on. Tell me more."

"Okay." Jed paused for a moment and continued. "Our jobs are the other part of it. They perfectly fit with each other, too. You're a detective, forced by years of training to look at the hard evidence and the details, to analyze a case through an objective, outside observer's viewpoint."

"And you're the opposite," Christie intoned.

"Exactly." Jed nodded. "I'm a therapist, someone whose entire job is to delve deep into the individual psychology of people. When I'm going through a case, I'm looking at it through exactly that lens: the individual-psychological one. Two entirely different ways of solving a problem. When you combine them together, you get a team like ours, which can accomplish everything thrice as fast and with triple the effectiveness."

Jed leaned back against the headrest after he had finished, and silence reigned in the car. Christie drove them quietly down the highway, her eyes only dimly paying enough attention to the road, the rest of her away somewhere else. Jed's words... they had not told her anything new. This was something she had recognized herself some time back. But the fact that Jed had noticed it, too, and decided to word it so properly, meant that it wasn't just Christie's imagination playing tricks on her. There was something here, between the two of them... something which made them such strong friends, partners....and, perhaps, more?

Stop it. You're overthinking. Christie reached forth impulsively with a hand and turned the volume up to drown out her thoughts. Jed looked at her quizzically for a second, then returned his gaze back outside the window, watching the endless concrete jungle of the city zoom past them in rivers of gray and brown.

The steel mill was located in a deserted, cracked parking lot, surrounded on all sides by imposing metal fences and armed guards. It was quite the contrast to the city and the vegetation surrounding it. A dry wind blew, whipping the sparse weeds slipping through cracks in the asphalt. Gravel crunched beneath Jed's boots as he walked alongside Christie, one hand raised before his eyes to shield him from the hurtling sheets of dust.

They had parked at the very edge of the property, and the mill resembled a giant aluminum can placed at the very center of a maze of fences and walkways. Jed and Christie approached the very first of these gates, striding toward a pair of guards who were standing stiffly, staring at them.

Alex used to come here for work every single day? Jed thought, standing to the side while Christie dealt with security, showing them her credentials. *Menial labor really is a life-draining burden for some people.*

They were granted access and continued on their course toward the building, walking a narrow strip of asphalt now. The wind raged and howled unceasingly around them, as if protesting their intrusion into its lands. The sun beat its slightly warm glare onto their necks and back. All the while, the steel mill slowly grew in size, its massive proportions unfolding before them the closer they got to it.

There were another two guards standing sentry at the entrance to the mill. They gave both Jed and Christie a preliminary screening before letting them in. As the pair stepped through the mill's steel gates, the turbulent weather outside ceased instantly and was replaced by the muggy interior of the mill. Here, the wind's howl was taken over by the much louder grinding and whirring and croaking of various kinds of machinery. Conveyor belts were stretched out in the main hall, and Jed saw workers leaning over it, their hands moving with practiced quickness as they continued their monotonous chores.

"May I help you?" A stout, bald man had come out of one of the side offices while they had been staring away. Jed glanced down at his shirt and saw a nametag there, reading: Mason.

"Hello, Mason," Christie spoke curtly, beating Jed to the deduction. "We're visiting this place as part of a murder investigation. You may have already received a call from our office today prior to our visit."

"Ah, yes, the police. Of course." Mason nodded. "You're here for that boy's death, right? What was his name? Alex Gray?

Both Christie and Jed inclined their heads in acknowledgement.

"What can I do for you?" Mason asked.

"Well, we need to speak to Alex's colleagues," Christie began. "Can you tell me which department he worked in?"

"Ah, see, that will be a problem." Mason regarded them both apologetically. "Alex was the only one in his department. He was in charge of stenciling all the pipes and vents here, labelling them according to the chemical they were carrying. It's pretty basic stuff—doesn't really require more than one person."

"So, you're saying…" Christie let her voice trail off.

"I'm saying Alex had no other colleagues." Mason scratched his nose. "And even if he did, I don't think they'd be able to tell you anything about him. That kid was the biggest introvert I've ever seen in my twenty-years here. Always kept to himself, either working quietly or taking cigarette breaks outside."

Jed spoke then, his voice firm and knowing. "He made more than an hour's commute to reach here every day, Mason. Then he spent nine hours working. People in such situations are bound to find, at the very least, acquaintances to pass the time. I'm positive Alex must have, also. Can you recall *any* occasion, any at all, when you saw him with someone else?"

Mason's large, hairless head furrowed with thought as he considered. "If you want, I can take you to Jameson," he admitted reluctantly. "I saw Alex once with him; they were sharing a cigarette together. Perhaps you'll be able to learn something from him, although I seriously doubt it."

"Jameson will be a good start," Christie answered firmly. "Why don't you take us to him, and then we'll handle it from there."

Jameson, also known as the janitor, was a dark-skinned, gangly fellow sporting a snow-white beard and hooded, shrewd eyes. A single toothpick jutted out from the corner of his lip, bobbing up and down with his speech.

"You got that right, mister," he slowly answered Jed's question in a thick Jamaican accent. "I knew the guy. Knew him better than most here, anyway."

"What can you tell us about him?' Christie pressed.

"What would you like to know?"

"What he did at work. What he did during his free time." Christie spread her hands out. "Anything you might think could help us solve your colleague's murder."

"He wasn't my colleague; he was my friend," Jameson answered, looking slightly affronted. "All he did here was work and smoke. We would speak a little while every day during lunch breaks, but it ain't hardly worth mentioning. That boy was a closed book, as closed as they come."

"Did something, *anything*, ever happen at work where you got a glimpse into his life?" Jed probed, staring hard at the man.

Jameson paused and squinted in the distance, as if he were trying to open a portal to see back through time.

"'Twas a month ago when I saw what you saying," he began, his toothpick leaning precariously on the edge of his mouth. "That time, Alex's friends came to pick him up. Otherwise, he'd always go by the bus." Jameson shook his head once, then looked back up at Jed and Christie with the toothpick firmly replanted between his clamped lips. "Those friends of his, they didn't look right. Something was off."

"What do you mean?" Christie asked.

Jameson gave her a sharp, knowing look. "You know what I mean, ma'am. You're a police officer. You're trained to find suspicious people by their appearances. I'm telling you, those people were not right. There's nothing more I can say."

Christie and Jed exchanged glances.

"Could you tell us anything you remember of their appearances or the vehicle they arrived in?" Jed inquired.

Jameson shook his head with certainty. "Faces are a blur. Typical white, Caucasian features, if you know what I mean. The car they drove in was a cherry red Camaro. 73' model, I'd reckon. It was a pretty sweet ride. I remember wondering how those deadbeats could have such a gem."

There was a moment of silence as Jed and Christie absorbed the information. Then, Jed stretched out his hand to shake, and the man took it.

"Thank you for your help, sir," Jed told him, turning around to leave with Christie. They made their winding way back to the building's entrance, then stepped outside into the wind's chaotic embrace, feeling the dull thudding of the machines behind them dying away as they walked to their car.

"Any thoughts for our next move?" Christie asked Jed, her face downturned to shield it from the sun's bright, prickling stare.

Jed grunted. His eyes were staring straight ahead into the empty, undulating fields stretching forth into the horizon.

"I have an idea."

Chapter 16

"THANK YOU, THAT WOULD be great. We'll be waiting for the footage to be sent to us." Christie hung up the phone and put it aside. She turned to Jed.

"In thirty minutes, I guess we'll be nearing the end of this case, one way or the other. We still haven't proven this is anything more than a freak accident. I spoke to the chief. He said this is our last shot at it. No more favors."

Jed let out a long breath, nodding slowly. He clasped his hands behind his back and leaned against them, closing his eyes. "Let me know when we've received it," he muttered.

Christie raised her eyebrows. "Are you sleeping?"

Jed shook his head once, his eyes still closed. "Just thinking."

Christie leaned forward and was almost about to put a hand on his knee before she caught herself. "Care to share your thoughts with me?"

Jed shook his head once again. "They're not worth sharing—at least, not yet. I'm trying to see if there's anything about this case I've missed, any angle we haven't explored yet."

"Gotcha. Guess I'll just grab a coffee in the meantime." There was just a tiny bit of resentment inside of Christie aimed at Jed for withdrawing into his own shell while in her company, but she didn't let it show. She didn't want him any more troubled than he already was.

It was the day after they had visited the mill. Jed had spent the entire previous night finishing his backlog of client-related work. He was finding this increasingly difficult to manage, juggling these two jobs side-by-side.

I might need to make a decision once this case is over, Jed thought to himself, feeling a sluggish weariness creeping into his mind, lulling the fast-flowing river of his thoughts. *Doing two jobs, and both of them so hectic, might not be the best idea long-term. I think I need to stick to one field if I want to remain sane.*

Despite his earlier declaration that he wasn't going to sleep, Jed felt himself sinking deeper and deeper into a fugue-like state as he reclined in that chair, his head resting in his palms. At first, the only thoughts he had were about Alex and the case. But then, his consciousness began to slip slowly away, and with each second, his mind turned more and more incoherent. Soon, before he knew it, Jed was asleep, with his hands somehow still magically twined behind his neck.

The dream came to him again.

It was the same as before. *Jed stood on the sidewalks of a bustling city, peering up at the high-rises scraping the sky, their giant metal bodies glimmering in the buttery sunlight. After that, everything progressed in similar fashion. There was a shimmer, like existence itself had blinked. The city stood deserted in its wake, as empty as a post-apocalyptic wasteland. The noisy chorus of voices was gone, and the wind whistled mournfully in its place, throwing Jed's hair haphazardly around while he gazed at his surroundings.*

Empty streets. Empty shops. Dead skies, with not a single bird soaring the pastel blue landscape. Every trace of life eroded away into nothingness, everything except for him and his stepbrother. Jed turned sideways and found Alex walking toward him from the coffeeshop's entrance, that same dreaded cup in his hand. His stepbrother's gait was eerily similar to the way it had been in the previous dream. Alex's eyes were dark and hooded, his face scrawled with an unreadable expression as his feet carried him toward the edge of the curb, where he raised the coffee to take his first sip.

"Alex!" Jed tried to cry out, knowing with absolute certainty that his mouth would not move. He tried fruitlessly to lunge toward his stepbrother, but some unknown cosmic power had filled his limbs with lead. Jed could do nothing, nothing except watch.

Alex took his sip. A moment later, his hand shot to his chest with frantic urgency, and the cup fell from his hands, spilling its dark brown contents all over the pavement. Then, Alex's eyes shot up toward Jed, pinning him in place with that look of piercing accusation.

"Shoot!" Alex spit out with venomous disappointment, the red lines on his face darkening and finally causing him to crumple to the ground, where he lay like a disjointed, leaking puzzle.

The dream ended, and Jed woke up with a jolt, almost falling out of his chair in his hurry to escape the grim scene he was in. His feet hit the linoleum floor with a loud whack, and the chair protested shrilly beneath him, begging him to have mercy on its rusted joints.

"Jed?"

Breathing hard, Jed turned around to find Christie staring at him. She was standing in the doorway with a look of concern on her face, holding her steaming cup of coffee.

"Are you okay?"

Jed nodded, not meeting Christie's gaze. He realized his hands were gripping the chair's armrests with an unusual tightness and loosened them before fixing his feet firmly on the ground.

"I'm fine." Jed cleared his throat and rose from the chair, grateful to find that his legs weren't wobbly. He looked at Christie now with his familiar, stolid expression. "Just had a bad dream, that's all."

"Uh-huh." Christie's face suggested that she didn't buy that explanation. She was too clever for that. But she also didn't pursue the matter any further, which was a testament to her wisdom. Jed was not at all in an arguing mood at that moment.

She knew how deep a wound this case had struck within him, the kind of wound you take years to forget about, but which begins aching again at the slightest touch. That ache was visible all over Jed's face. Christie just hoped he would open up and share some of his sorrow with her when he was ready.

"We've received the footage from the street," Christie informed him, following Jed out of the station's coffee room. "It's been set up in the conference area we went to last time. Are you ready?"

"As I'll ever be," Jed grunted grimly, walking with her to the door of the conference room and then inside it, where Derek and Graham had already put everything into place. The large monitor was whirring dully, vomiting its contents onto the screen that was placed in the front of the room. The video had been paused, its thumbnail showing a deserted street.

Jed took his place on a seat facing Graham, and Christie sat down beside him. They gestured to them to continue, and Derek picked up a white remote.

"This is footage of the street the Grays live on, an entire week prior to and including the day of Alex's death," Derek explained. "If anyone in the family left or came back to the house at any time, we will know." He pressed the play button, and the frozen image on the screen jerked into motion.

Jed and Christie sat and watched silently. The footage was on fast-forward, for obvious reasons. In the morning, at around 6:30 AM, Jed watched Alex come out of the house and stand on the sidewalk, his posture sagging with the bleariness of sleep. A few minutes later, a faded yellow taxi came to pick him up, and the boy stepped inside, his head bowed and his hands jammed into his pockets.

"That's him going to work," Christie murmured. This was most probably the taxi that would take Alex to one of the bus stops, from which he would catch the coach heading to his workplace.

The footage continued. Morning turned into afternoon, and the area was drenched in the merciless heat of the day. People came and went. Cars were parked and started. Jed saw the door to the Grays' house open multiple times as its other members went on with their different schedules. Cindi left once during the afternoon, returning a few hours later. His father exited at around 11:30 AM. Andy followed an hour or so later. The sun continued on its arcing path in the sky, and soon the day's brightness morphed slowly into the nebulous shadows of dusk. That faint twilight glow began to fade soon after, letting total darkness take its place. The streetlamps flickered to life then, one-by-one, and the street was bathed in their dirty sodium glow.

Jed shifted in his seat. Christie stirred slightly beside him, her sleeves rustling as they brushed the armrests. On the opposite side, Graham cleared his throat and Derek fiddled absently with the white remote. They all waited and watched the unfolding footage in silence.

After night had fallen, the family members all returned, one by one. First was Richard, then Alex soon after him, and Andy an hour after his brother. None of the Gray household members made any detours. They stepped straight into their homes, shutting the door behind them. When they entered the house and vanished inside it, Jed shot Christie a look.

"This is it." His voice was low. Christie bit her lip in tense acknowledgement and returned her eyes to the screen. Whatever evidence or suspicious activity they were looking for, it was going to happen in this timeframe, when Alex was back at home from work. If they were fortunate, their secret to solving this case lay buried somewhere within these few meagre hours of grainy footage.

Jed's thighs tensed with anticipation, and his eyes narrowed, focusing on the screen. His chest rose and fell in rapid breaths. The footage continued, showing the empty street facing the Gray house and nothing else. Seconds went by in the conference room, the clock's gentle ticking seeming to mock them all. Still, they watched, waiting, hoping.

Around 11:45 PM, the door to the Gray household opened, and a figure creeped out. Jed's heart surged within his chest in a rush of excitement.

This is it! he thought with barely contained energy, leaning forward on the seat. *We finally find out what Alex was up to!*

The figure standing outside the house closed the door with an unnatural level of care, as if he were trying not to wake anyone up. Then, he shuffled over to the edge of the street, and the lamp's gritty yellow light washed his face, revealing his features. It was, indeed, Alex.

Jed had to fight the urge to pump his fists in the air and cheer victoriously. Beside him, Christie didn't move an inch, but Jed could sense the same energy crackling within her, winding her up like a coiled spring.

They all watched, their faces wide and eager. Alex came to the edge of the street and simply stood there, his hands jammed into his pockets in his usual style. He looked left and right, like he was searching for someone, and then he took his phone out of his pocket and began swiping away on it.

Who is he meeting this late at night? Jed wondered. A minute later, his question was answered. From the right side of the road, a vehicle came forward, its single headlight like a bright, lidless eye scouring the darkness. It was a motorcycle, and it stopped right next to Alex. The man that was on it put the stand down, rose off the bike, and went toward its backside to open the large black bag that was strapped there. He tugged the zip down and pushed his hands inside, taking them out a moment later holding a white box, which was emblazoned with three red letters.

It was KFC.

The energy in the entire room seemed to fizzle and die. Jed stared at the screen in disbelief, as if in denial of the fact that all their effort had been leading up to this. He turned toward Christie, who was staring at the footage with a deflated face, her lips stretched in a thin, wretched line.

"Let it play," she said hopelessly, her voice hollow. "We have six more days of video. Maybe something will happen."

But nothing happened during those remaining six days, just as they had expected. The Grays followed their same schedules, leaving in the morning and returning after dusk. The house remained closed after that, with the exception of a single boy leaving its confines for a few minutes every day around midnight. Jed and Christie watched six more times as Alex stepped onto the street, looked around, and watched as his food deliveryman stopped beside him, took out his order, and handed it to him.

Derek powered off the monitor after that. He turned toward both of them, his gaze sympathetic.

"What will you do now?" he asked.

Jed met the man's gaze blankly. For the first time in his life, he shrugged with absolute uncertainty.

"I don't know."

Chapter 17

It had been a productive day. Jed decided to stay later at his office to catch up on his work since Alex's case had pulled him away lately.

The last, scant traces of twilight were fading from the city by the time Jed rose up from his chair, his work for the day concluded. He paused to stretch briefly, pushing his arms and torso as far as they would go, relishing the pleasurable sensations that coursed through his flesh as it was allowed to move after hours spent in a single seat. He walked leisurely over to the window, staring through its flat pane at the sky, which was now quickly shifting from a bruised purplish-blue to ebony.

Below the sky, the city was prepping itself for its night-time activities. Streetlamps had begun to ignite, spraying their chlorine-yellow glare onto sidewalks and street corners. Many of the cars on the roads had also turned on their head-lights, which appeared as nothing more than bright-yellow pinpricks from Jed's vantage point.

Inside the office, Jed's desk stood neat and organized. His black laptop was placed in the center, flanked on either side by stacks of papers and files. He cast another look that way and hummed softly in satisfaction. He had gotten a lot done today. At least two days' worth of backlog had been cleared, if not more. He had gone through and finalized more than two dozen client profiles, had completed the necessary research related to them, and most importantly, he had spoken to Max in what had been a long and revealing session.

A small smile creased the corners of Jed's lips now, as he recalled his conversation with the young man. Max had been doing well, much more than well, in fact. His stint at the burger joint was performing marvelously, and he had even taken Shanice out for a fancy dinner after a long, long while. The relationship between those two had also been improving slowly, with their frequency of fights diminishing with the passing of each day.

Jed chuckled softly as he remembered something Max had said to him during the session.

"Ya know, I never realized it properly before, but Shanice looks really beautiful when she's not shouting at me."

Jed had thrown his head back and laughed at that statement, unable to control himself. Max was, indeed, a most interesting and fascinating character. He was one of the people Jed really wanted to see succeed, with all his heart and soul.

Humming softly to himself now, Jed turned from the window and sauntered through the office, basking in the glow of a day well spent. It was one of those rare occasions when everything had gone just right for him.

Or almost everything.

The smile tugging at the corner of his lips sagged a little as that thought came to him. The pleasant gleam in Jed's eyes faded momentarily, while his mind tried to pry itself away from the subject it had swum toward yet again.

Alex.

Jed felt the sense of accomplishment built up within him beginning to crumble at the thought of the case. He had kept himself so busy today that his mind had hardly drifted toward Alex's death. But now that he was free and relaxed, he found himself unable to stop pondering upon it.

Two days had passed since they had seen that footage. They had been two days of zero progress made, zero insights gained about who the killer could be—if there even was a killer.

Is this a normal thing for police officers? Jed wondered, walking back to the window in the hopes that the city's nighttime lights would distract him. *Do they often come across cases they just cannot solve, no matter what, and then have to live with that fact forever?* Jed shuddered. He couldn't imagine doing that for the rest of his life. The idea of leaving a puzzle unsolved, and letting the curiosity gnaw forever... it was too agitating to even consider.

Unable to stop himself, unable to even put up a worthy fight against his mind's insistent calling, Jed let himself think about the case. He let his pent-up thoughts gush in its direction, like a river that could no longer be restrained and simply burst through its barriers.

How had the poison been administered? If it *was* a poison that they hadn't been able to test for yet. Or was it really just a freak accident? That was the central question of the case, assuming that it was a murder. Since they had not been able to deduce any straightforward answer, Jed and Christie had tried to approach it from a circuitous path, by trying to answer the following question instead: *Who* would want Alex dead?

Unfortunately, the furthest they had gotten on this road too had been that uneventful, infuriating footage Jed had laid eyes upon two days ago. That footage showed nothing except for a boy ordering a late midnight snack for himself.

Jed clacked his fingernails against the thick glass, his eyes absently tracking a car slowly coasting beneath his office, its bright fluorescent lights cutting through the darkness.

What were they missing? What angle were they overlooking? The frustration was too much. Every time Jed thought about the case, he felt like he was on the verge of making a game-changing discovery. But so far, he had never managed to make it beyond that. It seemed his feet had been glued there, resigning him to a fate of forever staring wistfully at the vague outline of an idea he could never truly grasp.

The clacking against the window increased as Jed's fingers moved with greater speed, as if he were playing a poignant piano note. He wondered, then, about the other possible outcome this case could have.

Was it possible that this was only an accident? That Alex had simply died of some freak natural causes even the coroner had been unable to discover? Certainly, it was possible. Such things happened in the world quite a lot, much more often than one would imagine.

And yet... *no.* Jed couldn't accept this entire ordeal as an accident. Something within him simply rebelled at the idea. He knew this feeling could just be him acting stupid, maybe being stubborn because this was his stepbrother and Jed felt like he had something to prove to himself, to his father, and to the world. But even this thought seemed false. No matter what Jed did, no matter how many times he approached the case with a renewed, unbiased stance, he couldn't shake the feeling that something was terribly suspicious.

Why can't I just find out what it is instead of running in circles, chasing my own tail? Jed sighed wearily. It was time for him to go home. The longer he stayed in his office, the quicker he would go crazy butting heads against this unyielding brick wall of a riddle.

He picked up his phone from the desk and rotated it playfully in his hand, deciding what he would do next. The apartment seemed like a nice idea; Jed could relax there, take a long, hot shower to unwind, and then maybe read one of those murder mystery novels aging on his shelf.

Or he could call Christie, and they could go out for a nice dinner. That was also a possibility. Jed's pulse quickened immediately at the idea. A wry grin twisted his lips. It was strange that even now, after so much time spent together working, he still reacted like this at the thought of meeting Christie in a non-work-related setting.

Why? Why did she make his heart beat in dizzying spirals? Jed did not know, and he never got to. He also didn't get to decide what course of action he should take tonight. Nor did he actually manage to crack the riddle. All three questions went unanswered in his mind and were brushed aside as his phone began ringing in his hand.

Jed's gaze flicked down to the screen. It was his mother. He answered the call after the first ring and put the phone's cool surface against his ear, speaking in a calm, unbothered voice which belied all the confusing turmoil in him.

"Hi, Mom. How are you?"

"I'm okay, Jed." Laurie's voice was oddly flat. "I called because I want to tell you something. But first, you must promise you won't instantly freak out. Promise me that, Jed."

"Okay, okay, Mom. I promise." Jed tried to keep his voice light but succeeded only halfway. His heart had suddenly tripled its activity inside his chest.

"So..." His mom paused, uncertain, and Jed wondered what it could be.

"It's okay, Mom." He forced a weak laugh to ease her nerves. "I already promised you I won't freak out. So, just give it to me straight."

"Right." Jed's mom cleared her throat. Then she added, in that same, flat voice. "Someone left a knife outside my apartment door."

Jed frowned. He didn't understand what his mom meant. "A knife? What do you mean?"

He heard his mother swallowing on the other end, trying to bite down on the emotion she didn't want to let seep into her voice. "Right outside my apartment, Jed. On the hallway's carpet. Someone left a big, silver knife, pointing at my door."

Realization dawned on Jed, crashing within him in a broiling wave of fear and panic.

"*What?*" He shot to his feet, all his previous promises forgotten, his eyes turned into slits and his jaw clenched. "What? Why didn't you tell me this before?"

"I just saw the knife right now!" Laurie protested, and then added, "You promised you wouldn't freak out, Jed! I'm okay! There was no one else in the hallway, and I just picked up the knife and carried it inside, locking the door behind me."

"I'm coming over to your place." Jed was breathing in heavy, guttural rasps, a single muscle twitching sporadically in his jaw.

"You don't need to," she replied quickly. "I'm perfectly fine. I don't want to let one stupid prank derail your entire night."

"Nonsense," Jed uttered in a flat, even tone which gave no room for argument. "I'm coming over right now. Until then, stay put and do not open the door for anyone but me."

Twenty-five minutes later, Jed was in his mom's apartment, sitting on her couch, with the knife held in his hands. He turned it over slowly, his heart sinking in his chest as he took in its wickedly sharp edge and monstrous size. This was a butcher knife, one meant for processing cows and elk. It was no joke.

"You know what this is related to, right?" Jed murmured softly, unable to tear his eyes away from the knife and its ghastly savagery.

His mother made a quizzical noise.

"This is about those threatening calls you were getting at night," Jed spoke, finally turning his face toward his mother and regarding her with darkened eyes, "the ones you wrote off as prank calls. Well, tonight, I think we can clearly see they were not just pranks. If this creep has the guts to come over right outside your door and leave such a conspicuous object there, then there's no reason to assume that he won't break into your place as well."

Laurie bit her lips in worry, not saying anything. She didn't need to. Jed had already made his decision.

"I'm calling Christie," Jed announced, rising from the couch and taking his phone out of his pocket. "I'm going to ask her to double the security outside this apartment. If this lunatic somehow managed a stunt like this with two officers stationed on the premises, then who knows what else he can do?" Jed raised the phone and began to dial it. He stopped halfway, though, and slowly turned around to face his mother.

"Actually, you know what..." his face had that distant gleam which overtook it whenever he was hatching a plan. "Mom, how do you feel about staying over at a friend's place for the next week?"

"A friend's place?" Laurie's forehead wrinkled. "What will that achieve?"

Jed took a long pause, working out the details of his strategy, then answered. "We can lure the stalker in this way. You won't be at your apartment, and we'll remove the security from here. Or rather, we'll place undercover cops on duty." He gave his mother a shrewd look. "That way, he will attack even more confidently, thinking no one's around. He won't realize your apartment's empty, and that the building has armed guards in it. If he makes a move, we'll get him."

Jed's mom opened her mouth to protest, saw the stern, shadowed look on Jed's face, and closed it again, realizing that her son would not listen.

"Think about it," Jed told her. "That way, I can rest easy, too, knowing you're completely safe. You can stay with one of your friends from the book club, that red head who keeps coming over."

"Clara?" Laurie laughed softly. "Hmmm. Now that you've mentioned it, it's not a bad idea. We've both stayed over at each other's place so many times it won't be awkward at all."

"That does it, then. We have a plan. Worst-case scenario? Your weird caller just doesn't show up. That's fine by me. Maybe it'll mean he's finally chickened out." Jed took the phone out of his pocket, dialed Christie's number, and then walked over to the empty dining room, his eyes narrowed into slits and his mouth set in a grim line.

"Hello, yes, Gray?"

"Christie." Just that single word and Christie immediately knew something really bad had happened.

"Jed, what is it?"

"It's my mother…" Jed paused, to steady his voice. "Someone left a knife outside her apartment door."

"*What?*" Christie practically hissed the words, and Jed heard the sound of a chair being thrown back against a desk.

"Calm down," he told her. "My mom's fine. I'm with her right now, and I'm just about to take her to stay over at her friend's place for the weekend. In the meantime, did you get any helpful intel from the phone trace?"

"No, we didn't." Christie's voice was apologetic. "The damn caller used a burner phone. He's clearly being very careful. But we'll get him, don't you worry. By the way, where is your mom's friend's place? I can station a guard there, too, just in case, you know."

"Yeah, that's probably a good idea. I'll text you the details." Jed snuck a glance back at the living room and saw that his mother was no longer there. She had probably gone to pack. He brought the phone closer against his mouth and

184

whispered. "She's trying to act brave, Christie, but I know she's scared. That knife has really upset her."

"Of course, Jed. Who wouldn't be terrified out of their wits in such a situation?" There was a pause on the other end. "I'll have a guard stationed at your mom's place as well. I'm thinking the caller doesn't know she's gone, so he might swing by again. This time, we'll use the apartment as a trap."

"Yeah, I was just about to suggest the same thing." Jed sighed. "You do that, Christie. I'll talk to you later, okay? I need to get my mom somewhere safe so I can stop worrying about her. We still have a case to solve, after all."

"Yeah, I get it. I'll speak to you later, Gray. Don't worry about Laurie. On behalf of the NYPD, I promise you no harm will come to her."

A faint smile crossed Jed's lips, a tiny needle of sunlight brightening his face's bleak landscape. "Thanks, Christie. Talk to you later."

"Take care, Jed." Christie spoke with genuine concern. "Bye."

Jed hung up the phone, took a moment to gather himself, then took his mother to her new place of residence for the next while, a place where she would, hopefully, be safe.

Chapter 18

Peace.

Everything in the area screamed that single word. Or, perhaps, scream wasn't the best way to describe a place as calming and soothing as Jed's retreat. Perhaps the better word would be whisper. Yes, the place seemed to whisper *peace*, its voice filled with the sweetness of an enchantress who could take away all your fears and worries for good.

Jed sat in the cabin, listening to the fire crackle and spit in its hearth. Right outside, if he strained his ears hard enough, he could hear the forest's soft rustle as its shed leaves stirred in the wind. *I should've done this a long time ago*, Jed thought, wrapping his woolen shawl around his shoulders and snuggling deeper into his cozy armchair. His eyes tracked the bright tongues of flames as they rollicked back and forth like mischievous imps, throwing stray embers in the air that swished slowly toward the floor.

Outside the cabin, beyond the wild patches of grass that poked up from the ground, there was a lake nestled by the foothills of the mountains. On this bright afternoon, the lake's surface lay absolutely still and clear, reflecting the blue skies in its silver depths. Inside the cabin, resting calmly in his chair, Jed's mind lay just as clear as that lake, his thoughts filled with a newfound clarity and perception like they had never seen before.

If I had done this earlier, Alex's body wouldn't have had to lie in the morgue for so long, Jed thought. He raised his cup of steaming hot chocolate to his lips and took a small sip, savoring the rich scent of cocoa filling his nostrils.

It was a day and a half following his mother's knife incident. After dropping her off at her friend's place, with a guard outside, Jed had felt some measure of calm return to him, knowing his mother was safe. Now, he could finally focus all his efforts on the problem at hand.

Last day to crack the case, Jed thought, taking another small sip. The thought didn't bother him the way it would have if he had still been within the city's twisted, noisy confines. No, now he felt confident, here in the vast openness of the wilderness, with nothing around him for miles but keening cold winds and trilling birds. Jed felt a strong certainty within him that he would make some kind of progress today. He could sense it. In just half a day of retreat, his mind already felt like a knife whose bluntness had fully been sharpened away.

Twenty-four hours. Out of which, six have already been used. Make the rest count. His inner voice pepped him up, and Jed nodded to himself. Today was the last day Alex's body was going to remain in the morgue. They had been delaying the Grays' requests for burial for quite a while, but no more. The family was getting agitated, eager to put their beloved to rest. Besides, the police were bound by law to honor the deceased's family's wishes after a certain period of time. After days upon days of fruitless banging against walls and running into dead ends, their time had finally run out. If they needed any further evidence from the body that they had not already collected, it would be gone forever.

Not yet, Jed corrected himself softly. *I still have this day. And I will make it count.* He chugged the remainder of his drink and put the mug on the side-table, readying his mind for its final excursion into the case.

But before that, Jed had some self-reflection of his own to do. Spending time here in the cabin's peaceful solitude had made him realize why his brain had been working so haltingly in this case: it was because of Jed's past memories. His memories of his father, and of his own days of substance abuse, were like thorns he had always tiptoed over. Now, it was time to walk through that field, full stride. That was the only way he would make it to the end of this mystery.

Jed closed his eyes. He made no effort to concentrate on a particular memory. He simply sat there, all his guards fully down, letting his mind wander wherever it wanted. It was a terrifying feeling of vulnerability, very much akin to swimming naked in a pool filled with hungry piranhas. But Jed did it. He forced aside all the barriers within himself and sat, statue-like, observing his mind's random motion, waiting to see where it would go. Jed's eyes were closed. His breathing was long and slow. Soon, his awareness faded from that room and the present moment, awakening in different, darker times.

He remembered.

A small, dingy bed. Its bed sheets were soiled, and the pitiful excuse for a pillow was caked with mud. A single fan croaked painfully overhead, blowing muggy gusts of wind downward. Two bulbs were fitted into the room's leftmost corner. One had stopped working, and the other was flickering, coating the walls and the floor in alternating hues of black and urine-yellow light.

Jed sat up.

He looked around. Or rather, he observed himself looking around, in his own memory. It was almost like watching a video someone had made of him. He was lying on the bed, his gangly limbs covered by a gauzy white sheet. There were two more beds in the room, and the remaining space was littered with mattresses. There were at least half-a-dozen people filling these empty spaces, and as Jed's gaze fell upon them, he saw and felt himself suck in a large breath.

There were wraiths lying everywhere—hollowed out, sunken faces, and bodies that were like twigs placed upon the mattresses and beds, their toothpick arms and legs twisted at odd angles. Vacant eyes stared up at the moldy ceiling, mouths stretched into hideous, dream-like smiles. In some of the people, their smiles exposed their teeth, and that was not a pretty sight. Each tooth was coated with a yellowish-green decay, resembling a crumbling tombstone that was just about to topple from its place. Jed looked around further.

The horror continued.

He saw the needles, spoons, and lighters lying on a steel tray on one of the corner tables. Each needle was rusted, worn with use. The spoons' middles were all a charred crisp, and their edges were coated with a flaky white powder. A bunch of lighters lay next to the spoons and needles. One was a vintage, bright pink lighter with a small joker's face engraved on it. Jed saw his own eyes zoom in on the picture; the joker seemed to be smiling at him, flashing his perfect white-teeth and those wide, laughing eyes in a taunting gesture.

Someone coughed in the room.

Jed's eyes flicked toward the person, who was a young woman that seemed to have aged two more decades in this place. Her face was a sack of weary bones, and her hair, which might have once been a thing of lustrous blonde splendor, now hung across her cheeks in limp, discolored rags.

The girl coughed again, her eyes closed, her hands clasped across her chest. A thin dribble of vomit oozed out from the corner of her lips and trickled down her chin. Jed watched her mutely, understanding with horror what was happening. The drugs had knocked her out, and she was choking on her own vomit now, suffocating to death unless someone turned her over onto her side.

He tried to rise off the bed to help the poor young woman, but he couldn't. Of course he couldn't. This was the past. It was unchangeable. It had already happened. He was just reliving it now, seeing all the details with a clearer eye.

The girl continued coughing, each cough louder and more choked than the last. Her body convulsed. Her chest spasmed. Bouts of vomit erupted from her splayed lips and splattered her neck and shoulders. Still, she continued to cough and wheeze violently, and Jed saw the color draining from her face.

His face turned to the side then, removing the girl from view, and Jed understood why he was not helping her. He was in no condition to. His own drug, a dull brown stub of lighted marijuana laced with heroin, was clamped between his two fingers. And behind him, on the sodden sheets, there were more than a dozen such stubs lying around, their buts crusted with smoke.

The girl coughed some more. Jed saw himself raise the joint to his lips and take in a large drag. His vision shimmered after that, and a cool blissfulness stole its way into his mind. Jed heard himself sighing with deep contentment. And then he felt his own body reclining back on that filthy bed, lying down to face the chipped ceiling. The last thing he saw of the room, before his eyes faced this hellish world's concrete sky, was the girl's twisting body, and a brown packet right next to her, across which the following had been labeled in bright yellow letters: Burger King.

The memory ended.

Merciful silence, at first. Then awakening.

Jed rose from the poisonous depths of that memory like a man clawing forth from a pool of ash-choked water. He sucked in a large, raspy breath, looking at the room around him, his hands tightened on the armrests of his chair. Everything was the same as it had been; the fire was still sputtering in the hearth, the light breeze was still gently plodding the planet's earthen chest, and the chill had only increased outside.

Calming down somewhat, Jed took in another lungful of fresh air. Was it his imagination, or was there a faint scent of mold in his nose? The bitter, lingering aftertaste of weed in his mouth? It was probably just his imagination. He threw his blanket aside and rose to his feet, the answer swimming in his head. He had found it. He had finally found it. It had been a miracle it hadn't occurred to him earlier, considering how obvious it had been.

"I knew there was something we were missing," Jed grimly murmured to himself, searching for his phone. He could not remember where he had kept it. Usually, when he went on these retreats, he kept all electronic devices aside during his stay, intending to connect with nature as much as he could.

As Jed discovered a frustrating fifteen minutes later, his phone was lying on the carpeted floor of his bedroom, hidden from view within a tangled heap of blankets.

"There you are, you little bugger." He plunged his hands into the blankets' messy folds and withdrew them, holding his phone. Jed began to dial a number then, his fingers moving swiftly. He knew exactly who he had to call. He should have done it a lot sooner, but it wasn't something he would normally do. Jed knew needed to be careful how he handled it.

The ringing tone buzzed in Jed's ears. He stood by his bedroom window like a man transfixed, staring at the lush sprawling greenness of the world outside.

The ringing continued. Once. Twice. Then thrice, and on and on even after that. By its sixth ring, Jed's left foot was tapping the floor impatiently. By the eighth ring, he had begun to remove the phone from his ear, thinking it would not be answered.

On the ninth ring, someone picked up.

"Mr. G?"

Jed jammed the phone back against his ear. His face widened into a victorious grin.

"Hello, Max. How are you?"

CHAPTER 19

"I'm hangin' okay, Mr. G." Max's amiable tone filtered in from the receiver's end. "What's up?"

"I'm alright," Jed answered, then scratched his chin thoughtfully before adding, "I'm doing well, actually, and will be doing even better depending upon how this conversation goes."

Silence from the other end. "… How's that?"

Jed walked to the end of his bed and sat down on it. With one hand, he propped a pillow behind his back and leaned against it. "I need your help, Max. *That* kind of help, the kind that relates to your past. You think it could happen?"

"Ohhh." Max chuckled. "I get it. You want the street deets from me."

Jed let out a small laugh of his own. "Sure, if that's what you want to call it. And only if you are comfortable talking to me about this. Don't feel that you have to answer my questions."

"Ask away, man."

Jed paused for a moment to gather his thoughts. Outside, the wind had increased in intensity. The grass was now letting out a dim susurration.

"What do you know about… smuggling drugs?" Jed asked slowly.

"Smuggling?" Max's frown could be felt through the phone. "Whatcha mean?"

"Excellent question." Jed tapped a finger against his thigh. "In a way that would not cast any suspicion. In a way that would even allow young kids and teenagers to become a part of the program, helping them earn a little income on the side."

"Sure." Max grunted. "That shit's happened a lot—and is still happening. The kids tape the packets of drugs to their stomachs and inside their boxers. Then they g—"

"—that's not what I'm talking about, Max," Jed cut in. "I'm talking about drugs being transported under the guise of… food deliveries. Say, someone is standing outside their house waiting for their Chick-fil-A order to show up. Then a guy arrives, on a bike wearing a black, nondescript rider's uniform. He takes out a box which does look identical to a Chick-fil-A box. He hands it over to the kid, in broad daylight, with the cameras watching. No one bats an eye because everyone assumes its actually food. But unbeknownst to them, the box contains a shipment of drugs the kid is supposed to store somewhere, and then smuggle onward when the situation arises."

There was a long and thick quiet that reigned on the other end. When Max finally spoke, it was in a surprised voice, one filled with grudging admiration.

"Damn, Mr. G. You figure that out all on your own? Geez, you should be a detective, man, I'm tellin' you."

I already am. Or at least trying to be. Jed bit back that reply, which would've derailed the conversation, and spoke patiently. "Do you get what I'm trying to explain to you, Max? Have you seen such a thing before?"

"Aye." Max clicked his tongue with regret. "During my… bad days, I was almost about to get all tangled up in it myself. But point being, what you've just said is real. I've seen it myself, with my own two eyes. And you'd be surprised to know, Mr. G, but it happens a lot more than you educated people think."

I don't doubt that. Jed leaned back on the bed, his face marred with lines of satisfaction, his lips chewing thoughtfully.

"You there, Mr. G?"

Jed almost started. He had sunk so deep into his own whirlpool of thoughts that Max's voice was like an alien hand plunging through the icy depths to yank him back into the real world. He adjusted the phone against his ear and spoke.

"I'm here, Max. Just thinking about what you said."

"You do that, man. You do that. Thinking is definitely your thing, not mine." Max sniggered lightly at his own joke. "In the meantime, you okay with me dashing off? I actually had plans to go to brunch with Shanice, and she's almost ready…"

"Oh, of course, don't let me keep you," Jed answered quickly, and then smiled. "Thank you for the confirmation you gave me today, Max. You may not realize it, but it seems that, as of late, you've been helping me a lot more than I've been of assistance to you."

"Aww, stop it, Mr. G." Max sounded embarrassed. "You know I'll never be able to make up for what you did for me. I was on a one-way train right toward destroying ma'self, and you gave me a new life. No matter what I do, I'll never be able to thank you enough for it."

Jed's smile was so wide and warm it could've melted the entire sheets of snow blanketing the ground outside, if there had there been any. But it was still too early in the winter for that.

"No need to thank me, Max. I just gave the advice. You're the one who acted on it. If you're searching for someone to pat on the back, then just take a look in the mirror."

"Uh huh," Max sounded like he was struggling to hold back his emotions. "You always know what the right thing to say is, huh? I'd guess that's what the whole point of being a therapist is. Well, anyways, I got to run now, Mr. G. Talk to ya later."

"Take care," Jed said before closing the call. He looked outside for a few more seconds, basking in the satisfaction that he finally had something to do, a road to pursue. Then, he picked up his phone again and dialed another number. This one answered on the second ring.

"Looks like someone's missing me on their little retreat." Christie's voice bubbled through from the speaker, as soft and warm as fresh spring water.

"You know me," Jed grinned wryly. "I don't enjoy anything unless my partner-in-crime is there with me."

"Partner-in-crime!" Christie whistled softly. "Oooh! I didn't realize our relationship had progressed to this stage." Her voice seemed to quiver slightly with nervousness.

"I—I meant that we catch criminals together," Jed explained a bit hurriedly, feeling his throat drying up somewhat. "So, we're partners-in-crime, technically."

"Of course, I get it. I was just messing with you." Christie turned serious. "So, how come you called? Or were you *actually* missing me?"

"No, I wanted to talk about the case," Jed answered immediately, and then, upon realizing how that sounded, he added quickly, "Not that I didn't want to talk to you. I do, always. You're one of the few people I genuinely enjoy conversing with."

"Hmmm." Christie's wide smile was practically visible through the phone. "Carry on."

"Right." The merriness faded from Jed's face as his thoughts shifted entirely to their puzzle. "I made an inroad into the investigation."

"Did you?" Even Christie sounded curious and business-like now. "Tell me what?"

"It wasn't KFC," Jed stated simply, and upon the confusing silence that came from the other end, he went on to explain. "The video footage we saw, of Alex stepping out at night and receiving his food. There's a chance, a good chance, in fact, that it wasn't KFC at all."

"… Then what was it?"

"Drugs," Jed told her grimly. "This is apparently another trick the gangs in the city are employing. They have their men dress up in black rider uniforms and drive a bike. The drugs are contained within the bag in the bike, stored securely in the container of any specific food outlet—like KFC." There was a pause, and Jed's eyes clouded over while he thought of the past. A couple of seconds passed, and then he added in a whispery tone, "or Burger King."

"So, you're saying Alex was doing the same thing?" Christie asked. "He was also involved in drug trafficking?"

"It's highly likely."

"Okay." Christie stopped and thought. A moment later, she spoke again, voicing her concerns. "That is a fantastic breakthrough, Jed. Unfortunately, the existence of a drug cartel such as this will not be enough to let us keep Alex's body in the morgue for an additional week. We need to give the superintendent some concrete intel to go on, a strong reason why we believe Alex is involved in this drug trafficking ring."

"Not one—we have two reasons," Jed uttered firmly. "One was his father's behavior when we asked him whether Alex was involved in any suspicious activities. The man said no when you asked him that, Christie, but he was clearly lying. And so was Andy. It was clear as day in their postures. Trust me, I know. I'm a therapist."

"Okay." Christie sounded a tad uncertain "And the second reason?"

"The second reason is in the footage itself," Jed began. "Alex steps out of his house and waits for the rider to arrive." He paused for a moment to let Christie grasp what he was trying to convey. "Think about it, Christie: who *waits* for a delivery man on their street?" Jed let out a harsh chuckle. "I can't believe we never noticed that before. Whenever anyone orders food, the most common course of action is to wait for the rider to call you once they've reached your house, and then step outside to get the food. Even people who are starving don't leave the house beforehand, standing on the sidewalk in the dead of night, all alone."

There was a long pause on the other end, after which Christie spoke slowly.

"You're right. You're absolutely right. The fact that Alex left his house beforehand should've sent up red flags immediately."

"Exactly," Jed agreed. "And him stepping outside earlier than usual also fits perfectly with our drug theory. Obviously, the man bringing him the drugs wouldn't want to stay parked in the street a second longer than necessary. Disguise or no disguise, smuggling is a tricky business, and you can get caught at any time. The smartest thing to do is get in and out as swiftly as possible."

"Yes, yes, correct." Christie's voice was low, whispery, tangled in the chaotic web of her own racing thoughts. She spoke again, and Jed heard the sound of a chair scraping, as if she was getting up to leave. "I'm going to go to the chief with this evidence and explain your theory to him. If you're correct, and if Alex was involved in a drug cartel that ultimately resulted in his death, then we will need to extend the time his body stays in the morgue to eventually establish the cause of his death.

"Yeah, you do that," Jed said, rising from the bed and walking over toward the window, where the rain was showering the ground with its tiny, pretty drops.

"Great. I'll talk to you soon." Christie paused, then. "When are you coming back, by the way?"

Jed continued staring outside, his eyes absently tracking a lone windblown leaf that was sailing through the air, its crunchy yellow body catching the faint sunbeams, seeming to be ablaze.

"I was planning to stay overnight and head back in the morning." His voice was a mix of reluctant acceptance and excitement. "But I guess due to current developments, I'll be returning home today."

"Oh, okay." Christie sounded pleased at this news, even though she had tried to come across as sympathetic. An amused smile tugged at the corner of Jed's lips.

"Well, I guess I'll see you tonight, then," Christie spoke.

"Indeed." Jed inclined his head in acknowledgement. "See you soon, Detective."

He hung up the phone and looked around at his room, where his suitcase lay, and his clothes lay neatly folded on the chest of drawers. Outside, in the lounge, were the remainder of his belongings: his charger, blanket, slippers, and even a packet of coffee beans.

It was time to leave. Letting out a prolonged sigh, Jed turned back and gave the mystical world outside his window a final, wistful look. Everything was glowing with a rich burst of color. The grass was a blazing orange, sleet clinging to its blades glimmering in the sun like glass. The trees stood straighter than usual, their barks damp and dark. The sky was a clear, unblemished canvas of azure. Everything seemed a perfectly drawn painting. Unfortunately, Jed would not be here to appreciate it.

He turned from the window and began to pack.

CHAPTER 20

THE CITY HAD NOT changed in Jed's short absence. It was the same as it had always been, a sprawling metropolis with its labyrinthine concrete streets and looming structures jutting from the ground like a buried giant's fingers. Cars filled every inch of the roads, horns blaring ceaselessly. In the remaining space of the sidewalks and curbs, a steady stream of people flowed back and forth. Jed witnessed a myriad of different colors, ethnicities, and faces all smudging together into a giant, blurred melting pot, too chaotic to ever make sense of.

How do so many people fit in one place? he thought with wonderment, idly gazing upon a woman in a beige fur jacket who was crossing the road, her eyes upturned haughtily. On the leftmost end of the sidewalk, a couple was walking their Chihuahua, and the tiny, rodent-like creature scurried to keep up with them, its beady black eyes rushing over a world it could never take in completely.

Jed leaned back in the driver's seat of his jeep for a moment to lessen the immense sensory input of the city's thrumming heart. He released a big sigh and let himself adjust to the constant din and activity of his home. He had been living in this place for many years now, but just a short break into the wilderness had rebooted his system completely, and now the city seemed almost overwhelming in its humongous size and scope.

Maybe I'm getting old, Jed mused, one corner of his mouth curling in a sour smile. That was not exactly true. He had still not hit his aging stage yet, not by a large margin. Besides, there was a lot left for him to do in his life—clients to help, puzzles to solve, perhaps even a special someone to settle down with one day...

Jed's stomach did a queasy cartwheel, with thoughts about Christie following on its heels. He twined his hands together on the steering wheel and stared down at the lines crisscrossing over his palms.

Was that why he was so nervous? Because he was meeting Christie after one days' break? Surely not. Surely, he couldn't have gotten so used to talking with his partner that an overnight away was enough to make him start missing her.

And yet, Jed couldn't think of any other reason to be so on edge. At first, he had assumed it to be just because of his return to the city's fast-paced atmosphere, but that was not quite it. There was something greater at play here. The more Jed pondered upon it, the more he realized that his racy pulse and slightly aching palms were because of his reunion with his partner.

When did I let her get such a strong hold over me? Jed wondered with a brief, humorless chuckle, his eyes fixed out the window as he turned a corner and began trundling down a less busy street toward the police station.

Regardless of how he felt, one thing was certain. A part of Jed was glad to be back because he could resume his work on Alex's case, which had taken on a fresh new tone after their discovery regarding the drugs. After Jed's initial call to her, Christie had phoned him back and told him they had been given permission to keep Alex's body in the morgue for an additional week. Christie had further added that the chief had informed her of the harsh reaction he had received from the Gray family upon informing them that their deceased's body would be kept at the morgue for an additional period.

"I was told that we need to wrap this up as soon as we possibly can," Christie had said to him. "The Chief even used the word *Godspeed*. When he says that, you know he means business."

Well, let's see how fast we can untangle this case. Jed saw the police station's imposing gray bulk approaching. He slowed the jeep down and quickly spotted a place to park. He eased into it, then got out.

He began to take long, slow strides forward, his knees suddenly feeling stiffer than normal. The wooden doors to the entrance swung open, and a woman walked out, her black ponytail swinging behind her. Jed gave her a curt nod as he passed, and then he was inside the station, walking toward Christie's office.

Christie was waiting for him inside.

Despite his best attempts to not think about the reunion, Jed had been unable to keep his mind entirely away from it. His imagination had conjured up various scenarios, each cheesier than the last. Now, as he stepped inside the cozy interior, his eyes fell upon Christie's smiling figure and all thoughts seemed to desert him.

Her hair was pinned behind her head in a high ponytail, which made her appear magnitudes more attractive than she had always looked. Or was it their twenty-four hour separation? There was a faint touch of rouge on her cheeks, and her lips were lightly dabbed with a cream-colored shade of lipstick. She was wearing white pants and a crisp blue shirt.

"Hello, Detective." Jed smiled at her, feeling the dryness in his mouth and the dizzying tremble of his heart.

"Hello to you, too." Christie stepped forward and, much to Jed's surprise, hugged him. It was a proper hug, not those formal kinds acquaintances give one another. Christie's arms went around Jed's shoulders and enveloped his back. Her chestnut hair tickled the nape of his neck, and her body lightly brushed his.

Jed had to exert a considerable level of willpower to remain steady on his feet. His entire body felt like it had been doused with saline and wrapped in coils of conductive wire. Energy, a buzzing and powerful energy, seemed to radiate right from his bones down to the very tips of his toes. Christie's perfume, a light and musky sandalwood scent, filled his nostrils, making him lightheaded where he stood. In that moment, though he would feel embarrassed about it later, Jed forgot entirely about the investigation and was aware only of his partner's proximity to him.

The moment, though it seemed to stretch eons long, finally ended. Christie pulled back, and Jed had to struggle to cover the look of disappointment that flashed across his features.

"I missed you," Christie murmured softly, shyly, then took a brisk step back to reestablish the distance between them.

Jed cleared his throat. He was afraid that if he spoke, his voice would come out high and squeaky.

"I missed you, too," he finally replied, grateful that there was nothing marking his tone except for a slight quiver.

They stood there for a tiny while longer, the shy awkwardness between them thickening the air far more than Christie's perfume. Finally, it was Jed who moved and got the ball rolling.

"So." He motioned vaguely with his hand. "Where are we with the investigation?"

"Right." Christie's eyes narrowed in their usual, business-like manner. "As I told you before," she gestured for him to sit, pulling out a chair of her own, "a body, even an embalmed one, can only be kept in a morgue for up to two weeks. All blood, urine, and hair samples are taken prior to the embalming, so it can be released to the family for burial as soon as possible.

"Okay." Jed sat down on his own chair and crossed his legs. "You already told me that the chief managed to get us an additional week, right?"

Christie nodded. "He did, but a week might not be enough for us to reach a conclusion." She raised a hand in response to Jed's look of surprise. "You managed to give us valuable intel, no doubt. But tracking that intel, tracing down the gang responsible for transporting these drugs, and then finding out how they are related to Alex," she spread both palms open, "... it's a long task. It will definitely take more than a week."

"So, you're saying..." Jed rubbed his chin pensively. "After this week ends, we can still keep Alex's body in the morgue?"

"We can keep it for another week or so," Christie repeated. "After that, it gets buried forever. We will have no way of determining if Alex was killed by a newly synthesized toxin or something similar, since we don't have his body to run the tests on."

"Won't his blood samples be enough?" Jed inquired.

"No. If we're dealing with an entirely new poisoning agent, some kind of concoction similar to what killed Joel, we need Alex's body to test our results. Muscle contraction, arterial blockage, and other such things can't be found in a blood sample. I spoke to one of the forensic analysts—they told me this." Christie drew in a tense breath. "So, this is our last shot to find a clue."

Jed nodded in understanding. "Well, looking for clues is something I might be good at. But tracking down drug-peddling gangs is something entirely out of my areas of expertise, I'm afraid."

Christie smiled thinly. "Don't worry, we know that. You've already made so much progress in this investigation all on your own." She sniffed and upturned her nose. "It's time the police department showed you what it's capable of. I will reach out to the drug squad to see if they have any intel about using delivery drivers as drug couriers."

Jed laughed briefly. "I'm sure your department can do wonders. I have just one request, though."

Christie stared at him. "Which is?"

"You need to take me along with you when you infiltrate the gang."

"Absolutely not." Christie shook her head vehemently, her eyes possessing that hard shine which Jed had glimpsed before in the eyes of other stern, uncompromising lawmen.

"Why not? Think about it; it makes sense." He leaned forward in the chair, his features morphing into that serious, penetrating therapist's gaze he used when making an important point to his clients. "I've been with this investigation from the very start. I know all its intricate details. Not only that, but I also know the victim's family personally!" He leaned back again. "It would only make sense if I'm made a part of this task, too. I might notice something the police have overlooked."

Christie stared hard at him, her expression inscrutable. "It's going to be dangerous."

Jed shrugged nonchalantly. "Life is dangerous."

"Someone might get hurt."

Jed shrugged again, with equal indifference. "Everyone's hurting in this world, in one way or another. That doesn't mean we should lock ourselves up and refuse to step outside."

Christie sighed, and now the unhappiness was clearly visible on her face. It shadowed the borders of her eyes in dark smudges of fear. "You're not going to give up, are you?"

"Never in a million years." Jed flashed her a sardonic grin. "So, it's settled then, right? I am to accompany you on this latest expedition, and wherever else you might go after that."

Christie nodded in reluctant defeat. "But on one condition only." Her face suddenly hardened, the lively color in her skin quickly solidifying into the icy sheen of marble. She held up a single, erect finger.

"What?" Jed asked.

"You do *exactly as I say, whenever I say it.*" Christie's voice was like a diamond, and her eyes allowed for no argument or complaint.

"Understood," Jed agreed instantly, crossing his arms across his chest. This side of Christie was one he seldom had the chance to witness, but it always made him slightly nervous and thrilled. His skin began tingling when she displayed such assertiveness. Jed suspected it was the kind of tingling that bordered right on arousal, if not outright being that. He cleared his throat loudly, hoping that would help clear the expression on his face. "Whatever you command, I'll follow in the field, without question. But then, you must also agree to keep me in the loop regarding any new developments—the very moment they're made."

"Agreed," Christie grunted and then leaned back, her face resuming its soft, gentle look as she relaxed. "Be up tomorrow at 6:00 AM. Or better yet, just reach the station by 6:30."

"6:30?" Jed echoed. He was an early riser himself, but not *this* early. "What are we going to do at that time of the morning?"

Christie's eyes twinkled dangerously. "Track down these drug suppliers," she responded with a sly grin.

CHAPTER 21

"HOW LONG IS THIS going to take, exactly?" Jed worded the question carefully, not wanting to show impatience while knowing he wasn't going to like the answer he received.

"How long?" Christie began to let out a big yawn, then stifled it halfway with one hand. She turned toward Jed, regarded him closely with her wide, sharp eyes. "Are you getting bored?"

"Of course not," Jed answered quickly and pushed back a yawn of his own. "I was just curious as to how much time these operations usually take."

"Well, realistically speaking, it could take the entire day or several days." Christie pushed back her driver's seat and pulled down the sunshade in front of her. She clasped both hands behind her neck and leaned back, closing her eyes briefly. "I would advise you not to hold your breath. When it comes to infiltrations of these kinds, patience is the name of the game."

I knew it. I'm going to spend the next twelve hours in this vehicle with Christie. Jed didn't know whether to be dismayed at that thought or start celebrating. He certainly felt like doing both at the same time. On the one hand, this would be the longest amount of time he would spend with his partner in a single go, and that, too, in such close proximity. On the other hand, sitting in a car in an obscure corner staring at nothing was not exactly Jed's idea of a thrilling police investigation. It had never occurred to him that capturing criminals could turn out to be so stale.

They were parked in the area where the Grays lived, a safe distance away from their home. Christie had smartly hidden her Ford Explorer in a shadowy patch nestled between two large Oakwood trees. From here, they could see a good portion of the empty street stretching out in front of them, its black asphalt shimmering like melted tar in the unholy brightness of the day.

The SUV's interior was cool, the tiny slit in the window letting in the air. They had put up sunshields on all four windows that would keep out any inquisitive glances they received from the area's inhabitants. So far, however, no one had bothered to give them a single look. That was partly because Jed had seen only two people come and go in the last three hours, both of whom had been aged men, slowly shuffling toward their vehicle with bent backs.

He opened his mouth to sigh again but closed it promptly, realizing Christie was in the SUV with him. She was so quiet that Jed could practically close his eyes and pretend there was no one inside except for himself. He shot a sidelong look Christie's way and found her face stitched into that familiar look of dull concentration, her eyes fixed on the empty street before them.

Should I say something? Or am I going to disrupt her workflow and irritate her? Jed pondered those thoughts for a few moments, watching Christie out of the corner of his eyes. Her hair had come unpinned from the back and hung in loose, cascading curls around her shoulders and neck. Her lips lay loosely pressed in a faint pink line, the small cleft in her chin rising to prominence while she continued scanning the street.

"You can say what you're thinking, Jed," Christie murmured absently, not moving her face an inch.

"I—uh, what?" Jed stammered. He felt heat rising in his cheeks. Goddamn, what was he thinking, staring at his partner while she was sitting right next to him?

Christie turned to give Jed a brief, playfully chastising look. Her eyes shone with a sardonic gleam.

"I could see you checking me out," she told him in a soft voice, smirking. "Whatever's on your mind, you can say it. It won't spoil my focus or anything; I can promise you that."

Damn, she's clever. Jed couldn't help it. He chuckled, massaging both eyes with his fingers.

"I was just wondering if we're doing the right thing," he began, leaning against his own seat. "I mean, it seems more like a game of chance than anything else—hiding here, waiting for a deliveryman to show up who looks like he could be transporting drugs, then intercepting him midway."

"Jed, I understand you're having doubts." Christie didn't seem offended in the slightest that someone might be questioning her ability to do her job. "But get this: the kind of intel we have *only* allows us to do this. There's no other path we can take." She jabbed a thumb in the direction of the deserted street before them.

"If we want to find and interrogate a deliveryman who's transporting drugs, then we need to catch him in the act. That's the only way we'll have the legal right to apprehend him and take him to the station. Most of police work isn't as exciting as on tv or in books. A large part of it takes patience and perseverance."

"Hmmm, yeah," Jed murmured an agreement. He knew Christie was talking sense. She always did. It was just this waiting... it gnawed at him. As an ex-addict, the need for immediate gratification was still a struggle to overcome sometimes. He felt that every second spent idly was another moment where Alex's killer slipped further out of their grasp. A sense of urgency had gripped him now, ever since he had made that last breakthrough in the case, and the prospect of waiting for hours in the hopes that their target man *might* show up made Jed uneasy.

But there was nothing else to be done, unfortunately. His partner had spoken, and Jed was not one to interfere in areas that were not his expertise. He rubbed a weary arm across his eyes and stared at the empty street before him with renewed focus.

The houses lay quiet, their indifferent, stone-faces revealing nothing. Rays from the sun continued to shine weakly down at the street with its single, open eye, as if locked in a staring contest with the planet. The cool air in the vehicle continued buffeting Jed's face gently, and beside him, every minute or so, Christie made absent clicking noises.

The minutes passed with agonizing slowness, as if they were wading through syrup. Jed purposefully stopped himself from checking the time; he didn't want to open his phone after an exhausting eternity only to find out minutes had passed. That would only further dampen his enthusiasm, which was already pretty low.

A crow cawed somewhere nearby, then projected itself into flight, its body nothing more than a tiny black speck against the sky's vast blue backdrop. While it circled the houses below it, another car came to a stop on the street. It was a dirty green sedan, which parked before one of the houses on the leftmost corner.

Jed watched with interest as the sedan's front and back doors both opened, and a man and a child disembarked. The man was old, or maybe just didn't take care of himself. He had a slight potbelly and hair that had dwindled away to a wispy black puff which stood motionless in the center of his shining head. A thick handlebar mustache covered his upper lip, and the man frowned hatefully at the empty street around him, as if taking personal offense at the cold.

The kid, a lanky teenager with a shock of blonde hair on his head, got out next after the man, and Jed observed him carefully.

Are you the one? he asked the kid wordlessly, his eyes watching while the sedan's back door was thrown shut. The kid looked around in a daze for a second or two, seeming to be struck dumb by the winter day, then followed the man—probably his father—inside the house. Jed watched him go, tracking his gangly figure until it had disappeared inside the house's interior.

Christie made a noise. "What do you think? That kid look like a druggie to you?"

After a moment's consideration, Jed reluctantly agreed. "Yeah. But most kids today look like druggies, what with spending the entire day glued to their iPhones or PlayStations. It doesn't really mean anything."

"Yeah. Guess you're right." Christie's head turned sideways toward him. Her eyes were curious. "What did *you* do in your childhood, Jed? Were you the nerdy kid who played video games all day or the jock who was always outside, pushing other people around?"

"Neither of those and both of those." Jed blinked, his eyes still on the empty street where that lone crow continued to soar in the air in circles. "Before I made some really bad choices, I was an athlete with so many possibilities and a gamer in my free time. Then I was the idiotic kid who did drugs and brought his life to the brink of destruction."

The silence in the SUV changed into one of a different kind. Jed was aware that his breathing had altered slightly, too. It was coming out with a louder rasp now, even though he was trying very hard to be normal.

"Jed." He felt Christie's hand lightly on his own. Jed didn't look her way, not immediately. He didn't want her to see the emotions swirling in his eyes, but he couldn't ignore the jolt of energy surging from Christie's hand to his.

"You know, considering the childhood you had," Christie began, "you should be even more proud of yourself. I know many adults who were stellar performers as kids, but even they couldn't create a life as impactful as yours."

Jed finally turned toward Christie. By then, his face was once more a mask of cool composure. "I don't help people the way you think, Christie," he mumbled. "Technically, I only help them to help themselves."

Christie's brows rose. "Even better," she confessed with admiration before giving him a cute, little smile. "To quote that adage: give a man a fish, and you feed him for a day. Teach a man how to fish, and you feed him for a lifetime."

Jed snickered. He couldn't help himself; he had always found that quote so cheesy. "Yeah, I guess you could say I'm a fisherman of a kind."

"You're a fisherman's coach!" Christie exclaimed, eyes flashing. She laughed quietly, a hand held to her mouth, and Jed laughed with her.

They returned their gazes to the front and resumed their silent watchfulness of the street. Jed's eyes flicked up and he saw that the crow had disappeared from the sky. Now, it was just the two of them again.

Some more time passed. The minutes marched on with a steady laziness. Another car appeared on the street, a black Honda Civic that came to a stop right in the middle. A man and a woman stepped out from the front seats, both of them young, both of them pointedly not talking to one another.

"What's your assessment of this couple? Lover's spat?" Christie sounded bemused.

"Probably." Jed watched as the man locked the car door, and the pair took a step toward the house when the woman suddenly seemed to remember something she had left in the car. She spoke a few words and made a gesture to the man. Jed watched as the man's face twisted into a scowl. He stepped out once more, unlocked the car, and stepped aside to let the woman fetch her possession. Two minutes later, the couple were gone, the man's stride pronouncedly angrier as he stepped inside his house.

"Wow, they seem so happy together." Christie's voice held a tinge of sarcasm. "Why do people like that stay together? I don't get it."

Jed glanced her way and shrugged. "Kids, probably."

"Nah." Christie shook her head, staring at the house the couple had just walked into. "They look too young to have kids."

Jed shrugged again, tired. "Could be a bunch of reasons, you know? They could be scared to try to start all over again with someone new. Maybe they value the love that once existed between them and are trying to save whatever of it is left. Maybe they don't want to take the easy way out, which is just abandoning ship at the first sign of trouble. Maybe they love and cherish their ship enough to stay on it until the very last moment, when all hope is truly lost. I mean, that is what love is, isn't it? Risking drowning in the hope of being able to fly."

Christie's lips parted slightly in surprise. She did not say anything. She just continued to stare long and hard at Jed, her eyes glimmering. Embarrassed, Jed averted his gaze, feeling heat rushing to his cheeks.

"Apologies. I tend to give long speeches when asked about people and the reasoning behind their behavior. Comes with the job, I'm afraid." Jed forced a chuckle and wiped his hand through his hair.

"No… that was…" Christie's voice somewhat resembled a high squeak. It brimmed with an unidentifiable emotion. "That was a very wise thing you said, Jed. Very wise and mature. Whoever you get into a relationship with, I can tell that you will be a great partner."

The heat rushing to Jed's cheeks intensified. He reached out a hand and turned down the heater a notch. His eyes were still gazing absently at the street, wary of turning toward Christie.

"Jed," Christie spoke softly again.

"Yeah, I heard you," Jed murmured. He felt awkward inside. He never knew how to respond to such compliments. "I think you're being silly, praising me when there's no reason to. But since you've already given the compliment, I shall graciously accept it a—"

"—No, Jed, *look*."

The harsh, whispery tone in which Christie spoke pulled Jed's attention her way. He turned sideways and found Christie's body taut with tension. Her eyes were slits gazing to the left.

"Look, Jed," Christie spoke again in that sandpapery whisper, then thrust a finger to the front. Jed followed its direction to see what she was pointing at. He froze.

It was the boy—the boy they had seen step out of the car with his father. He was back on the street now, standing on the porch just outside his house. A phone was held to his ear. The boy's lips were moving. A second later, he cut the call and fidgeted impatiently, looking to the left with one hand cupped over his eyes. Jed followed the boy's gaze, already knowing what he would see. His heart coiled in his chest like a caged animal as his eyes fell upon the bike heading the boy's way, being driven by a deliveryman wearing a white helmet.

"Get ready." Christie's voice was brisk, businesslike. Her eyes were the hardened pupils of a veteran. She kicked the SUV into drive and sat, waiting, her hands clenched over the steering wheel.

The bike travelled down the road swiftly, kicking up a plume of dust and smoke in its wake. The driver was staring straight ahead, his face cloaked in the shadows thrown by his helmet. The boy stood on the sidewalk, his bony arms and legs moving impatiently. Somewhere far above, the crow cawed again and circled the scene like a vulture waiting for disaster to strike. Jed watched with hypnotized eyes.

Thirty meters. Then twenty. And ten… then, the bike had reached the boy, and Christie had gunned the accelerator at the same time. With a tortured screech, the Ford Explorer burst into motion, tires skidding against the tarmac as they scrambled briefly to retain their grip before rushing down the road.

Both the boy and the rider turned at the sound, but that was all they were given time to do. The Ford had already reached them by then, and it screeched madly once more while braking.

Christie already had the door open before the car had fully stopped, the pistol cocked and ready in her hand. She yanked the handbrake upward and jumped out, pointing her weapon straight at the deliveryman.

"Hands in the air!" Christie shouted, stopping short of the man and planting her feet wide apart on the asphalt. "NYPD! Get on your knees and put your hands in the air!"

The deliveryman stood stunned for a second, the delivery box dangling from his hands, his lips parted stupidly. Christie repeated her command, and it seemed to finally break the spell of paralysis. The man moved. He dropped the box to the pavement and almost fell to his knees, his hands shooting above him. Jed stared at it all, horribly transfixed. Somewhere in his periphery, he saw the boy fleeing back up the steps of his house, shutting the door behind him.

Once the man was down, Christie moved instantly, the gun still up and pointing. It was then that Jed opened the door and stepped out as well. Taking careful steps forward, Jed crossed in front of the vehicle and went toward the man, whom Christie was checking for weapons. The delivery box lay discarded to the side.

That's it. That's what we were looking for. Jed half-jogged, half-walked toward the box. His nerves jangled with tense excitement. His hands were tingly. He bent down, picked up the box, and flung open the lid. All his excitement deserted him right then and there as he saw what was inside. Defeat and shame came crushing down on him as he stood there, gaping at the opened carton, his eyes almost bulging from their sockets, his mind refusing to accept what it was seeing.

It couldn't be. It couldn't be.

But it was. No matter how much he tried to deny it or run away from it, it was.

There was nothing in the box.

Nothing except for food.

Chapter 22

"I still don't feel comfortable leaving you here alone, Mom."

"Oh, Jed." Laurie sighed, her face creasing with concern for her son. "I'm going to be fine; don't worry. And besides, how long can I really expect to hide away from the world at my friend's place?"

"I know, but still," Jed grunted with dissatisfaction. He didn't like this. The idea of his mother living alone after that knife incident filled him with dread. He also knew that dread was the last thing he needed right now, with the case hanging over his head. Jed wouldn't be able to concentrate one bit while half his mind was worrying about his mother.

"Jed, look at me." Laurie came and sat down next to her son on the couch. She looked into his serious face, the brooding shadows underlining his eyes, and the clenched muscle in his lower jaw. Her heart ached for him then, with the thought that he was going through so much trouble all for her sake. He didn't need it, especially not at a time as crucial as this.

"I'll be fine." Laurie tried to pour as much conviction into her voice as she possibly could. She looked straight into Jed's eyes, trying to persuade him to believe her. "The door will be closed and bolted at all times, and at the very first sign of trouble, I'll call you immediately, just like I promised."

A few of the lines marring Jed's features seemed to dissipate upon hearing that, and his shoulders sagged a bit with relief. His mother's mysterious caller had made no return since the knife incident. Maybe the creep had chickened out. Jed fervently hoped it was true. Nevertheless, the police officers would be stationed outside this apartment for five more days, just in case. Jed really hoped they wouldn't be needed.

He rose from the couch and began pacing the living room, his feet making barely audible thumps on the carpet.

"What if I came to stay with you every alternate day, after the guards outside are gone?" Jed almost seemed to be speaking to himself. "It would be better than leaving you alone entirely. It would also help both of us sleep at night more soundly, I'm sure."

Laurie shook her head firmly. "If we do any of those things, we're letting this mysterious man win. That's exactly what he wants: to frighten us, to keep us cowering inside our homes, unable to live our lives fully."

Jed stopped midway during one of his pacing rounds. The light from an overhead bulb painted his face the color of gold. "But we do have a reason to be frightened, don't we?" he spoke softly. "That dagger outside your door... that was a statement, Mom." He took a deep breath. "It was the man telling us he's not afraid to come to your apartment, and that, too, with a weapon."

Laurie shrugged. "So, what? Let him come. I have a guard standing outside this week. And once he's gone, I will still have your number on speed dial." She smiled at him. "What more security could I want?"

Jed returned his mother's smile with one of his own. "That's sweet, Mom, but I'm not always going to be there to answer your call. What if I'm with a client or in the shower or…" his voice trailed off, and Jed exhaled harshly.

"Then I'll deal with that damn man myself," Laurie stated calmly. She added in a joking voice, "I'm not the helpless damsel in distress you think I am, okay?"

Jed gave his mom a look. He saw the hardened, determined glint in his mom's eyes and knew she wasn't going to give in, no matter what.

"You know you can be quite stubborn at times, right?" He flopped down with defeat on the sofa next to her.

"Yes, I do. It's one quality of mine I take pride in." The grin still on her face, Laurie reached forward with one hand and tapped her son on the shoulder. "Now, enough about me. Let's talk about you. How did that stake out of yours go, the one with Christie?"

Jed flinched as his mother uttered those words. That memory was still floating at the surface of his mind, smarting like a fresh bruise. Each time he recalled it, he felt a new wave of embarrassment roll through him.

"Terribly," Jed answered his mother, putting his palms over his face. "It went terribly. We caught a guy according to the intel I had provided them, and he turned out to be completely innocent."

"What, really?" His mother seemed surprised. "You had sounded so certain about your hunch the last time we spoke."

"I was," Jed groaned, his face still buried in his hands, his voice coming out muffled from between his fingers. "But after the terrible mishap today, I don't know if Christie is going to pursue that line of investigation any further. I mean, we scared the rider so badly it took him a good fifteen minutes to settle down; the poor man just couldn't stop shaking. We had to stay with him the entire time and make sure he was okay before he left."

"Oh, that's horrible!" Laurie exclaimed. She added, "But keeping that in mind, would you like some advice regarding what to do next? I know you keep your work pretty close to your chest, Jed, with everything being classified and all that, but I still feel there's something important you need to hear right now."

Jed's face slowly rose from his cupped hands. His eyes were bleary, but a look of hope marked his features. Advice was *exactly* what he was looking for.

"What is it?" he asked his mother.

Laurie was silent for a moment. When she spoke, it was in a confident tone. "Don't give up on your hunch just because it's become difficult to prove. I know you, Jed. You don't arrive at a conclusion unless you have a rock-solid feeling in your gut that it's the right one. I haven't ever told you this, but even as a child you showed a glimmer of that deductive ability living within you."

"Really?" Jed was genuinely surprised. His mother had never mentioned that to him before.

"Yes. There aren't many people in the world who have been given the cognitive gifts you have, Jed. What I'm saying is that you should place your trust in those gifts. Believe that they will guide you toward the end of your case, even if you can't see that end right now."

Jed's eyes were wide open now. They had a faraway look in them. "Believe," Jed repeated softly.

His mother made a noise of agreement. "Exactly. When it comes to that one thing, we all need a bit of encouragement sometimes." She smiled gently.

"Yes, we do," Jed replied, smiling back at her. More of the stress lines had disappeared from his face, and his eyes seemed to have risen from their weary, shadowy depths. "Thanks, Mom. I really needed to hear that. I have a meeting with Christie today at 5:30, and I had been wondering the entire afternoon how I would face her after this morning's calamity."

"Your partner is a smart woman," his mother said. "She knows that not all guesses turn out to be right immediately. She won't blame you for this morning, Jed. The only one doing that is yourself."

Jed bit his lip. "You think so?"

"I *know* so. You can take my word for it." His mother held out a hand with a ten-dollar bill lying in it. "Want to bet?" she asked jokingly.

Jed chuckled. "Sure. We'll find out in a few hours, anyways."

Later that day, sitting in a roadside cafe with Christie, Jed realized that he had, in fact, lost the bet. His mother had been right in her assessment of the situation. Christie didn't blame him. In fact, she didn't even seem irritated or put out about what had happened that morning. All of this came off as so surprising to Jed that he was unable to hold himself back from asking Christie about it. When the question left his mouth, she just shrugged.

"You made a call," Christie said simply, revolving the steaming mug of coffee before her with one hand. "It turned out false. That happens."

"Yes," Jed admitted, "but the entire investigation had been staked on my hunch. Because of my guess, we terrified a poor delivery guy right out of his skin."

"All part of the job," Christie confirmed. "Look, Jed. When you're investigating a case as tricky as this one, the only option you have left is to make hunches. It's a given that not all those hunches will prove to be right all the time. Instead of fretting senselessly over them, it's better we start thinking about what to do next. We always learn something when our hunches don't pay off. Now we know that direction has been investigated, so where should we look next? We still have a murder to solve."

"Okay." Jed was nonplussed by the ease with which Christie had moved on after the day's events. "What if I suggested that we continue this morning's investigation? We may have caught the wrong rider this time, but that doesn't mean there aren't actually ones out there carrying drugs."

Christie gave him an even stare. "You're right. Continuing the investigation was something I'd thought of myself. If that's what you want to do, too, then we can resume where we left off tomorrow morning. Night obviously is too conspicuous—we'll stick out like a sore thumb in this suburban neighborhood, where everyone knows everyone. Unless we make zero progress in our daytime venture, we'll stick to working when there's plenty of light. Makes us far less likely to get noticed that way."

"Wow." Jed leaned back in his chair. "Back to business that quick, huh? My mom was right about you."

Christie frowned. "About me?"

"Yeah." Jed smiled lightly. "She said that you would understand that following dead ends is part of the job and that you wouldn't get too hung up over it."

"Oh." Christie paused and chewed over the information. Then, suddenly, a mischievous sparkle entered her eyes.

"What?" Jed asked, spotting it.

Christie looked at him slyly. "So, you talk about me to your mother, huh?" Her voice was innocent, but the way she batted her eyelashes was far from that.

Jed swallowed. Suddenly, the coffee he was drinking seemed to have turned into wet sand clinging to the walls of his throat. "I—mention of you sometimes arises," he stammered weakly. "You're my partner, after all, and sometimes I briefly mention my work to my mom."

"Uh huh." Christie didn't say anything further. That devilish gleam was still in her eyes. It made Jed's stomach twist in uneasy knots. He knew he was outmatched when it came to wits right now. They were tracking down a drug ring, which was basically Christie's home ground. She had years of experience and successful incarcerations under her belt. No wonder her confidence was at an all-time high.

"What?" he asked again.

Christie shook her head slightly. "Is that all I am to you?" she inquired, staring him straight in the eyes. "Just work?"

Jed opened his mouth and was about to give one of his safe, diplomatic answers when something suddenly made him stop. On impulse, he leaned forward slightly and met Christie's gaze.

"You're a lot more than that," he responded, before adding, "how *much* more you want to be… well, that depends on you, I guess."

A tidal wave of surprise swept across Christie's face, washing away all other emotions. Jed felt his heart suddenly jack hammering in his chest, and he realized what he had done. For the first time since their partnership began, he had been openly upfront with Christie, or at least more upfront than he had ever been. He had told her what existed between them... and what more could exist.

What more could exist.

Jed shivered slightly at the electrifying possibility those four short words represented. He was still looking at Christie, who hadn't yet responded to his comments. Her face had turned hooded, and she was playing with her fingers.

"That's a good question you asked," Christie murmured softly, staring at the table, wisps of steam rising from the mug and dancing across her face like tiny, ghostly sprites. "Once this case ends, you think we should sit down and discuss this further?" She looked up at him then, conflicting tides of hope and uncertainty clashing across her features.

That nervous ache had returned to Jed's palms. At the same time, though, he felt excited, immensely excited, as if something he had long been tangled up in was finally approaching a resolution. His mind thought of the future, and much to his surprise, Jed found himself looking forward to it. A smile crossed his lips.

"Yes, Christie," he answered in an equally hopeful voice. "I think we should."

CHAPTER 23

THAT SAME DREAM, AGAIN.

The city stood bustling with mad, impatient, chaotic life. Jed stood in its midst, staring around him, waiting for it all to disappear. Once again, it did, just like he had expected. One quick blink, and when his eyelids fluttered open again, a desolate graveyard rushed in toward him.

Empty streets. Empty skies. Even buildings that stood so utterly quiet that they resembled gigantic tombstones brought back from some dystopian future. Jed took it all in, knowing none of it was real, yet deeply unsettled anyway. He felt the dying remains of a listless wind brush against his face and blow a strand or two of his hair sideways. He tried to move, to shift forward a millimeter even, but his feet would not let him. They stayed firmly rooted to the spot, intent on making him witness the next part of the dream from his preassigned seat.

The city's eerie quiet was broken by a sound: the swing of a door opening. Jed's eyes flicked to the left, and he saw his stepbrother exiting the coffee shop with a rehearsed smoothness. His hand held that same horrible container of death. He ambled forward absently, coming to a halt at the edge of the curb, staring distractedly at his surroundings, as if there were hordes upon hordes of people streaming through the streets which Jed's own eyes could not see.

Jed was sweating now, feeling the rough palpitations of his pulse even though he had seen this exact same scene play out too many times to count. But each time he found himself in it, the terror returned to haunt him with a renewed vigor. Once again, his heart lurched like a wildly braking vehicle, and his hand attempted to rise up in a gesture of alarm. His lips tried vainly to split open so that the shrill cry contained within them could finally be released out into this dry, dead husk of a world. But none of those things happened, of course. Jed's mouth remained sewn shut. His hands continued to hang by his sides like inanimate blocks of marble. Only his eyes were alive, eyes which could do nothing except to watch helplessly.

Alex took a sip—that same, tiny, seemingly harmless sip. His mouth twisted in a grimace, as if the coffee was too strong. Or maybe it was the venom floating around in it. It didn't matter.

Now came the worst part, the one Jed dreaded the most. His stepbrother's face twisted with confusion, as if he were trying to remember something important but just couldn't. Red lines began to appear across his face, zigzagging and crisscrossing in angry red spurts across the vast paleness of his features. The lines grew thicker, and the reddish hue grew darker, until it was no longer a hue but actual blood oozing from the cracks like treacle.

Alex turned his confused, broken face toward Jed, and Jed tried desperately to close his eyes. He did not want to look again into those angry, accusing eyes. He did not want to feel the blame being hurled his way or hear that sharp final word Alex would spit in his direction. But what Jed wanted did not matter—not in this dream, at least. In this dream, he was a helpless witness who simply went on witnessing.

Alex looked at his stepbrother. His mouth opened like a jagged red hole, and that single, inexplicable retort shot out. It was filled with disappointment.

"Shoot."

Then he was gone, crumpling to the ground like a deflated balloon, his gangly limbs twisting in on each other, his face mercifully hidden from view.

The dream ended.

Jed awoke with a low gasp, one hand reflexively throwing the comforter off him. He laid a palm against one cheek and felt his sweat-riddled skin turned hot and feverish.

"This has got to stop." Jed rose with a stifled curse from his bed and walked over to the nightstand. He poured himself a tall glass of water and chugged it in one gulp, sighing with relief as the water's coolness spread through his neck and chest. Then, feeling somewhat more composed, he turned on the room's lights and went to stand in front of the mirror.

"Wow, I look like one of my patients," Jed murmured, then snorted with irony. His pasty, sweaty reflection stared back at him. His skin was glazed with a thin sheen of sweat and glowed unhealthily in the light. His eyes were rimmed with shadows, and a muscle in his lower jaw quivered slightly.

Jed snorted again, unable to contain himself. The irony of it was truly hilarious. Here he was, a therapist trained in helping other people deal with their nightmares, and yet he couldn't even make his own go away! To top it all off, the nightmare he had didn't even make much sense! It wasn't related to his days of substance abuse or to his damaged relationship with his father. No, for some reason, this recurring dream centered around a person Jed had hardly known or thought of much before his death: Alex. Why? Why had some secret part of his subconscious mind latched onto Alex? And what was it trying to tell him, if anything, through this strangely discomfiting vision Jed was now having on an almost regular basis?

In the quiet of his room, all answers evaded him. The heater continued whirring softly. Jed gave himself a final ponderous look in the mirror, and then darted a glance the clock's way. It showed 4:37 AM in its radial green letters.

"Perfect timing," Jed muttered to himself. "There goes a healthy night of sleep again." He had another long day planned with Christie, which was scheduled to begin at 7:30 sharp, which meant that there were three empty hours left for him to pass. Sleep was out of the question, obviously. Even the thought of reentering that dream made Jed's stomach queasy. He realized that his best bet now was to busy himself with work. It would mean beginning the morning already tired, but that was his only option. Hopefully, a couple cups of black coffee would keep him on his toes.

As soon as the thought of coffee entered his mind, Jed thought back to that white Styrofoam cup in his dream. His appetite did a nosedive right then, and he realized with a sinking feeling that he would have to get through today without the help of his favorite black brew. Perhaps it would be a good idea to go for a short run instead.

"Oh, Universe," Jed murmured, heading out into his living room, where his running shoes lay. "You really test me sometimes."

Later, sitting in the Ford Explorer with Christie and sharing the breakfast he had brought for them with her, Jed's mood was still somewhat rotten. Part of his mind was half-drowsy with unfinished sleep, and the rest continued to revolve around his dream and its meaning. Every few seconds, he had to yank his attention back to the present moment and the case at hand.

"You're not having a very good day today, are you?" Christie gave him a sidelong glance. The box of scrambled eggs and mortadella cheese before them lay half-eaten, "You look like you've been burning the midnight oil."

"I have, somewhat." Jed smiled weakly. "But against my own wishes."

Things had changed between Jed and Christie since their last conversation at that café. It was a subtle, hidden change, and yet it underlined all their interactions now. There was a closeness to them, an intimacy that hadn't existed before. It had been kindled to life by the indirect confessions both had made in the cafe, and now they were far more than partners, their bond visible not just to them but to others. And both were now eager to solve this case and put it aside, so they could finally have that conversation they should have had a long while ago.

"How's your mother doing?" Christie inquired, her eyes facing the front. She closed the breakfast box and put it away. Neither of them seemed to be particularly hungry this morning, for some reason. "After that knife incident, I mean. You said she went back to her apartment?"

Jed stared at a squirrel scurrying across a freshly-mown lawn. "Uh huh. She went home yesterday, actually. She's doing fine—at least so far." He sighed and scratched his nose with irritation. "I don't like her living alone, so far from me. But what can I do? When my mother sets her stubborn mind on something, even God can't persuade her otherwise."

Christie let out a low, tinkling laugh. "That sounds like an independent, strong-headed woman. You should be proud of her, considering how courageously she's handling this entire situation."

"I am proud..." Jed's voice trailed off for a moment. "But courage sometimes leads to foolhardiness, and that can have disastrous consequences." He gave Christie a look. "I don't want my mom in danger just because she has to prove her courage."

"I understand, but she's not proving her courage to anyone." Christie smiled faintly. "That's just who she is."

"Yeah, well, sometimes I wish she was someone else. It's annoying handling so much bravery."

Christie laughed again. "I can imagine. But you'll do fine; don't worry. I've seen you interacting with people when you're with me. You have a knack for handling even the toughest nuts with grace. You'll do fine with your mom, too, and *she'll* be fine as well. I promise." Christie gave Jed's hand a light, reassuring pat.

"I hope you're right." Jed gazed out at the pastel blue sky stretching above the homes and suddenly winced as its emptiness reminded him of another sky, the one seen in his dream. He rubbed his forehead with his palm gingerly, trying to rub away a headache which was in its early stages. After a few moments, almost on impulse, he spoke:

"I've been having nightmares.'

Christie's eyes darted toward him, surprise flowering across her features which she wasn't able to hide quickly enough. She didn't need to, though. The surprise was justified. For the first time since she had met him, Jed had *voluntarily shared* something deeply personal about his own life. Wow! Christie felt like she had just crossed a major milestone.

"What kind of nightmares?" she asked carefully.

Jed bit his lips, wondering if his impulsiveness had made him act rashly. "It's a dream about Alex," he finally admitted, his voice reluctant. "I'm in the city, watching him come out of the coffee shop and take *the* sip. Then he looks at me, mutters the word *shoot* in disappointment, like I've let him down, and simply dies. I can't do anything to stop it or warn him. I just have to stand there, helpless, and watch it happen."

Christie was quiet for a moment. "That must be horrible for you"

"Yeah, that's the crux of it." Jed ran a weary hand through his hair. "It's been occurring fairly regularly now, enough to become bothersome."

"So, that's why you're looking so exhausted today!" Christie exclaimed, realizing.

"Yeah."

"Hmmm. Maybe you just need to let the dream play out?" Christie looked at him questioningly. "Isn't that a thing in human psychology, that bad dreams carry a certain amount of fuel and simply stop occurring once they've burned all of it?"

Jed chuckled. "Even if that's true, the problem is that this dream has decided to interfere with my sleep at a very crucial time. I won't be able to concentrate fully on the case if I'm running on just a couple hours of rest."

"That is true." Christie nodded sympathetically. "Maybe I can co—"

—her voice died right then as her eyes spotted something on the street. Christie's posture stiffened.

"Look," she told Jed, pointing. Jed followed her gaze and saw what had grabbed her attention.

It was just like the previous day. They were parked on another street now, one that was also close to the Grays' home. This was how they had conducted yesterday's operation. A fleet of five undercover police cars had been strategically positioned in a circle near the Grays' home, creating a perimeter that would spot any suspicious riders heading in. Each car in this circle was continually revolving at regular intervals, shifting from one strategic spot to another so that the entire area could be surveyed at maximum capacity. The result of this arrangement was an observational circle that was constantly in motion, keeping a large chunk of the blocks around the Grays' home within its watchful eye.

Now that eye was finally seeing something.

There was another rider coming.

CHAPTER 24

THIS TIME, CHRISTIE DID not explode into action. She waited patiently in the Explorer instead, watching the man approach on his motorbike. He was a young, well-built fellow with sharp eyes and fuzzy, golden stubble coating his cheeks.

The man came to a slow stop near one of the leftmost houses, where a young boy already stood, waiting for him. He kicked down his bike's stand and disembarked, walking casually toward the bag that was tied to the bike's back. As the man's fingers found the zipper and began to pull it open, Christie started the ignition, and their SUV went forward. It didn't race across the tarmac like it had previously; this time, the Ford Explorer calmly coasted in their direction, as if it was simply passing by and wanted nothing to do with them.

By the time they reached the two, their exchange had already happened. The boy who had stepped out of the house was holding his food parcel in both hands and was in the midst of turning back around. The bike rider was back on his vehicle, kicking it to a start. He flashed the Ford Explorer trundling toward him a single disinterested glance before bowing his head again, his hands gripping the throttle.

The Ford Explorer came to an abrupt halt beside them. Its black metal body and tinted windows gleamed in the sun. A single window slid down, and Christie's calm, stern face peered out.

"Excuse me!" she called out, and the boy who had been walking back toward the house turned, his carton of food resting in upturned palms. He saw Christie's face and frowned with confusion.

"Could you come here, please? We're the police." Christie thrust forth an arm through her open window and held her badge out before the boy. It glittered, the emblazoned letters on it standing out clearly.

All the confusion disappeared from the boy's face in an instant. His eyes widened like saucers. Terror stole across his features in a flood, turning his already pale skin bone white. The box he was holding dropped from his shaking hands, hit the ground sideways, and spilled forth its contents—which definitely didn't look like food.

Jed stared at the small, transparent plastic bag that had rolled out of the food carton and now lay sprawled on the curb, its whitish-blue contents catching the light and shining like tiny crystals. He raised his head and saw the boy fleeing back into the house with large, galloping strides.

"Chri—" Jed began to say but was cut off by a shout.

"Stop! Police!" Christie cried, but she wasn't looking at the boy. Her eyes were trained in front, and Jed followed her gaze to find the bike rider racing forward on the street and away from them, a plume of smoke gushing from his motorcycle's exhaust.

Christie gunned the accelerator, and the SUV's engine roared like a sleeping giant that had just been poked awake. Jed's head was thrown back against his seat as the Ford Explorer shot forward, leaving skid marks in its wake.

The biker was already at the end of the street. He barely slowed before turning left and disappearing from their view. Christie cursed and pushed down even harder on the accelerator, and their vehicle streaked forward with maniacal rage, turning everything around them into a blur of colors.

"Christie, there's a turn coming up ahead," Jed spoke hastily. "You need to slo—Ahhh!"

The tires screeched and groped against the asphalt in a mad competition for control as Christie rounded the corner without slowing down even a bit. For a horrifying second, the Ford Explorer was sliding sideways, and Jed waited for them to either topple over or crash into a house. But neither of those things happened. Christie was in control. They rounded the corner with perfect speed and continued forward again, the rider now not very far from them.

They had almost reached the bike's tail-end when it swerved madly to the left, crossing an empty lawn and entering through a slit between two houses that was more of a slightly big alleyway than a road. Christie cursed and kicked down on the brakes while twisting the steering wheel in that same direction. The Explorer swung toward the bike's path while its tires let out another tortured cry. There was a light bump as they left the road and went up to the tarmac, heading straight behind the bike and toward the tiny slit between the two houses.

"Christie, no!" Jed felt fear crack in his heart like thunder. "There isn't enough space for us. Christie, no. NO, DO—"

He held his hands over his face with a wild cry, bracing himself for impact. But there was none—just a dull thud as the SUV dropped down from the tarmac onto a grassy lawn and slipped through the crack between the houses. Jed heard a dim shattering sound a moment later and peeked through his fingers to find that the Ford Explorer's right-side mirror had been left behind in a splintered mess.

They continued racing forward, trampling unknown people's lawns and tearing down fences in their wake. The bike was just a couple meters ahead of them now, and there were no more alleyways or lanes for it to escape into. Christie pressed down on the pedal with a final grunt of strength, and the vehicle shot forward, its fender lightly tapping the bike's tail-end. That light tap was all it took. The bike wobbled madly before them, careening to the left in a mad arc before finally toppling sideways, throwing its rider onto another patch of lawn.

Christie braked, undid her seatbelt, and jumped out of the SUV, drawing her gun in the process. Jed followed after her, walking behind her with his heart thudding dully in his chest. Christie went to the man who was lying on the lawn, one of his legs scratched and slightly bloodied, his face twisted into a grimace.

The man looked up as Christie approached. His face was tired and defeated, his eyes crinkled more with frustration than pain. He watched mutely as she came to a stop right over him and bent down with a cold smile gleaming in her eyes.

"How about we have a talk, huh?" Christie asked.

The inside of the police station was cool and dark. He sat on a chair by the water cooler and nursed a paper cup of the chilled liquid in his hands, taking small sips.

"Bit of a day, huh?" He turned to see Christie standing over him, smiling thinly.

"Yeah, you could say that," Jed mumbled and scratched his head thoughtfully. "I realized something: this only looks cool in the movies."

"What does?"

"What we just did." Jed stared up at her with a shaky smile of his own. "Those cool car chases are only nice when you're watching them on a screen, knowing you can't get hurt." He winced, then, as the memory came rushing back. "But in real life? No way. I think I've had enough to last a lifetime."

Christie chuckled, laying a hand on his shoulder. "You do realize that I was always in control, right? I wasn't just madly risking our lives to catch a criminal."

"Yeah," Jed muttered. "But still." He finished the water and put the cup aside, standing up from his chair. "Now what?"

Derek and Carter, who had been staked out on the adjacent block, were able to retrieve the drugs as evidence, and they brought the boy in for questioning. They were waiting for a parent to arrive since he was a minor.

Christie turned sideways to look at the room adjacent to theirs, which was covered with blinds. "Now, we go interrogate this guy and find out what he knows. They'll call us in once they've slapped a few bandages on the minor cuts he received."

Jed snickered softly. "You gave him quite a fall, didn't you?"

Christie couldn't help but grin. "It's his fault. He should've stopped where he was when I held up my badge."

"Hmm. Wouldn't be much of a criminal now would he, if he didn't try to run from you?" Jed muttered, watching the two police officers and a paramedic heading their way. They stopped at the room's entrance and gestured at Christie.

"Come—the guy's ready." Christie nudged Jed with an elbow. "Let's find out what he knows."

Five minutes later, they were seated in the interrogation room, facing the young rider who stared at them both with sullen eyes.

"How's the leg, Owen?" Christie asked him.

Resentment flashed across Owen's features. "It'll heal," he grunted.

"Hmmm. Wish I could say the same for your criminal record." Christie opened a thin file which lay before her and began thumbing through it, tutting softly as she did. "Supplying drugs to a teenager; now, that's a major felony. Especially if that drug is methamphetamine." She looked up at him. "We recovered the packet you gave that boy, Owen. It was no less than two kilograms of pure crystal meth." She narrowed her eyes. "You know what that means, right? A minimum of ten to fifteen years in prison."

Fear scurried across Owen's face, although he tried hard to hide it. A single vein throbbed in his temple.

"What do you want?" he asked.

Christie spread her hands before him. "Everything. I want you to tell me everything." She leaned back in her seat. "Starting with who is in charge of this drug syndicate and how much territory your operation is covering."

Owen shook his head once. "I can't tell you all of that." His voice was low and resigned. "I'm just the deliveryman. I don't meet the bosses, and I don't know any important details. I'm just told to deliver the merchandise, and I do. That's all."

There was a moment of silence in the room. Christie spoke again.

"Who gives you your orders?"

Owen hesitated, fear of becoming a rat colliding with the fear of a long jail sentence. Finally, the latter fear won.

"My handler," he answered, eyes downcast. "His name is Zane. He texts me the addresses, and I go to them."

"Where do you get the drugs from?" Christie inquired.

Owen's fingers danced across the sheets with wild unease. "There's a warehouse," he mumbled. "I'm told to come outside its gates whenever Zane tells me to, and a man arrives to hand me my delivery."

"Well, we're going to need you to write down that warehouse's address before you leave, Owen." Christie gave him an icy smile, "so that we can tell the prosecutor how cooperative you've been and plead with the judge to give you a more lenient sentence."

"Sure," Owen replied dully. "I'll do that."

"Great." Christie turned toward Jed. "You have any questions for him?"

Jed had been standing silently all this time, observing the man before him. Upon Christie prompting him, he stepped forward.

"How many people would you say you've delivered drugs to, Owen?" he asked. "Could you give me a ballpark figure?"

Owen did not reply immediately. His forehead creased with lines while he thought about the answer.

"Umm, around fifteen to seventeen, maybe?"

Jed nodded curtly. He held out his hand then, in which he held his phone, facing outward. Alex's picture was open on the phone, a clear, front-facing image of his stepbrother.

"Do you remember ever delivering to this man, Owen?"

Owen stared hard at the picture. No recognition flared in his eyes. A moment later, he shook his head firmly.

"No. That face doesn't look familiar at all."

Jed exhaled in disappointment before withdrawing his hand. He pushed the phone back into his pocket.

"Okay. That's it from my side."

Christie pushed a yellow legal pad across the table to Owen. "Write down all the details you know, including the warehouse address and the phone number your handler texts you from."

Once Owen finished scribbling on the pad, he pushed it back toward Christie. She picked up the pad and pen. She and Jed left the room. She instructed the guard that was waiting outside the interrogation room to take Owen down and get him processed.

"So, I guess your hunch about Alex being involved in a drug ring was right," Christie commented.

"Yeah, I guess it was." Jed didn't sound very pleased. "But I thought it would clear things up, not complicate them further. It doesn't seem like we're any close to catching Alex's killer."

CHAPTER 25

CHRISTIE STARED AT THE warehouse through the van's tinted windows. "There doesn't seem to be a lot of security stationed here," she observed.

Jed breathed a sigh of relief. Sitting here in the van's back, with the team of six trained policemen wearing balaclavas and combat gear around him, he felt like an obsolete toy, clunky and out of place.

"I think we can get this done on our own," Christie murmured, turning away from the window to survey her team waiting quietly behind her—Derek, Graham, Carter, Jason, and Joseph. She eyed each of them, turn-by-turn, staring at their hardened, flinty expressions. "Are you guys ready?"

The men all nodded and muttered their yeses. Jed glanced at the sleek, black Heckler and Koch submachine guns that were balanced on their laps, the muzzles fitted with silencers. He swallowed.

"Jed?" Christie asked.

Jed turned toward her. "Yes?"

"You'll be staying here with the driver," Christie instructed him. She consulted her watch. "Judging by the dismal protection this place has, it shouldn't take us longer than thirty-minutes to complete the entire operation and have this warehouse seized."

"Understood," Jed answered, feeling his voice quaver slightly. His gaze drifted to Christie's own outfit, a gray camo bulletproof vest with the police department's logo on it, and his heart shrank with fear. The idea of letting her infiltrate a drug den that could possibly be teeming with armed guards was too horrific to consider. It was making him physically ill. His vision swam with nauseating motion, and his veins were sculptures of ice. Jed swallowed again, more deeply this time, and yet he couldn't get rid of the lump in his throat—nor could he relieve the parched dryness which marked his mouth. His tongue was like a sandpapery weight in his mouth, lying stiff with fear.

"Please be careful," Jed managed to get out, staring intently at Christie, at her chestnut hair which was pinned tightly behind her head, with a single strand dangling loose.

Christie gave him a faint half-smile. "Don't worry; we'll all be fine. I have a feeling this operation is going to conclude sooner than expected." She turned back toward the men. "Let's go, team."

The van's backdoors slid open soundlessly, and Christie slipped out into the night, her team following quietly behind her. The whole team inspected their guns one last time, then began to creep toward the warehouse from the side.

Jed watched them go. In the evening's dusky light, they were nothing more than shadowy wraiths gliding through an ocean of silken darkness, their guns melting into the black of their clothes. After they had gone ahead a few meters, they seemed to lose their individual forms and meld into a single, threatening silhouette which slowly approached the warehouse from its western side.

The minutes ticked by. Jed sat in a quiet tenseness, hearing the rattled rasp of his own frightened breath while his eyes scoured the blackness before him. He could no longer see Christie and the team now; they had disappeared entirely. The only thing visible through the van's front windows was the warehouse's hulking outline in the distance. The mere sight of it made Jed queasy. He bit his lip and twisted his fingers into knots, beginning to count backward from one thousand.

An unknown while later, Jed reached the end of his count and let out a small breath. Still, the silence remained—that awful, unnerving silence which was pregnant with a sense of impending doom. It hung all around him, cloaking the world in its infinite folds. How much time had passed? Jed could not tell, and he did not have the nerve to check his phone. It felt like he had been sitting in this cramped leather seat for an eternity, staring out at the mute, black world that seemed devoid of all life. Sucking in another deep breath, Jed began to count back once more from one thousand. He strained to look into the darkness. He couldn't see anything. The more he searched the dark, the more his eyes began to play tricks on him—were those shadows? Were they moving? Could he see anything at all?

A gunshot shattered his thoughts.

The sound of it was a sharp, deafening crack, as if some invisible, cosmic giant standing over the planet had just clapped his hands together. Jed's heart jumped to his throat, and he leaned forward in his seat, staring blindly out at a dead world.

No further noise came.

What was that? Did someone get shot? Was it... Jed forced the dreadful thought from his mind. It would paralyze him if he let himself dwell on it. He sat stiffly in place, his arms clasped together, his legs leaden. It took every ounce inside of him to stay in the van. Every part of his body wanted to run in and make sure Christie was ok.

More minutes passed. The silence returned to reestablish its rightful foothold on this cloaked, desolate area of the city. Jed continued staring out through the window, his eyes unmoving, his attention unyielding.

It seemed like another eternity passed before the team finally returned, their pale forms emerging from the shadowy womb as if they had just been born. At the head of the team was Christie, and Jed noted with wonderful, dizzying relief that she seemed to be fine. The men following behind her seemed to be fine as well. They approached the van and slid open its back doors.

"Operation successful," Christie exclaimed, settling into the seat opposite Jed. "Cavalry's here to take care of things. We can leave." Her forehead was slick with sweat, and a few strands of her hair clung to it.

"We secured the warehouse and immobilized the men inside. We waited for support to arrive and they will detain them and escort them back to the police station for interrogation." Christie explained to Jed as she climbed into the vehicle. Her face was buzzing and alive.

"It was a pathetically guarded place," she told him. "There were only two guards there, and they were just some random old buzzards who had been hired on minimum wage. We barely had to do anything to get them to drop their weapons."

"And the men inside?" Jed asked, fascinated.

Christie made a disappointed face. "Equally pathetic." She bit her lower lip in thought. "We were expecting this to be some kind of grand drug-peddling ring, run by some fearsome mafia boss, but it was the exact opposite." She wiped a hand across her brows. "The people running this whole thing were a bunch of washed-up scam artists who thought they were being clever. We just fired one shot at the ceiling in a display of threat, and they were all on their knees, their hands up in the air."

"Huh." Jed's eyes acquired a faraway look. The news Christie was giving him was good… and also *bad*.

"You don't look very happy," Christie observed, staring at him.

Jed met her gaze. "We're dealing with a murder," he began in a puzzled voice. "If these people aren't even equipped to handle the police, and if they're really as pathetic as you say, then..." he let his voice trail off. "It just sounds weird that they would be ready and willing to murder Alex, if he really did work for them."

"Let's just wait until the interrogation," Christie assured him. "Then, we can make our conclusions."

An hour-and-a-half later, after some more impatient waiting, Jed was seated alongside Christie in the interrogation room once more, facing the man who had been in charge of the drug operation. As Jed looked at him, he felt his hopes sinking.

Carl was the man's name, and he resembled a grizzled homeless person more than a cunning drug lord. His face was pudgy and stained with dirt and sweat, his hair an unruly tangle of frizz which rested on his head and stuck out awkwardly from behind his elvish ears.

This can't be it. Jed felt a wave of disappointment crashing over him. It was mixed with a sense of anger. Jed found himself silently urging the man to show some power, to prove to him and Christie that he was capable of cold-blooded murder.

"Mr. Carl Stoneman," Christie began, raising her head from the file lying before her. A tinge of disdain colored her features as she took in the trembling, pitiful figure of the suspect sitting in front of her.

"I—I'm so very sorry, officer," Carl stammered in a squeaky, nasal voice, his lips shivering and his eyes wide open with fear. "I was just trying to make some money on the side, th—that's all. I—I never wanted any—"

"—please be quiet one moment," Christie snapped, unable to control her annoyance. She picked up a document with Alex's picture printed on it and thrust it in Carl's direction. "Do you know this boy?"

Carl took one look at the picture and began to nod earnestly. "Y—yes, I do. He used to work for us a while back. Poor chap died a few weeks ago, I think. Terrible."

"Died... or was murdered?" Christie asked softly.

"What?" Carl stared at her uncomprehendingly. When Christie's implied accusation finally hit him, his jaw dropped open, and his eyes bulged from their sockets with almost cartoonish terror.

"*What? Me?*" Carl was practically hyperventilating now, his lips quivering blurs of pink. "I didn't kill him! I have never harmed a soul in my life! What are you talking about?"

He's telling the truth, Jed realized dimly, watching Carl's explosive reaction. *Every fiber of his being is screaming that he's telling the truth. Now either this man is an Oscar-worthy actor, or our investigation has hit a dead-end once again.*

"Mr. Stoneman," Christie stated, unperturbed by the man's outburst. "We already have reason enough to know you were involved. You just admitted that Alex was involved in your operation. He must've done something wrong. Maybe he told somebody something he wasn't supposed to, or maybe he just wanted out, and then you killed him."

"Nooo!" Carl wailed, his hands flying to his mouth, and Jed had to fight off a mad impulse to break into laughter. This man was clearly no killer. Jed doubted he had ever even seen the inside of a police station before in his life.

"I didn't do it! I didn't do it!" Carl swore, grabbing his neck with his thumb and forefinger as if he were taking a solemn oath. That urge to cackle crazily bubbled up within Jed again, and he bit his lip hard to suppress it.

"If you can tell us what poison you used to kill the boy," Christie continued, ignoring all of Carl's antics. "Then we can put this investigation to rest and, maybe, have the judge consider a more lenient sentence for you."

"*Poison?*" Carl spat. "What poison? I don't even know where you can buy poison!" He let out a despairing laugh and buried his face in his hands.

Jed rose quietly from his seat, beginning to leave.

"Hey, where are you going?" Christie asked him.

Jed gave her a sad smile. "Outside. There's nothing more left to do here." He walked over to the door, opened it and then stepped outside, hearing Christie's own chair scrape backward as she followed him.

"Hey! Hey!" Christie called. Jed turned around and found her storming in his direction, anger flashing in her eyes.

"You don't just walk out of an interrogation like that!" Christie exclaimed hotly, hands on her hips. "What's wrong with you?"

Jed said nothing in response. He didn't need to. The defeated sag of his shoulders was answer enough.

"I'm sorry, Christie, but I'm going home," he told her wearily. "We've tried and tried and tried, and yet we haven't been able to crack this case. Now our final lead, the only one we had, has also led to a dead end. There's nothing more to do. I'm sorry, but I have failed." He turned around and began walking toward the exit.

"What, so you're just going to leave, just like that?" Christie called after him, angry and betrayed. "Are you giving up?"

Jed continued walking, not responding to her. There was nothing left to say.

CHAPTER 26

IT WAS A BUSY day.

Jed was in his office, dressed neatly in a formal shirt and pants, typing away on his laptop. His hair, which had grown long in the past month or so, was now smartly trimmed and parted from the side. His face glowed with a freshly-shaven look. His eyes were alert and focused intently on the screen in front of him, and his fingers typed away with furious energy, intent on making up for weeks of missed work.

There were three emptied cups of black coffee placed symmetrically on the edge of Jed's desk. He had gone through them all in the last half-hour, and now his veins were buzzing with caffeinated energy. His plan was to complete at least 75% of his pending work today and deal with the rest tomorrow. It was a good plan, and after making it, he had dived headfirst into client profiles, losing himself entirely in them.

Beyond and below his office, as seen from his floor-to-ceiling windows, the city seemed to be bustling with the same energy. It was only a quarter past noon, and already the crowds of bodies and cars had filled the streets, their individual noises all melding together into a single, incoherent, unceasing clamor. The sun had escaped from its prison of clouds and was gilding the skyscrapers with its radiant presence.

Jed continued to type with a robotic concentration. Every now and then, he would come across a detail of particular interest and jot it down in the notebook before him. On the wall to his left, a clock ticked slowly, but Jed seemed oblivious to it. He seemed oblivious to everything now—everything except for his work. The seconds and minutes and hours all passed him by, but Jed did not notice them. His eyes were fixed like glue to the screen, and his fingers continued their tireless dance over the keyboard.

It was the ringing of his phone that caused him to finally break from his trance. Jed blinked once, twice, and then a third time, returning to reality. His gaze shifted toward his phone on the desk. It was vibrating. Jed picked it up and answered the call.

"Hi, Mom. How are you?" His voice sounded cheery and distracted.

"Hello, Jed. I'm good." Laurie paused. "I hope I'm not calling you at a bad time. I know you must be neck-deep in that confusing case of yours—the one you told me about."

The smile on Jed's face wavered briefly. A single muscle in his jaw twitched. For a brief, fleeting instant, the busyness clouding his eyes seemed to wane and was replaced by a look of restless defeat. But then, Jed regained control over himself and clenched his hand over the phone. That smile reappeared on his lips, and the shadows covering his eyes were driven back.

"I've actually moved on from that case now, Mom," Jed answered. "I'm doing some of my regular therapist work. But anyways, you didn't call at a bad time. Tell me, what's up?"

"Oh, you've already solved that case?" Laurie sounded surprised. "Wow, that's nice to hear. Only a couple of days ago, you looked so exhausted and worn out because of it."

Jed didn't answer. He just continued staring at the wall, the phone clenched in his hands and that sick smile forced across his face.

"Anyways," his mother continued, "I actually called you because you told me to."

"I told you to?" Jed frowned. "When?"

There was a pause on the other end. "Remember when you told me to inform you the second I received another threatening phone call?" His mother spoke with a forced cheerfulness. "Well, I just did."

"Oh, no." Jed rose from his chair, pushing back his work both mentally and physically. He walked over to the window and stared at the seething mass of bodies below him, a single palm pressed against the windowpane. "What did he say?"

"Oh, you know." His mother let out a tiny, unconcerned chuckle. "That I was going to pay for my sins. That the knife he left outside my door was only the beginning, and that soon that same knife would be inside my heart."

"Mom!" Jed cried. "That's not a small thing!" He cursed. "I told you to let me stay at your place!

"Jed, it's okay!" Laurie protested. "I'm fine, really. I've gotten used to this sicko's warnings. They don't really bother me anymore."

"What about the day he actually decides to show up and stick a knife in you?" Jed demanded. "Will it bother you then? Huh?"

"That won't happen, Jed," his mother assured him. "The people who make the most threats are also the ones who act on them the least. Really, I'm not even that bothered by this call. The only reason I told you is because you made me swear to do it when I insisted on coming home."

Jed didn't respond. He was breathing hard. His eyes stared down at the people below him, as if he believed that if he stared hard enough, he would be able to pick out the face of the mysterious caller from the thronging mass lining the streets.

"I'm coming over to your place, Mom." Jed said with finality. His face was set with grim, grey lines. "We have to do something about these calls. Enough is enough."

"Jed…" his mother began weakly, and then didn't speak more. She guessed that arguing would serve no purpose. Instead, she let out a long sigh. "Okay, then. Come."

Jed hung up the phone and moved toward his desk. He put away the confidential documents lying there and closed his laptop. Then, he grabbed his wallet and keys from the side-drawer and began to leave. He brought out his phone while he walked and opened his messages. One of the messages at the top was from Christie, asking him where he was and to call whenever he had time.

Jed paused, his fingers hovering above the screen, his chest rising and falling rapidly. After a few moments of indecision, he typed out a quick reply, telling Christie he was going to visit his mom and that he would call her afterward. When that afterward came, though, he did not know if he would actually have the strength or the courage to make that call. He had failed her in the case, let her down as a partner. All his hunches had done nothing but waste the police's time, and they had not been able to make any progress in the investigation, no matter how hard they tried. What was left to talk about? This case seemed to be a sign from the universe telling Jed to return to his area of expertise. Maybe some riddles could never be solved. Maybe some murders would always remain a mystery.

All these jumbled thoughts raced through Jed's mind during the split second in which he raised the phone in front of him and cast his wary eyes down at its screen. An instant later, he inhaled a sharp breath.

It was not Christie calling.

It was his father.

What does he want? Confusion and uncertainty flooded Jed. He stood there with dizzying stillness, looking down at the name *Richard Gray* flashing on his mobile like a siren light, instructing him to answer its call. After a few seconds of nervous indecision, Jed did. He pressed the phone against his ear and spoke:

"Hello?"

"Who the hell do you think you are?" His father's fuming, volcanic voice gushed over him in its molten anger. Jed winced, feeling the harshness of the words pricking him like poisonous barbs.

"What do you mean?"

"You know exactly what I mean," his father swore. "Were two deaths in my family not enough for you? Did you have to embark on a crusade to tarnish my dead son's reputation as well?"

"What are you talk—" Jed stopped midway. Realization finally dawned. "Are you referring to Alex's involvement in a drug ring?"

"That has nothing to do with you, you sonofabitch!" his father shouted, then cursed furiously. "Everyone knows now! They're saying things behind my back! Word of your investigation has slipped out, and the people you interviewed at Alex's workplace are spreading things about him! Are you happy now? Isn't that what you wanted?"

Jed paused for a moment and took a deep breath to calm the maelstrom of emotions rising within him. "If you had just told us what Alex was involved in," he began slowly, "we wouldn't have had to try and figure it out on our own. Besides, this is a police investigation. We have to do our duty, no matter what people think or say."

"Your duty," his father scoffed, laughing mockingly. "Have you done it then? Can you tell me who killed Alex?"

Jed said nothing to that. Each taunt by his father was a whip lashing at his heart, leaving deep, permanent gashes across it. "We're trying," he finally managed to utter through gritted teeth.

"*Trying*." Richard scoffed again. Jed could feel his father's sneer through the phone. "You're a good-for-nothing little twat. Always have been, always will be." He paused, then added with ice-cold softness. "You will pay for this, for what you have done to my family. You and your mother both."

"Don't you dare talk about Mom," Jed snarled, the rage finally breaking free and shooting through him in a geyser. "Don't you dare u—" His voice cut off. He listened to the dial tone beeping in his ear, soft and sympathetic.

His father had cut the call.

Jed let out a deep, shuddering breath. His legs suddenly did not seem like they could support him. Wobbling slightly on his feet, he shuffled over to his desk and threw himself down on the chair, breathing in harsh, ragged bursts. His palms were clammy with sweat. His body was, too, and his shirt clung to it uncomfortably. He ran a hand over his forehead and wiped away the accumulated sweat there.

What was happening? Too much was happening; that was the entire problem. It was all happening at once, giving him no room to breathe. First, this godforsaken investigation.

Then, his mother's threatening phone calls. Now, his father's mad anger, too…

Jed picked up the phone and went to his call log. He stared wistfully at the four missed calls from Christie, deeply longing to call her back and speak to her. He knew the sound of her soft, understanding voice would calm him, would act like a balm to the wounds his father inflicted.

But Jed couldn't talk to Christie, not now. Not after he had walked out of the investigation. Not after he had let her down—and the entire police department by extension—in this case. For both their sakes, it was best that they returned to their own lives and their own professions.

Jed continued sitting there for a while longer. He let his heartbeat return to normal, allowed the tingling ache in his palms to disappear, and waited for his breathing to turn from shallow to regular. Once his entire body had reestablished control over itself, he put both hands against his seat's armrests and pushed himself back onto his feet. He stood there for a second or two, checking his balance, allowing his senses to reorient themselves. Then, he began walking forward and out of the office.

The phone did not ring again as Jed walked down the stairs and got into his Jeep. It did not ring while he fastened his seatbelt and turned the ignition. Christie did not call, and neither did his father or mother. Jed welcomed the silence. It was the only thing keeping him sane at this point, he guessed.

Chapter 27

Jed tossed and turned in bed. The aged springs beneath the mattress protested with feeble creaks every time he changed his posture, as if angrily demanding he lay still. But Jed couldn't do that; he had been trying to for the past hour and failing miserably at it. All the techniques had failed. He had tried counting to one hundred, had gone and taken a warm shower in the hope of relaxing himself, and had even made an effort to listen to soothing nature sounds with his headphones. Nothing had worked. Sleep continued to evade him like he was the plague.

It was some ungodly hour past midnight, and the spare room was seeped in darkness. He had drawn the curtains on the windows in order to blot out the moonlight. But even this pitch-black void wasn't strong enough to lull him to sleep. It wasn't even making him drowsy. His mind sat in his skull like a high-strung cocaine addict, brimming with manic energy.

His mother's apartment, however, lay quiet and peaceful, just like a house should be in the dead of night. Jed was the odd one out here, the only inhabitant within these walls who was neither quiet nor at peace. His thoughts rambled on and on, traveling in a dozen different directions at once.

At least I'm not worried about my mom being attacked and being alone, Jed told himself and found the thought somewhat calming. It was true. Staying over at his mom's place had at least given him one benefit: he no longer feared for her safety. In fact, he was so awake and energized that he felt ready to take on any assailant that should come bursting through the door—more than one, actually. Jed felt capable of handling a dozen intruders right now. *After such a battle, I might actually be able to sleep,* he chuffed.

After another long spell of fruitless tossing and turning, he sighed with defeat and rose from his bed, padding over to the window. A stream of silvery moonlight struck his face as soon as he pulled the curtains apart. Jed blinked rapidly a few times, adjusting to the brightness. His eyes traveled below the window and landed upon the narrow alleyway which lay there sparkling, draped in the moonbeam's gossamer strands.

A dull nostalgia flickered within him then, as an old memory came rushing back. Jed saw himself as a young boy, brooding and somber even in his teenage years, sitting on the sofa by the window and reading a book at night. His childhood self's image appeared in his mind, and he noticed with amusement its finer details: the tousled, poufy hair he had sported back then, and the way he would purse his lips while concentrating on something.

"How fast time flies," Jed observed with dry amusement, unable to move his eyes from that small alleyway. More images came flooding to him, all of them disjointed and unrelated, like scenes from different movies. He saw himself as a boy running through an alley during the day, his left foot slipping on a banana peel and sending him flying forward, face-first. Jed rubbed his cheek absently, almost feeling the ghostly ache of that bruise reaching forth from the past.

There was another memory after that. This one was of his father, and it was a surprisingly happy one. Or at least, it wasn't a miserable one. Jed was in his room, staring down through the window at his father's walking figure. Midway through his stride, his father seemed to sense someone's gaze on him and turned sideways, raising his face up. His eyes met Jed's in the afternoon glare, and Richard Gray gave his son a brief wave, his lips parting into the beginnings of a very thin smile.

Jed stood by the window, reliving the past, feeling con-flicted on all levels. Where had his father been going on that day? He couldn't remember. But if he had to wager a guess, it would probably be Cindi's house. Yes, their affair had already begun when Jed was young. He had been too innocent to notice it back then, his mind incapable of understanding that the duration of his father's increasingly frequent absences bordered on outright suspicious. He had never even imagined as a boy that his dad would do something as horrid and dirty as cheating on his mother. But that hadn't mattered. Jed's belief in his father hadn't mattered at all. Richard had gone ahead all the same and done what he wanted anyway.

Reaching out with a tentative hand, Jed touched the glass of the room's window. It was cool beneath his skin, cool and unyielding. There were more memories bubbling up from within him now, more jumbled snapshots of his past which he had taken such care to hide away.

Unable to move from the window, and part of him not even wanting to, Jed stood where he was and let the memories capture him. He closed his eyes, and the colors washed in, so very vivid and lifelike.

Now, he was with his mother, playing Scrabble in the living room. Laurie was beautiful in her youth, with a full, well-defined face and bright, laughing eyes. Her hair lay around her shoulders in a tumble of lustrous curls. She was smiling at Jed, her teeth showing through her parted lips as she raised a square and placed it on the board, securing more points. Little Jed peered at the word she had made and frowned, his lower lip disappearing beneath his upper one.

"What's *resplendent?*" he asked.

His mother laughed. It was a beautiful sound, like the tinkling of glasses. "It describes you," she told him, leaning close and messing up his hair with one hand. Jed shrank back from her hand with an annoyed sound and began fixing his hair with the godlike vanity of an adolescent right on the brink of teen-hood. His mother laughed harder.

Another memory, after that one. This one was not as nice. Jed was peeking from his room, listening to his mother and father arguing hotly. It was about Richard's *work-related absences*, which Jed hadn't been able to understand back then. His mother was practically standing on her tiptoes, her eyes burning with accusation, her chest rising and falling rapidly. And Jed's father? He just stood there, taking it all with the resigned indifference of a man who has already made a decision and would stick by it, no matter what. Jed watched it all unfold from the doorway of his room, his tiny, frail heart thumping erratically in his chest. He heard his mom's voice rise higher and higher, becoming shrill and taut, like it was about to break. He saw his father standing with that same impassiveness, his eyes hardened and his lips pressed together.

Mom's going to cry soon, little Jed thought from his corner, right before the scene ended and the final memory rose up in its place.

He was sitting on a park bench now. It was evening time, and a nice wind was blowing. His mother was sitting beside him. Jed looked up at her and saw her gazing into the distance, her eyes so far away they seemed to be in another dimension. There weren't a lot of people around them—just two kids running in circles and a young couple sitting under a tree, secretly stealing kisses.

"Jed," his mom said. She turned down to look at her little son, at his wide saucer-like eyes. She smiled, but it was a sad smile. "I have something to tell you."

"What is it, Mom?" Jed asked with interest, his gaze never leaving his mother.

Laurie took a deep breath. Her eyes became watery, and the edge of a teardrop hung down from her left eye, dangling precariously over her cheek.

"What is it?" Jed asked again. He placed a small, reassuring hand over his mother's own. "You can tell me; it'll be okay." Even though he was only eight years old, he tried to be bigger than he was.

Laurie looked down at her son again. She smiled for the second time, this smile even sadder than the previous one, and the teardrop jumped from the ledge of her eyeball, falling to her cheek and trailing a wet path downward. She spoke then, in a tired, muffled voice:

"Daddy won't be living with us anymore."

The memories ended, and Jed opened his eyes. He was slightly surprised to find that his own cheeks were wet with tears. But apart from that, everything else about him felt rinsed and cleaned. The slight headache in the back of his skull was gone, and his rambling thoughts had died down entirely. Jed understood immediately that it was these memories which had been blocking his sleep. He wasn't shocked to reach that realization. Once more, his past had turned into an obstacle, and simply reliving it without fear had done the trick.

Jed went back to his bed and laid down on it, pulling the blankets up to his chin. He knew that sleep would whisk him away the moment he closed his eyes; he could feel every muscle in him finally relaxing, preparing for rest. His mind felt the most relaxed of all. All the rust of the past had been rubbed from it, and now it shone like a honed blade.

Tomorrow, I'm going to give Alex's case a fresh look, Jed thought, feeling a sudden surge of new hope flare within him. He smiled slightly and closed his eyes. As he had been expecting, sleep swooped in instantly and carried him away on its wings.

The dream returned.

Once more, the dead street. The silence. The buildings which resembled gravestones for Pharaohs of the future. Once more, the swinging of the door and the sound of Alex's footsteps. Jed turned his eyes, completely unafraid now, and watched his stepbrother walk toward him. He watched without fear as his stepbrother took the fatal sip. He watched without fear as the lines of blood appeared on Alex's face, and then he met his stepbrother's accusing stare with that same resolute fearlessness. Alex's mouth opened, and the word came out.

"Shoot."

He fell to the ground.

It all clicked into place.

Jed awoke from his dream with a gasp. Suddenly, it all made perfect sense to him—perfect, crystal-clear sense. Of course, *that* was why he had been having the dream! What other reason could there have been? Now, there was only one thing left to do.

Christie.

Jed jammed his hands into the tangled folds of his sheets and frantically began searching for his phone. Where was it? His fingers groped through the blanket's soft folds and found nothing. God dammit, where was the stupid device when you actually need—

"Found it!" Jed exclaimed with triumph, withdrawing his hands with the phone in them and holding it up in the air momentarily like a prized trophy. He opened the phone and began dialing Christie's number, his fingers moving fast.

It was 4:37 AM—not the right time by any stretch to make a normal call. But this wasn't a normal call at all. No, this was a call that simply couldn't wait until morning.

Jed pressed the phone against his ear and heard ringing. Each ring was a clear indicator that Christie was fast asleep, that now wasn't the appropriate time to contact her. But Jed didn't care. He sat on his bed patiently, his posture fully alert.

Three rings.

Four.

Five.

Six.

Seven.

Eight.

Ni—

"—Hello?" Christie's groggy, half-asleep voice appeared. Jed had to resist the urge to celebrate.

"Christie, it's me," he spoke urgently. "Jed."

There was a moment's pause, where he only heard heavy breathing.

"Jed?" First there was confusion in Christie's voice, which quickly transformed into anger. "First, you don't pick up my calls. Then you think you can just call me in the mi—"

"—I figured it out, Christie," Jed cut in.

Another pause. "Figured out what?"

Jed smiled with grim satisfaction.

"I know how Alex was killed."

CHAPTER 28

"PLAY THE FOOTAGE, PLEASE."

Derek pressed a button on the remote, and the frozen image started moving. Everyone sat and watched, their eyes fixed on the video they had already seen many times before. It began with an overhead view of the sidewalk, crowded with briskly moving strangers of all ages and ethnicities. They went back and forth in constant, unceasing motion, their heads upturned and their strides purposeful. A few minutes later, the door to a coffee shop opened, and a young man stepped out.

Jed shifted slightly in his seat, feeling his heartbeat quicken. He leaned toward the screen, frowning. This was it. It was going to happen any second now, if he was right.

As they had observed before, the video showed Alex walking from the coffee shop's door to the sidewalk, holding a Styrofoam cup in his hands. He stopped at the curb and took a tiny sip. Right afterward, his hand shot to his chest, and his mouth contorted into a grimace.

"Stop." Jed instructed quickly, his voice high and strained.

Derek paused the video. The frozen image now showed Alex standing at the sidewalk's edge, a drink his hand, and his mouth open in a wide-O, as if the beverage he had gotten was terrible in taste.

"This is it," Jed began, turning to Christie and the two officers sitting opposite him. "This is where it all went wrong. But not just for Alex. For us, too."

They all sat and listened to him, their faces rapt with attention.

"Since the beginning of this case," Jed continued, "we've been continuing all our investigation based upon the certainty of a single premise, a premise which necessitates that Alex was poisoned—or less likely that he suffered cardiac arrest that made him collapse and land on the rake. It has dictated our decisions and hunches from the very start." He paused, giving the three a moment to absorb his words, and then he finished his sentence.

"But what if that premise was wrong?"

Brows furrowed with confusion. Eyes crinkled, staring at him skeptically. Jed wasn't bothered. He had expected it.

"Hear me out." He splayed his hands forward in a gesture saying, *humor me.* "What if Alex *was* killed but not by being poisoned?"

"Then..." Christie looked at him hard, her eyes dark and filled with emotion. "How?"

This was it. This was the moment Jed had been waiting for. It was time to drop his theory on them and see how it went. He took a deep breath and finally gave the answer he had been holding in.

"What if Alex was shot?"

A small wave of murmurs went through the room. The confusion and doubt in everyone's eyes deepened, and they turned their gaze once more toward the frozen screen, as if expecting to obtain some clarity by looking there.

"Let me explain." Jed followed their gazes. "Look closely at the image in front of you. This is the most crucial moment of this case, when whatever happened to Alex happened."

They all soundlessly stared at the frozen thumbnail image of Alex standing on the sidewalk, his mouth open in surprise, his hand on his way to his chest.

"This image." Jed pointed a finger at Alex. "All of us saw this, and we immediately assumed that Alex had been poisoned. It made the greatest sense, of course. A guy gets a coffee from a store, takes only one sip, and then instantly clutches his chest in pain a moment after?" He shook his head, chuckling softly to himself at how easily they had been duped. "But that's not what happened here."

"Then what?" Christie pressed. "You need to explain yourself."

"I'm about to." Jed took a deep breath, gathered his thoughts and strengthened his nerves, before continuing. "What you see on the screen in front of you is Alex grimacing in pain, with one hand on its way to clutch his chest. We all think that's because the toxin has taken effect inside his body. But let's discard that theory entirely for one moment." He paused, taking in the sea of intrigued eyes staring at him.

"What if," Jed uttered, pointing his finger at the screen again, "*this* is the exact moment he was shot?"

A few murmurs arose, but mostly there was silence—a confused, uncomprehending silence.

"What do you mean?" Christie asked at last.

"Look at the screen," Jed told her. "What if the video we're seeing is showing us Alex getting shot *while* he's sipping his coffee? What if the moment he grimaces is when the bullet enters his body?"

Christie was frowning. Everyone was frowning. They were all staring at the screen, their expressions marred with skepticism and confusion.

"Shot," Christie repeated slowly, her face still turned toward the paused image of Alex. "Hmmm. But where's the shooter, then? Why don't we see him standing somewhere with a gun? This is an open street, after all, and the camera is giving us a wide-angled view. If someone shot Alex, they would have had to shoot him from up close, considering the thick crowd of people surrounding him. Firing from a distance would practically be impossible in this situation." She turned back to Jed. "Where's the shooter, then?"

"Excellent question," Jed confirmed.

Christie narrowed her eyes at him. "You've already thought of this, haven't you?"

Jed nodded. "Indeed. What you're saying is correct. It would be impossible for someone to shoot Alex in this crowd from a distance." He smiled slightly, his eyes twinkling. "But who said the shooter had to do it from the street?"

"Then where e—" Christie's voice cut off midway. Her jaw fell slightly open, and Jed saw the understanding dawning in her eyes.

"Oh." Christie's voice was a soft whisper. "You're saying… Alex was killed by a *sniper*?"

Jed leaned back in his chair with grim satisfaction. They had finally reached the heart of the issue.

"Yes," he answered Christie, his voice confident. "It fits with everything. It's the only reason we ran into so many dead ends." He shook his head and chuckled briefly again. It was a dry, humorless sound. "Alex may have been involved in a drug dealing ring of some kind, but that had nothing to do with his death. Nothing at all. The real truth of his murder lies here, with the person who shot him."

"Wait a minute," Graham interrupted, tapping the wooden desk with his hands. "I have a question."

Jed looked at him. "Yes?"

"If Alex was shot," Graham drummed his fingers on the table, "then why didn't we see the bullet wound in his body? It should've been the first thing to spring up in the autopsy."

Jed opened his mouth to answer but Christie filled in for him.

"Because of how Alex died," she said, her face crowded with deep, thoughtful lines and a faraway look in her eyes. "When he was shot, he stumbled back and fell onto the rake lying behind him. The rake's tines pierced Alex's chest and back. It was a mad stroke of luck. The witnesses reported him convulsing on the rake, and the ME said that was very destructive to his heart, which could have destroyed all evidence of the bullet."

"Correct, although we will have to confirm this with the medical examiner, of course," Jed answered softly, watching the brooding shadows covering Christie's face. Her hands were twined together, and she was twiddling her thumbs repeatedly, absently scratching at the desk's wooden surface with them.

A thin silence filled the room while everyone digested this new theory. Only the clock ticked on the wall, and the screen flickered with the image of Alex frozen on it. Jed sat in his seat and quietly watched the others, especially Christie, who seemed to have taken this news the hardest.

The silence persisted. Each second went by slowly, stretching out like taffy, making its presence last as long as possible. Jed continued sitting in his seat, waiting for someone to speak. Finally, a considerable while later, Christie's tight and strained voice filled the room.

"We've been played." She looked up at them all, her eyes hardened with anger, her face a mask of cold marble. "All this while, we've been played. The killer openly shot Alex in the middle of a busy street in daylight, and instead of catching him, we were busy chasing down irrelevant drug dealers and questioning the victim's family with no rhyme or reason. It's time to pull up our socks. We inadvertently shut down an entire drug ring, which isn't too shabby. Now, let's find Alex's killer!""

There were nods from all around. Christie rose up from her chair, harshly pushing it back, and went to stand in the middle of the room.

"Okay, so now we have Jed's theory to work with. I have a strong feeling that this is exactly what happened to Alex." She gave Jed a brief nod of appreciation before returning her focus to Derek and Graham sitting on the other side. "We need to canvas the entire area where Alex was killed—every single inch. Speak with Gary in forensics. He specializes in sniper trajectory and can tell you all the possible angles that could have been used in this shot. We need to find out every potential vantage point the shooter could have fired from."

Derek and Graham nodded. Chairs scraped back as they began to rise from their seats.

"One more thing," Christie added, her voice sharpening. "We've already wasted too much time as it is. I expect us all to be working at triple speed. If the individual who shot Alex hasn't already disappeared forever, he'll be right on the verge of doing so. Every second counts. Understood?"

"Understood," they all replied together.

"Good." Christie seemed to relax a bit. "Go on, then. I want the location where Alex died canvassed by the end of today, if possible. Bring me a list of places the shooter could have fired from. I'll be waiting." She waved a hand to dismiss them, and the men left, the door closing in their wake.

Silence returned to the room. Christie looked at Jed.

"That was quite a brilliant deduction," she muttered, sliding back a chair and sitting down on it. "We never even thought of the case from that perspective."

"I guess that's why you hired me," Jed answered, biting his lip and looking closely at Christie. "Because I'm not from the police force, I can look at situations from an angle that might not occur to you."

"Uh huh." Christie was frowning down at the desk, playing absently with the hem of her shirt. "If it hadn't been for you, we would still be here butting our heads against the wall."

Jed said nothing to that. He just continued watching Christie, observing her hands as they fiddled with the white cloth of her shirt. Finally, when he just couldn't take it anymore, he spoke.

"Christie."

She looked up at him.

"I'm sorry." Jed uttered the words softly and with honesty, looking straight into her eyes.

Christie met his gaze head-on, her expression impassive. Her eyes were twin clouds of haze which showed nothing.

"For what?" she finally asked.

"You know," Jed sighed deeply when she didn't say anything, "for walking out of that interrogation the way I did."

A single muscle twitched in Christie's jaw. The smoke in her eyes seemed to swirl faster. "You shouldn't have done that," she told him softly.

Jed spread his hands out on the desk in an open admission of guilt. "I know. It was my fault entirely, and I'm not going to try and make excuses for it." He cleared his throat. "I embarrassed you that night, in front of our suspect. I shouldn't have done that. I apologize."

Christie sniffed. She turned her face back down toward her lap, not saying anything for a while. Jed didn't push her any further. He let her deal with her own emotions and handle his apology the way she wanted. Just because he had said he was sorry didn't mean he was now owed her immediate forgiveness. That was not how it worked.

They both sat quietly for a long, long while. The clock continued to tick, and the monitor lay dead and silent. Finally, after Jed's back had begun to ache slightly from reclining in the chair, Christie looked up at him. She gave him a faint but real smile.

"Apology accepted," she stated gently. "I know this case has been especially hard on you. Let's move on and put an end to this case, once and for all."

Jed sighed with relief. Christie's smile was like a burst of fresh air gracing his skin after years spent in a damp, moldy cell.

"Yes, let's." He frowned, then. "I just hope we're not too late. What if the killer has already disappeared?"

"He hasn't." Christie spoke with certainty. "I know it."

Jed looked at her, a question forming on his brow. "How?"

She flashed him another faint grin. "I can feel it in my bones. We've worked far too hard for it all to end with failure."

"Hmmm. Do you think it's a contract killer?" Jed mused. "Or just someone with a vendetta?"

"Contract killer," Christie spoke quickly. "It's not easy shooting someone on a crowded street with a sniper rifle. There are so many things you have to consider. Wind speed and direction. Distance. The bullet's curving arc." She shook her head slowly. "Whoever did this was an expert."

"Speaking of bullets," Jed began, frowning as he considered the possibility, "we know that it went straight through Alex's body, which is why it wasn't found in the autopsy. There's no way a bullet would have enough momentum to pierce a human body and then embed itself in concrete." He looked at Christie. "Do you think it could still be lying somewhere on the street?"

Christie chuckled. "You have too much optimism, Jed. And to answer your question, no." She looked at him. "If one of the thousand walking pedestrians on that street didn't unknowingly kick it away, and if it wasn't crushed beneath one of the dozen cars which are always crowding the road, then it probably just fell through one of the sewer grates and was carried away by the city's sewer system." She shrugged. "The only chance we have now is catching the killer who did this. That's it."

"How will you get him to confess," Jed asked, "if you have no evidence to link him to the crime?"

Christie smiled. It was a dangerous smile, beautiful like the glint of a tiger's wickedly sharp teeth. "You leave that to me. There are certain things we police officers are trained in which even you, with all your Sherlock Holmes abilities, can't figure out."

Jed laughed, throwing up his hands in defeat. "Understood, madam. I'll make sure to stay out of your way when it comes to that." He rose from his seat, picking up his phone and putting it in his pocket. "I think I'll go back to my apartment for a quick break. You call me as soon as there's any update, okay?"

"Of course." Christie rose up to hug him goodbye, her arms going round his back, her hair tickling the nape of his neck as she pressed into him. Jed sighed softly, feeling the sheer relief and peace he always felt when she was so close to him, her warmth wrapped around him like a comforting blanket. They stayed that way for a few seconds, seeking solace in each other's closeness, and then Jed stepped out of the conference room, walking through the police station's corridors toward the exit, his mind buzzing with energy and excitement.

CHAPTER 29

"MOM, I'M GOING TO have to phone you back. I'm getting a
call from Christie." Jed disconnected the line and answered
Christie's call.

"Hello, yes?" He couldn't keep the eagerness out of his
voice. His heart was pumping rapidly.

"Come to the station, Jed." Christie's voice was strangely
even. It showed almost no emotion, except for a tiny flutter
of excitement creeping through it. It only made Jed's pulse
race faster.

"Did you find something?" he asked, unable to hold himself
back.

There was a pause. "Yes. Come fast." Then the line disconnected.

Jed was already dressed. He sprang to his feet and practically
raced out of the living room, his feet flying forward.

Once on the road, he had to practice a remarkable amount
of self-restraint to stop himself from gunning the Jeep down
the street. Evening had arrived, and at this hour, the traffic in
the city was at its peak. It was a truly infuriating test of Jed's

patience, as his vehicle trickled forward in the clogged sea of their vehicles.

A grueling half-hour later, he was sitting in the conference room with Christie, the team, and some uniformed officers. Everyone looked visibly more exhausted.

"Okay, then. Let's get started." Christie closed the door to the room and went up to the head of the table. She surveyed the men sitting there.

"First off, great job from Derek and Graham for pulling this off in record time." She gave them both a small salute. "It's made everything so much easier." She motioned toward Derek, and he connected his laptop with the large TV in the room so that everyone could see easily.

Jed watched the screen blink to life, and a list of names appeared there. There were five names in total, and he could not recognize any of them.

"What are these?" he inquired.

"These," Christie straightened up with a grin, "are called our good luck."

"What?" Jed frowned.

"Thanks to their lightning-fast canvassing of the area with the help of some officers, we've managed to get these names." Christie jabbed a thumb at the screen. "These are the only five buildings our killer could've shot Alex from."

"Only five?" Jed's voice was dubious. "That street is so large and filled with so many buildings. Are you sure it can only be five?"

"Positive," Christie confirmed. "Not every building in the vicinity is accessible. Not every building offers the right vantage point to shoot from. Not every building is just lying vacant for a sniper to use. After a careful and thorough examination by Gary, our expert in the department on bullet trajectory and snipers, these five names are all we have."

"Oh, wow." Jed couldn't believe their luck, and he voiced his sentiment. "Seems like we've gotten lucky."

A half-smile broke out on Christie's face. She looked at him with sharp, gleaming eyes. "It gets better. Boys, your time to shine."

Jed watched as Derek and Graham rose from their chairs and walked toward the head of the table. Derek carried his laptop with him.

"This first building," Derek began, "is called Pronzas Residencia. Our killer couldn't have done his dirty deed from here because all its top floors are occupied. There are families living on each floor, all of whom were present in their apartments during the time Alex was killed."

"What about the rooftop?" Jed inquired.

"Out of bounds. There are doormen and security stationed at the entrance and at the topmost floor to identify any unwanted intruders. If you don't live there, you need to sign in and be announced by security to get buzzed up."

"Okay." Jed leaned back in his seat and nodded once, satisfied.

"Right. Let's go on." Derek leaned forward again and pressed another button. The second name on the list was crossed out as well.

"These are the Sivanz Towers," he began. "Another residential complex. And impossible to use for the same reasons as the first one. Any questions or doubts?"

Jed shook his head.

Derek continued. He pressed the button again, and the fourth name was crossed out this time.

"This is a corporate workplace," he said. "Belongs to the data management company Frexo." A short chuckle escaped his lips. "The company's employees work six days a week, from morning to evening. All floors are fully in use every day, and you need an ID badge and fingerprint scan to gain access—which is why we shall rule this out, too."

There were just two names left now. The third one and the last one on the list. Derek pressed down on the laptop again, and the fifth name was crossed out.

"Paulo and Co. headquarters," he explained to Jed quickly. "Another corporate office, which was impossible to use for the reasons I just mentioned. That leaves us with our one and only suspect on this list."

Jed stared at the name scrawled in black on the screen, and a tiny shiver fluttered across his spine. He felt the hair on his arms rising on its ends as his eyes traveled over the letters. Suddenly, and with an inexplicable surety, Jed knew this was it. Without a shadow of a doubt, this was it. They had reached their killer's attacking spot.

"Sunflower Garden Residences," Graham announced, taking over, his gruff voice startlingly different from Derek's mild tone. "They've been given that name because—surprise, surprise—they have sunflowers growing on their roof, in a small greenhouse which is constantly attended to."

"That means the roof couldn't have been used as the firing location," Jed guessed.

"Correct. The plants would have been disturbed if anyone had even made an attempt. That only leaves the top floors, which is where our suspect finally enters the scene." Graham sucked in a big breath, and Jed saw for the first time how tautly drawn he was at the mention of the elusive killer who had been evading them from the moment this case began.

"All the apartments in the Sunflower Garden Residences are also fully occupied," Graham said, pausing to let Jed absorb his words, "but not every apartment has a family living in it."

"How many?" Jed asked quickly, feeling the sickly fast beat of his pulse now. His palms were tingling painfully. He felt a strong impulse to rise to his feet and suppressed it.

Graham paused again, and although it was only a fleeting pause, Jed found himself in the grips of a maddening impatience. He needed to know. He needed to know *now*.

"Three of the apartments had been rented by bachelors." It was Christie who answered him.

"Three?" Jed took in the information. That wasn't bad. That wasn't bad at all. "So, we have three suspects, then?"

A secret grin tugged at the corners of Christie's lips. She shook her head. "Out of those three suspects, we spoke to two. One is an elderly man who has trouble rising from the sofa and putting his fake dentures in place, much less operating a lethal weapon. The second is an accountant from Minneapolis who has an alibi for the time of Alex's murder. We checked his alibi out, and it was rock solid."

"Which leaves only one." Jed's voice was like a ghost of a sigh in the room's entombed silence. It fluttered off his lips and dissipated instantly. "Only one suspect. Who is he?"

"Jack Stanley," Christie said, and the temperature in the room seemed to drop a degree or two at the mention of that name.

"Jack Stanley," Jed murmured to himself, feeling the strangeness of the name rolling around on his tongue. He swallowed once, twice, but the lump in his throat remained. He looked at Christie, and that was when the realization came to him.

"Wait a minute." Jed frowned. "You said you questioned two out of the three suspects. Why didn't you question this Jack Stanley?"

Christie had been waiting for Jed to ask that. Her lips pressed together into a firm, victorious line as she answered.

"Because he wasn't at the apartment. The guard at the front desk said he hadn't seen him since the day of Alex's death."

The words dropped like bombshells in the room, detonating and letting the truth strike Jed with a deafening certainty. He blinked rapidly multiple times and had to remind himself to breathe.

This is it. We found him. The killer. The one who murdered Alex.

"Please tell me we've managed to get a lead on this guy." Jed's voice was inflected with a small, pleading note. "Please don't tell me that he's disappeared forever and that the case ends here."

Christie's eyes shone, and that was answer enough for him. "I wouldn't have called you here if that had been the case, now, would I?"

Jed's shoulders sagged with relief. He let out a huge, pent-up breath. "Okay, continue."

Derek leaned forward and closed the laptop. The display on the screen behind her winked out a second later. Both men returned to their seats.

"The moment this guy entered our radar," Christie began, "the first thing we did was call all airports and train stations and try and find out whether any flight or train was booked under the name of Jack Stanley."

"And ... did you find anything?"

"Uh huh." Christie picked up her phone and idly looked at something. Jed realized a few seconds later she was inspecting a ticket.

"Congratulations to Jed and everyone else." She clapped briefly. "Thanks to your exceptional effort, we managed to crack this case *just* in the nick of time." She held her thumb and forefinger apart to illustrate how close it had been. Jed could barely see any space between her two fingers.

"Jack Stanley is scheduled to depart for Montreal tomorrow at 6:30 PM," Christie informed them all. "I've assembled a team, and it should be a simple and easy operation. Jack Stanley will be nabbed right before he enters the airport gates. We'll be waiting for him in a disguised van."

"I'll be coming with you," Jed added.

"No way." Christie shook her head sharply. "This is not like that raid at the warehouse, Jed. There will be civilians present at the scene, dozens of them. Even the tiniest mishap can put innocent lives at risk. I won't have that."

Under normal circumstances, Jed would have simply agreed. But this time, something within him rose up in defiant insistence.

"I'm coming with you, Christie," he spoke adamantly. "I have to… I have to see this man when you first catch him. I just… I have to." He shook his head, unable to articulate that thick emotion swirling within him. "I'll be at the back of the van like last time, entirely hidden from view. I won't disrupt your operation in any way. I promise."

Christie pursed her lips, hesitating. "I don't think the chief will give us permission to take you along for a second time, Jed."

"He will. Tell him the case is at its closing and that I need to be there when that happens." Jed paused, and that thick, swirling emotion within him finally rose toward the light, revealing itself. "I have a gut feeling that something is going to happen at the airport—something very important that I need to see."

That did it. The doubt in Christie's eyes disappeared instantly upon hearing those words. She knew how valuable Jed's ability to read people was.

"Fine. You're coming, then," she told him. "I'll plead a special case for you myself. Besides, this case isn't over until we've caught the guy and made him confess. Until that happens, I need my investigative partner with me at all times."

"Yep, you got that right," Jed answered softly, leaning back.

"Right, then. I guess that concludes our meeting." Christie nodded to the men all around her. "See you tomorrow, gentlemen, at 5:00 PM sharp. Please get a good night's sleep and make sure you're well fed and alert. We can't risk screwing up in any way now. This is our one and only shot."

"Understood, Christie. See you tomorrow." The team rose up from their seats and left the room, Jed following behind them. He gave Christie a final handshake before leaving through the open door and turning away from the two officers to make his way to the exit.

As Jed walked, his mind reeled with thoughts. He felt a storm of conflicting emotions raging inside him and had no clue how to make sense of it. There was a rushing excitement about tomorrow, a dim, glowing satisfaction at the case having been cracked, and beyond those two emotions… something else as well. A hidden, cloaked prick of apprehension sat in his belly, secretly whispering to him that it wasn't all over yet. The final act still remained.

Pushing those troubling thoughts out of his mind, Jed opened the station's doors and walked out into the night.

CHAPTER 30

THE DAY HAD ARRIVED.

It was time.

Jed sat in the back seat of the van, his boots restlessly tapping the floor. All around him, the team of five Christie had assembled readied itself for the task at hand. Jason, Carter, Derek, Graham, and Joseph were busy completing their preparations. Guns were checked and double-checked, bulletproof vests refitted properly, shoes laced and double tied.

There was a tiny digital clock lying askew on one of the seats. It showed that only fifteen minutes were left until their moment of action. Jed kept looking at it, feeling his stomach rolling queasily inside him. Through the tinted side window, he could see people walking to and from on the concourse outside, lugging their suitcases behind them.

How would it all play out, exactly? Jed did not know, and that only tightened the nervous knot inside him. He was a therapist, not a police officer. He had no clue how such operations unfolded. All he could do was place his trust in Christie and follow whatever instructions she gave him.

"Jed." Christie's voice startled Jed out of his thoughts. He snapped his head up to look at her, and she smiled.

All good? she mouthed at him while her team assembled its equipment.

Jed nodded numbly. He did not want to worry her right now. There were bigger things at play here. Swallowing the dryness in his mouth, he returned her smile with a weak one of his own. Christie saw it and resumed her preparations.

Ten minutes left, now. How quickly time went by when you felt like a taut guitar string being plucked repeatedly, every nerve within you jangling with anxiety. Jed glanced out the side window again and saw that the crowd was beginning to slowly thicken. Of course. Evening flights were the most popular ones of all, he had read somewhere. Soon, these steady streams of people would turn into chaotic tides.

There was a phone lying next to the clock on the seat, its screen silent and dark. Jed glanced at it and wondered dimly when it would ring. A call from this phone would alert them to Jack Stanley's arrival at the airport. His name had already been placed on the exit control list, and the guards within the terminals were silently watching out for him. The moment he arrived, Christie would be notified, and the team would spring into action.

They had also spoken to the guard at the building where Stanley had lived, and he had provided them with a description of Jack Stanley's features. Christie had had a rough sketch drawn based on the guard's description, along with his DMV photo, and their entire search and capture operation would be based on it.

Jed had taken a look at the drawn sketch, and he had shivered slightly upon seeing it. The drawn picture showed a regular, nondescript man with a thin face and a light, scraggly beard—the kind of man you passed on the street without a second glance. It was this kind of man who served as the perfect criminal because no one noticed him. He was invisible.

Five minutes left, now.

The crowd had thickened even more outside, and Jed could see the beginnings of that surging tide of people appearing. Cars were parked in a straight line at the edge of the concourse: taxis, Volkswagens, Chevrolets, and cabs all loitering near the sidewalk in a burst of colors. People were disembarking from them even as he watched, hauling their heavy suitcases and bags underneath heaving arms, their expressions strained and busy. People were embracing and saying their goodbyes.

Someone's phone rang in the van, and Jed froze instantly, his heart jumping into his throat. A second later, he realized it was a personal cell, not the one lying on the seat. He relaxed again, and the ringing noise was cut off a few seconds later. Joseph looked a bit sheepish as he tucked his cell away.

"Guys." Christie's voice filled the van's cramped quarters, and all activity ceased. Six pairs of eyes flicked in her direction—Jed's included. He gave the clock on the seat a final look and understood.

Time was up.

"Final briefing before we begin." Christie was sitting upright, her hair tied behind her in a tight bun, the sickly fluorescent light in the van's roof giving her skin an unnatural sheen. "We'll receive the call any moment now, so please listen up as I repeat your responsibilities one more time."

They all listened quietly.

"I will be leading the team, and the rest of you will be following behind me in two different pairs, flanking both my sides." She gave the men sitting before her a scrutinizing look, her eyes traveling over their casual clothing. "Remember, we're going undercover, so don't attract any undue attention. Act as natural as you can. We should all appear as separate individuals, never as one big group. Understood?"

They all nodded.

"Good. Now you, Jed." Christie turned toward him. "You will remain ten feet behind us at all times, regardless of what happens. Just observe from the outskirts, even once we've apprehended the man. This operation is not over until we've securely gotten him inside the van. Until then, all of us must follow procedure. It's entirely possible that there might be other allies of his at the airport. The last thing we want is a shootout near civilians, or for one of our men to be taken captive. Understood?"

Jed nodded, the remaining men murmuring their agreement.

"Good. Now that that's settled, we ca—" Christie's voice broke off midway. Or rather, it was interrupted by a shrill ringing sound. Jed glanced at the seat and saw the phone there buzzing with life, vibrating on the cushion while its screen blinked brightly.

Jack Stanley was here.

"Let's go, team!" The side door opened, and the men stepped out, one-by-one. They were all dressed in casual attire, sporting bulletproof vests and pistols beneath their faded flannel shirts and cargo jeans. Silently following behind them, Jed marveled at how easily they blended into the crowd, ambling forward like bored travelers who had arrived early for a flight.

They made their way across the concourse and toward the departure doors, where a uniformed guard stood waiting for them, twitching nervously. As soon as he saw Christie approaching, he stiffened and beckoned for her to follow.

They traced a curving path around the departure doors and toward the side of the building, where there was another tiny door manned by two armed personnel. Christie approached them, and Jed saw her speak a few words. He glimpsed the backside of her badge as she took it out of her pocket and showed it to the two men. A moment later, the doors had opened, and they were through.

They walked through a long, winding, marbled corridor which was entirely empty and lit up by bright, penetrating lights. All the men formed a line behind Christie, with Jed at its tail.

Eventually, after a minute or so of walking, the corridor led to another set of doors, which were manned by two more guards. They spotted Christie approaching them, her team behind her, and fished in their pockets for a keycard, which they used to open the door. Christie slipped in, and the remaining men followed, the door clicking shut behind them.

They were inside the airport now, on the other side of security, near the departure terminal Jack Stanley would be using.

The tomblike silence was gone immediately, and now the airport's noisy, incoherent din greeted them. There were people everywhere, sprawled on seats, buying food from McDonalds, browsing books in kiosks, and chattering away on their phones. They had bypassed the security checkpoints and arrived within the lounge. Somewhere within this noisy, lit hall, Jack Stanley sat.

This part was the true challenge. They had to stay together as a group but not let it show. Each person had to walk separately from the others, with his own unique gait.

Jed lagged behind the team and furtively observed the men adopt their own different postures. Graham strode forward with that sagging, avuncular stride which fitted him so much. Next to him, Derek walked in a completely opposite fashion, appearing like a young, ambitious professional heading for his first international conference. Joseph dragged his feet, as if he were being made to leave the country against his will. Carter just trotted briskly, blending in perfectly. Jason walked with his usual swagger—or at least pretended to, as best as he could.

They all silently trailed Christie, who had the phone against her ear and was winding through the maze of seats and people. They went from lounge thirteen to lounge twenty-one, and it was here that Christie stopped dead in her tracks, waiting for the others to see what she had seen. Jed peered over everyone's shoulders, and his eyes spotted him a second later. His heartbeat increased.

There he was.

Jack Stanley.

Christie walked closer, and the men followed, approaching the killer. He was reclining lazily on a seat, a magazine held in his hands. The sketch made by the police artist did not do him justice. Up close, Jack Stanley appeared even more harmless and pathetic. He was a bony, reedy fellow, with a peach-colored fuzz of hair on his head and a similar, slightly golden beard. His face was sharp and angled, his eyes almost sleepy as he studied the magazine with a barely displayed interest.

This is Alex's killer? Jed wondered dubiously. But then, he pushed down that thought. He knew how deceiving looks could be.

They all casually took their seats at a sufficient distance from the man, surrounding him from all sides, yet ensuring they went unnoticed. Jack did not raise his head from his magazine as they passed by him.

Once they were seated, they waited. Christie held the phone in her hands, her eyes glued to the screen. They had arranged this next part with the help of the airport personnel. An official would call Jack and ask him to come to a designated counter regarding a ticket problem, leading him to one of the empty hallways that were not currently connected to any plane. Jack would go to the counter and trailing much further behind him, hidden entirely from view, would be the team. They would accost Jack in the empty hallway and take him to the van from there, without anyone in the airport being disturbed.

Sure enough, Jack Stanley raised his phone to his ears a few moments later. A moment after that, he was on his feet, walking toward a distant counter.

Jed sat in his seat and fidgeted, noticing a man in a blue aviation uniform approaching Jack from the counter. The man walked casually, easily, as if he actually was on an errand to fix an issue with someone's ticket and not to lure a homicidal maniac into a trap.

The man stopped right before Jack and spoke something softly. Jed watched from the corner of one eye, his pulse thrumming in his ears like a gushing river. Jack turned. A frown creased his forehead, and he leaned forward. The official bent forward and politely repeated what he was saying. A moment after that, Jed saw Jack nod and follow behind the man, who was heading into an empty corridor.

This was it.

Once the pair was a fair distance away, Christie rose, and the rest of her team rose after her. They followed Jack, who was following the man in blue, who led them all past several twists and turns and into an empty and quiet hallway. It was then that Christie exploded into action.

"Freeze!" she shouted, her voice burning with iron command, her Beretta held in her hands, pointed straight at Jack.

Jack Stanley turned, frowning. He saw the pistol in Christie's hands, and his frown deepened. He saw the other men approaching from behind Christie, all of them with their weapons trained on him, and he fell to his knees, raising his hands above his head.

Jed watched it all unfold. His eyes were fixed on the man like lasers, observing him carefully. There were many things he noticed—things which unnerved him deeply and truly made him wonder who was playing who here.

"Jack Stanley," Christie grunted, stepping up to the man and handcuffing him, "you're under arrest for the murder of Alex Gray."

Chapter 31

"Mr. Jack Stanley."

Christie's voice filled the room, flinty like ice. There was a grinding noise of her chair being deliberately scraped backwards, and then the dull thud of the files she dropped onto the desk with a purposeful force. "How are you doing today?"

The man sitting across from Jed and Christie gazed at them with an expressionless face. He appeared perfectly at ease, his shoulders relaxed, his hands resting in his lap. The light from the overhead bulb pierced his eyes and washed over his skin in unhealthy white waves.

"Surviving." His voice sounded tired and flat. He spoke no more.

"Surviving," Christie mused, staring intently at him. "Wish I could say the same for Alex Gray. Why did you kill him?

Stanley said nothing, did nothing. Every inch of him remained perfectly still, including his slit eyes.

"Is that how you want to play it then, Jack?" Christie huffed out a laugh. "Okay, then. But I would urge you to think again. The courts here have very strict laws concerning premeditated murder—life without parole, almost always."

Still, Jack Stanley did not speak. His face was corpse-like and waxy, his thin lips pressed shut in what looked to be a vow of eternal silence.

"Do you think we don't have evidence to convict you?" Christie regarded him closely. "Is that why you're refusing to speak?" She chuckled, then. "If you wanted that to happen, Mr. Stanley, then you shouldn't have planned such a shoddy murder."

Christie's hand went to the right pocket of her jacket, and she withdrew a tiny evidence bag from its depths, with something twisted and crumpled nestling inside it, its bronze surface glinting in the room's light. She put the wrapped object on the table, right in front of Stanley. It hit the table's metal surface with a sharp tinkle.

"That is the bullet you used to kill Alex Gray."

Christie folded her arms and leaned over the table. "We found a pair of fingerprints on it, Stanley. When we try to match them with yours, what result do you think we'll get?" Her voice was soft, gloating.

Jed sat quietly in the corner and observed Christie carry out her little play. Of course, the bullet was a fake. The real one had never been found. But Jack Stanley didn't know that. The way Christie was convincingly carrying out this ploy, even Jed found himself starting to believe her lie.

Yet, his unease remained.

The source of that unease was nothing other than the man sitting opposite him. Something about him was just... off, deeply unsettling. Jed's internal alarms had begun flashing the moment he had seen Jack get arrested at the airport. They were still flashing now, half-an-hour later, inside this interrogation room. An icy dread was beginning to seep into him, filling him with a strange sense of impending doom he couldn't quite pinpoint.

"You know, your best bet is to simply confess to what you did to prove your cooperation, and the courts may take pity on you." Christie spoke in a reasonable, friendly voice, her demeanor quickly shifting from enemy to ally. "If you tell us what you did, we'll plead a special case with the judge. Who knows? You might even get a chance at parole."

Jack Stanley continued staring at her with those carved marble features. His eyes stood motionless, like gems embedded within a granite skull. The seconds ticked by, quiet and unnerving. Christie said nothing more, continuing to look at Jack with her arms folded across the table, waiting for him to talk.

And then, he did.

"I'll confess to the murder on one condition." His voice was nothing more than the faint rustle of papers being shuffled, but it caused both Jed and Christie to stir in their seats.

"What's that?" Christie asked.

Jack Stanley smiled at her. It was a horrid, hideous thing, like the terrifying rictus of a grin on a skeleton's face. His lips seemed to peel back from his face, as if the flesh was being torn off, and he bared his teeth at Christie in a mad, feral grin.

"If you remove that fake bullet from the table, then I'll confess to my crimes."

Shock rippled across Jed's features, such a sudden and powerful shock he was unable to hide it. He turned toward Christie and was impressed to see her staring back at Jack with that same stony face.

"What are you talking about?" she asked flatly.

Jack's smile widened. His lips pulled back further from his teeth, crowding his cheeks with wrinkles. Those deadened, vacant eyes flickered with amusement.

"You heard me, detective."

Christie pursed her lips, like she was disappointed. "You think this bullet is fake?"

Jack Stanley shook his head. "I *know* this bullet is fake." He tilted his head, looking at her with intrigue. "Do you think I'm lying? Do you think I won't admit to the murder if you accept that this bullet is not real?" He tutted softly, like a parent disappointed by a child's deceptive behavior. "Okay, then. How about this? I'll confess to the murder first, *then* you remove this bullet from the table. How about that? Does that sound better?"

This time, even Christie wasn't able to fully keep the surprise from showing on her face. Her lips twitched with a tiny, almost imperceptible movement, and her nostrils flared slightly. She paused for a moment, thrown off guard by this most unexpected offer.

"Okay, then." She tried to sound casual. "Let's start with your confession."

Jack Stanley nodded at her with satisfaction. He leaned back in his chair, twined both hands together, and spoke:

"Yes. I killed Alex Gray. I rented a room in the Sunflower Garden Residences." He spoke with the smooth calmness of someone who seemed to be discussing nothing more important than the weather. "I used a VSS Vintorez Russian compact precision rifle for the act. I equipped it with a suppressor to block out its subsonic boom and set it up just inside my window the day before the murder. On the morning Alex arrived at the coffee shop and stepped outside with his beverage, I took aim and shot him in the chest, killing him."

Silence filled the room. Even the sound of their breathing seemed to have died away. Jed and Christie sat and stared mutely at the man calmly observing them, his lips clamped shut once again.

"Why did you kill him?" Christie asked finally.

"Uh-uh." Stanley let out a noise of disapproval. He gestured with his face toward the mangled bullet lying on the table. "You made a promise, detective."

Christie's face hardened. Her eyes narrowed, and a flicker of red-hot anger sliced through them at having been beaten so easily. She reached out with two stiff fingers and plucked the bag with the fake bullet in it off the table, pushing it roughly back into her pocket.

"Why did you kill Alex?" she asked again, her voice steely now, with all the friendless evaporated from it.

"I'm a contract killer," Stanley simply said, as if that was answer enough. "I was asked to do a job, and I did it." He paused, and the corners of his lips quirked upward. "Just like I was asked to kill Joel with a poisoned dart."

All the air seemed to rush out of the room at those words. Jed's mouth sealed shut, and he was afraid that if he tried to breathe he would let out a choked gasp. Beside him, he sensed Christie go utterly still.

"What did you say?" Christie's voice was frighteningly low and fragile.

Jack Stanley continued to slouch in his chair, unperturbed by their reactions. "You heard me, *detectives*." A soft snicker escaped his lips. "I killed Joel. Since the two of you were doing such a marvelous job of tracking down the killer, I thought I'd have another go and hope that the second time around, you'd do better." He shrugged. "All according to the orders I was given, of course."

"Given by whom?"

"Ahhh. Now we get to the rub. Finally." Stanley leaned forward again. For the first time in the interview, the blank canvas of his face colored with an emotion. That emotion seemed to be interest.

"Detective, I think it's time you paid some attention to your partner." Stanley looked toward Jed, giving him an appraising look. "I think he has a few questions for me which will prove far more incisive than the dull ones you've been asking."

"What?" Christie turned to Jed, frowning. "Jed? Do you have something to ask?"

Jed bit his lip, his mind racing. Ever since that arrest at the airport, he had known this moment was coming. He had seen it in Jack Stanley's entire demeanor, and in those soulless eyes of his. Now, that moment was here, and there was no more running from it. It was time to face the truth.

"You were expecting us at the airport," Jed spoke with reluctance, his eyes never leaving the man before him. "You *wanted* to be arrested. Everything was planned."

Christie stirred with surprise as she heard Jed's revelation. Jack Stanley's eyes widened with what clearly resembled happiness. He raised both hands in the air and began to clap slowly.

"Good job, Jed Gray," he spoke, smiling at him. "He told me not to worry too much, that you were going to make all the deductions yourself. I was a bit doubtful, but you have just proven him right."

Him. The nape of Jed's neck prickled with fear. He bit back the urge to ask Stanley who that mysterious *him* was. That would come later.

"The guard at the apartment you rented," Jed continued. "You paid him to tell you when we came there searching. You paid that guard to give the police your description. You told him to inform you the moment we deduced you were the killer. Then, and only then, did you book your ticket out of this city because you knew that we would catch you at the airport."

"Marvelous!" Stanley broke out into full-fledged applause, his eyes gleaming with delight. "Simply marvelous, Jed! I have to say, you have truly lived up to the description I was given of you."

"Wait, hold on," Christie broke in, unable to hold herself back. Her voice was boiling with confused frustration. She had lost all control of this interview and had no idea where it was headed. "Why did you want to get yourself arrested?"

Stanley didn't even look at her. He continued staring at Jed, his eyes studying him with curious admiration. "Go on, Jed. Complete the deduction. Tell your partner why I wanted to be caught for my crimes."

Jed sighed. He was tired now, tired of all these games, wanting them to come to an end. But he could tell the end was still far, far away from him.

"You're dying," Jed spoke dully, his voice resigned. "It's evident by the unhealthy shine of your skin, the noticeable yellowness in your eyes, and the fact that you're as a thin as a stork." He paused. "You have some sort of terminal illness, and its slowly killing you."

Stanley stared at Jed with fascination, his hands twitching in his lap as if they wanted to clap again. "Good job, Jed Gray. You've guessed right." He patted the right side of his abdomen gently, wincing as he did so. "My liver is failing. Doctors have given me no more than a few months."

Silence seeped into the room again. Stanley leaned back in his seat, Christie fidgeted uncomfortably, and Jed sat utterly still, trying to build up the courage to continue this investigation. Finally, when he had gathered enough, he spoke.

"Who hired you? And why are they targeting me?"

"You have a fan, Jed." Stanley grinned to himself, as if he had made a joke. "Don't you remember?"

"Remember? Remember what?"

"Oh, don't be like that." Stanley let out a sigh of disappointment. "I suppose I shouldn't be surprised, considering you've tucked away that part of your life."

"What?" Jed's breath caught in his throat. A flush of ice filled his chest. "Are you..."

"Yes." Stanley nodded once in confirmation. "I am, indeed, talking about your past, Jed. Your glorious, beautiful past, the one you've been trying so hard to run away from all your life."

Stanley leaned forward then, and a chilly breeze seemed to waft through the room, although every window and door was closed.

"I'm here to tell you that you weren't able to run fast enough, Jed." Stanley's voice came out in a whisper, dripping with menace. "You weren't fast enough, and now your past has caught up with you. If you don't reflect soon enough, it's going to catch you." He made a vicious grabbing motion with both hands before leaning back and withdrawing into silence.

Jed sat in his seat in stunned silence. Christie scowled at Stanley, her hands twitching on the desk as if she were trying to hold herself back from throttling him.

"You need to be up front and clear with us right now," she demanded in a razor-sharp voice. "Tell us who sent you. Tell us why you agreed to work for him. Tell us everything, including his name and wher—"

"—Or what?" Stanley interrupted her. His expression was icy. "Are you going to put me in jail? Do it, then. I've already confessed voluntarily. Are you going to kill me?" He snickered. "Go ahead. You're only doing what's inevitably going to happen in a few months."

The scowl remained on Christie's face, but she did not speak further. She knew the man was right, and that was what infuriated her so much.

"I'm done talking now," Stanley murmured, relaxing back against his seat and clasping his hands together. Before either Christie or Jed could do anything, Jack Stanley broke his vow of silence and burst into an eerie fit of giggles. The sound of his laughter was like leaking ventilation pipes—not something you'd want to hear in a closed room. It went on for a good fifteen seconds. When Stanley was done, he abruptly straightened and wiped away a tear from his left eye. "Sorry about that. It's just that this whole thing is so much fun! Now, where was I? Right! I was just stating that no matter what you say, do, or threaten me with, I won't talk. In fact, I'd like to be taken to my cell now, if you'll allow. The day has been quite tiring." He stretched his face back and feigned a deep yawn.

Jed continued staring at the man, at a complete loss for words. That unease within him only rose higher and higher, making his muscles stiffen tensely. He knew Stanley was right about everything—about his past being related to this murder and about Stanley's decision to not speak further.

He had no idea what to do about either of those things.

CHAPTER 32

JED SAT ALONE IN his apartment.

It was evening, but he had still turned all the lights off. He found the brightness intrusive and distracting. Right now, no such distractions could be afforded.

His apartment lay quiet and steeped in shadows. It was a funny thing, Jed noticed, how darkness seemed to turn everything threatening, even the most mundane of objects. He could see the evidence before him as he sat on the edge of his bed. The door to the room was open, and the fridge peeked from the corner of the living room—except that it didn't really look like a fridge in this dimness. It looked like the crouching body of some kind of beast knit from the blackness of space that had finally arrived to devour Jed. Even the chair in the corner of the room appeared to be a demon, waiting for the moment to pounce.

Yes, the darkness made everything terrifying.

Especially the past.

Unfortunately for Jed, he had kept that part of his life locked away in a lightless, musty room for too long—far too long. It had been almost a decade since he had opened that room.

He had peeked through its keyhole from time to time and even put his ear against the door on rare occasions to listen. But Jed had never, ever turned the doorknob and thrown that door open. Even the thought of it had terrified him. What unholy, crawling horrors might be lurking there in the moldy darkness, biding their time, waiting for him? What abominations from the memories of his past had survived and were clinging to that room's ceiling, their appetites ravenous after so many years of patient waiting? No, that room had been a Pandora's box for Jed his entire life. He had done his level best to steer clear of it at all times.

Until now.

Jed had known this day was coming. He had known it deep in his bones. He was a therapist, after all. Who better to understand that a person could never outrun their past? It had to be faced, sooner or later. The longer you waited, the more rotten and mutated the contents of that locked room became, twisting and hideously building upon themselves in all those years of isolation.

Jed sucked in a deep, shivering breath. His hands curled into fists on his lap. His thigh muscles clenched in apprehension. He sat there on the edge of the bed for a few more seconds, a hunched, weary outline in the dark. Then he exhaled long and deep before kicking off his shoes and lying straight back on his bed, his eyes facing the ceiling. It was time to enter that room.

Jed closed his eyes.

His mind's hand gripped the doorknob and turned it, swinging the door open.

He entered.

He is sitting on a gurney, in a hall that reeks of disinfectant and sanitizer. Bright, sterile lights glare down at him from above. In the distance, people dressed in white clothes are hurrying to and fro.

Jed is in the rehabilitation center.

He knows why he has been brought here. The white gown hanging off his skeleton-like body and the heart-rate monitor clipped to his finger are answer enough. Even if they weren't, he would have still known. The traces of his actions are present in his body. He can feel the frail, dizzying beat of his heart, the lightheadedness which grips him every few seconds, and a thin, slicing pain in his abdomen, like pins and needles scurrying back and forth.

Jed has overdosed.

He has survived, thankfully—or perhaps unthankfully; he does not yet know. His mind is a mess. There are so many worries and fears teeming in it that it's hard to believe so much darkness can fit so snugly within his skull. He looks up and sees another boy coming from the distance.

Jed recognizes the boy instantly. His name is Jeff, and he is going to become one of Jed's closest friends at this clinic. It hasn't happened yet, but it's about to.

Jeff is a tall, skinny boy with long hair that is parted in the middle and hangs over both his ears like a limp curtain. The bottom ends of his hair have been dyed a seaweed green. There is a ring glinting in his nose.

Jed watches Jeff approach. The boy's head is down-turned, and he is dragging his feet forward rather than simply placing them ahead of him. His hospital gown is open at the bottom, and three stark ribs peek through it.

Jeff raises his head as he passes by Jed. His eyes fall on Jed and the heartrate monitor attached to him. He slows, coming to a stop.

"Hello," Jeff mumbles, looking at the floor.

"Hey," Jed answers him back. His own voice sounds strained and weak to his ears. He looks at Jeff, who is staring intently at the floor. Later, after they have become friends, Jed will one day ask why Jeff does not look at people while talking to them. Jeff will answer him truthfully, telling Jed that his parents shamed him too cruelly after discovering his heroin addiction, that he has trouble looking anyone in the eyes now without feeling that despairing guilt creeping back in. Jed will nod somberly in understanding, intrigued and saddened at the same time. He will not know it then, but the seed will already have been planted in his mind at that moment. It will blossom later, eventually guiding him toward becoming a therapist.

But all of that is to come in the future. Right now, Jeff is looking at a light fixture on a nearby wall and saying something to Jed. But Jed can't hear him because he's suddenly being pulled back, into an endlessly black corridor, with the hospital shrinking to a speck before him. The memory is receding, he understands. Another one is coming to take its place.

On the bed, Jed's sleeping form stirs.

They're in the rehabilitation courtyard, all of them. It is a cloudless, sunny day, and the overhead brightness is painting the basketball court in buttery, golden strokes. Somewhere nearby, a bird trills. The scraggly plants at the courtyard's edge are swaying in the grip of a light breeze.

Jed is standing there with Jeff, Rowan, and Mindy. There are others, too—many more patients loitering in the open space, breathing in the air and basking in the sun. But Jed is standing a bit to the side with his friends, the three closest ones he's made at this place.

Mindy is a short, slight girl with raven eyes and equally dark bangs that brush against her jawbones. She always wears dark mascara and eyeliner whenever she's awake and moving. There is a tattoo of a three-headed dog on her wrist. In her loose-fitting hospital gown, Mindy seems to resemble a normal, healthy girl. But of course, she is not. No one here is. The demon she has been destined to wrestle with is anorexia, and ever since she was admitted to this rehab clinic, she has slowly been winning that battle. Every day, Jed notices her looking a little healthier. And it makes him happy.

Rowan is the oldest of their group. He's a heroin addict like Jeff and has sandy hair and a pair of permanent, scowling eyes. Out of the four of them, Rowan has been finding his battle the toughest. There are dark circles beneath his eyes, and his lips quiver with the effects of withdrawal. The breeze blowing around them isn't that cool, yet Rowan's hands are wrapped around his chest, and he is shivering.

All four of them are playing a game. It is the only one they play, a game full of bittersweet fun.

"I'm going to get a hotdog for myself when I first get out," Mindy says. She licks her lips in anticipation and rubs her hands together, her dark eyes shining with excitement. "Oh, yes, one of those big, juicy hotdogs that comes in a buttered, toasted bun, drizzled with all kinds of heavenly sauces." She rolls her eyes and pretends to swoon at the idea.

They all laugh.

"I'm going to go watch a movie a week at the cinema," Jeff answers, gazing wistfully at the barren landscape stretching out beyond the clinic fence. "I'm going to go alone and just sit in a theater with a bunch of normal people around me, doing the most normal thing possible. With no one giving me sidelong glances or thinking the word 'junkie' when they look at me." He rubs his hands together earnestly. "Yes, that will be a dream come true."

"And I'm going to take all that money in my account and finally start the restaurant I've been thinking of," Rowan chimes in, his voice quavering with effort. "It's going to be a green salad bar, full of the healthiest foods imaginable—avocados, nuts, you name it! Even smoking won't be allowed within the premises!" He chuckles, and everyone joins in.

"What about you, Jed?" Mindy asks, looking at him inquiringly.

Jed is staring at the crowd of people around them when the question reaches his ears. He turns toward Mindy and the rest.

"I'm going to try my level best to make sure that others don't end up where we did—and that they don't have to learn their lessons the hard way." His voice is filled with surety.

The others stare back at him in admiring silence.

"Jed, the beacon of altruism!" Jeff crows, and they all laugh. Mindy says something then, and it begins an excited, heated conversation.

But Jed isn't listening. Or, at least, the Jed revisiting this memory is not paying any attention to his friends talking. He's looking at the throng of people around him… feeling unsettled.

There's something here… something connected in some way to Alex's murder. He can feel it.

But what is it? Jed cannot pinpoint it. There are so many patients filling up the yard, so many drawn and sickly faces. Lurking within those sea of faces, or perhaps somewhere near them, is an answer—the key to this riddle. What could it possibly be?

He cannot tell, and there is not much time left. The whole scene before him is beginning to recede, fleeing into the distance like that previous memory did. Knowing he doesn't have long, Jed squints at the sunlit courtyard, searching for that unknown prick of recognition he felt. What caused it? What's lurking here, in his past, which is connected to Alex's death, and to Jack Stanley?

He does not know.

Time is up.

Once more, Jed is falling through that endless black corridor, going from one memory to the next like an astronaut switching space stations. This time, he's in the cafeteria, sitting with Jeff, talking about the stale food. Here, too, that prick of awareness remains, telling him that the answer is close…

Jed is unable to find out what it is. That memory races away, and now he is in another one—standing in a room in the hospital clinic, with Jeff and Mindy, watching Rowan convulse and writhe on the bed, caught in the agonizing throes of withdrawal after he somehow got a hold of something and relapsed. Rowan will survive; Jed already knows that. His mind is on the room, trying to see if he can spot something... anything...

But no. Now the memories are rushing past him in floods. So many of them—too many to count. Images are flashing before him like the shutter of a demonically possessed camera, clicking left and right, hurling pictures and scenes his way. Jed opens his arms and takes them all in, no longer afraid.

Throughout those recurring flashes of remembrance, as he once more tours the pasty white insides of his rehabilitation clinic, Jed continues to feel that prick of recognition bothering him. But he is unable to understand what it could be. No matter how hard he tries, it steers clear of his grasp, continuing to taunt him with its infuriating jabs.

When the memories end, finally having exhausted themselves, and Jed sits up straight in his bed, feeling a mix of powerful emotions swirling within him, the lingering ache of that jab remains. It haunts him like a phantom pain, telling him that there is still one last riddle remaining, one last answer he has yet to figure out.

CHAPTER 33

"Hello, sir. How can I help you?"

Jed stared back at the receptionist's smiling face and was momentarily at a loss for words. How could she help him? He didn't know. He didn't even know how to help himself.

"Uh, I was wondering if I could take a look inside," Jed spoke, swallowing. His own words bounced into his ears, and he realized how suspicious they sounded. "I stayed here for a long while when I was a kid," he added hastily. "Just wanted to… come back and see how this place was doing. It… I—I made some good memories here, you know."

That frozen, artificial smile on the receptionist's face melted into an understanding one. Jed wasn't the first of his kind to visit this place, of course. Many like him had come before, wanting to give back to the place which had given so much to them.

"Could you come back tomorrow, sir?" she requested gently. "I'll have to speak with the dean here and ask for formal approval before allowing you inside the premises. Since its already quite late, the dean has left for the day. He'll be back tomorrow morning at 8:00 AM sharp. You can come back then."

Jed paused. "Would it not be possible to allow me a quick look inside? I probably won't be able to come back Monday morning because I'll be tangled up in work. This place is on the other side of the city—took me a good three hours to drive over here."

"I..." The receptionist, whose name was Linda, considered his request for an uncertain second. This place wasn't Fort Knox, not like all those flashy, expensive-as-hell rehab clinics made especially for movie stars and musicians who had fallen off the wagon. This was a far tinier, far more modest place, barely keeping itself afloat with the funding it received. It wasn't that unusual for unexpected guests to be given a quick, improvised tour of the common areas. All the patients were in their rooms at this hour, so she didn't need to be concerned with patient confidentiality. She had done it before, but then again, it was also quite late.

"No need to feel pressured by my request." Jed smiled amiably at her. "I understand completely if you're unable to accommodate me. It's just that..." he paused again and exhaled softly, "... I literally owe this place my life. Not only that, but I owe my career to it, too. I'm a therapist, by the way."

"Wow." Linda was surprised. She hadn't been expecting that bit of news.

"Yeah." Jed chuckled dryly to himself. "This place taught me the value of helping people, which is why I just decided tonight that I would give it a visit. See if a look inside would jog my memory and bring back the old days." He laughed briefly before turning around. "But it's okay if you're not allowed to let me in. I guess I'll just come back some other time, when I'm free." He started walking toward the exit.

"Wait," Linda called out.

Jed turned back and found the receptionist looking at him, her fingers drumming the countertop.

"It's fine," Linda gave in. "You can go in for a quick tour. Fifteen minutes, no more than that. Just the common areas, where none of the patients currently are. Does that sound okay?"

Jed grinned with gratitude. "That sounds wonderful, Linda."

He waited before the counter while Linda fetched a temporary visitor card for him, which he hung around his neck. She then picked up the telephone by her side and called and spoke to someone on the other end of the line.

"Hello, Mathew. Could you come over to reception, please? We have a guest here who just needs a quick look around for ten to fifteen minutes. He's waiting for you." She set the phone down and scribbled Jed's name in a register lying before her.

"Mathew should be here any minute now. He's one of our security guards during the night shift," she explained.

Jed did not have to wait long. A pair of wooden dou-ble-doors to his left swung open moments later, and a bald, brawny man sporting thick black stubble stepped out. He was dressed in a dark blue security uniform.

"Hello, I'm Mathew," the young man spoke with a thick southern accent, clasping Jed's hand in his own. "Come with me, sir."

Jed followed Mathew through the wooden doors, who closed them once they were inside. He began leading Jed forward, toward another door at the end which led to the rehab clinic's interior.

I know this place, Jed thought dimly to himself, looking around at the dull white walls and the tiled floor. His heartbeat was quickening with every step he took. He felt like he had returned to the street which lay outside his childhood home. His entire body tingled with a faint familiarity, and goosebumps prickled the nape of his neck.

The second door they reached was a metal one, and its handle let out a startled screech as Mathew turned it clock-wise, pushing the metal barrier outward on its hinges. A large, circular waiting room came into view.

Jed froze where he was. His legs came to an abrupt stop, one foot placed right in front of the other. He kept looking at the room peeking through the door before him—those tiny, wooden chairs, the wall with its pastel blue paint, and that small reception area made out of teakwood, which stood vacant. All of it slapped him in the face with the strength of a familiar stranger. Everything looked new, and yet, at the same time, seemed as old as the face of his mother.

This was my home, Jed thought dully, *my sanctuary as a young man.*

"Sir?" Mathew was standing at the door, looking at him quizzically.

Jed started. "I'm coming," he answered quickly, clearing his throat and walking forward. He went past the held door, and it swung shut behind him. The marble in this part of the clinic was cleaner and shinier. Even the lights had changed from bright white to a warm, disarming yellow. He felt like he was in a friendly dentist's lounge.

Matthew continued walking. There was another pair of double doors at the lounge's end, and he used a keycard to swipe them open. The doors swung inward to reveal another hallway, this one lined with closed rooms on both sides.

Once more, Jed could not move. This time, he even found breathing difficult. He stood there, gawking at the rooms stretching out till the end, his mind reeling with a jarring sense of déjà vu.

The withdrawal clinics, Jed thought numbly, going forward, *where the patients of this place go through the worst phase of their cleansing process—where I saw Rowan go through his worst phase and reach the point where we all thought he was going to die, him included.*

In contrast to the lounge, the waiting room was dimmer and shadowy. Perhaps it had been done on purpose by the clinic staff, to somehow symbolize the excruciating purging process people went through within these walls, a process which wrung out every bit of darkness from their bodies. Maybe that darkness was what he was seeing right now, clinging to the walls and the ceiling like fungi.

Jed's loud footsteps echoed in his ears like ghostly claps as he continued down the hallway, stopping at its very end, near the last door to his left. Something about it had caught his eye. He peeked through the narrow glass slit in the corner and saw nothing but a draped curtain. A metal slat beneath the door stated that it currently lay vacant.

"One second, Mathew," Jed called out, unable to move from where he stood. "I just need a moment to… figure something out."

"Take your time," Mathew called out, turning his back toward the troubled-looking man. This was not the first time he had seen one of this clinic's old patients travelling through its corridors and having vivid flashbacks. He understood.

Jed, meanwhile, was *not* having flashbacks. In fact, he was having the opposite. He was trying to *force* a flashback to happen, but it just wasn't happening. Something in his mind had clicked upon seeing this door, something he knew was closely connected to his current case. He just needed to figure out what it was. That tiny glass slit in the door… he had seen something through it once, a long time ago, when he had been a patient here. What could it be?

After a couple minutes of futile effort, Jed continued past the door, knowing the answer would not come to him right then. But that was okay. He had fed his brain the visuals. His subconscious mind would work on it in quiet privacy and inform him when it had reached an answer. That was how things had been happening with him lately for this case.

They continued on, going past the withdrawal clinics and stepping left through a forking corridor into the cafeteria. Jed gazed upon the oaken tables and chairs laid out here, and contrasted what he saw with the steel benches and stools he had seen in his flashback. Even the aluminum counter had been replaced with a marbled one. This place had clearly been renovated, and it was almost nothing like his memories anymore. Nevertheless, that didn't stop the nostalgia from rushing over him with tidal force, as he swept his eyes around the cafeteria's large, oval-shaped interior. Once more, just like with the withdrawal rooms, he felt a premonition of fear prick him while studying the area. He knew there was something about this place he was missing too… but his mind refused to drudge up the memory.

Jed continued with the tour, he and Matthew moving at a brisk speed now. They had only five minutes left, and it was quite late in the night. All the patients were in their rooms, probably asleep or trying to be.

They went through the remaining areas faster than before, Jed only giving them a cursory glance before moving on. The recognition within him continued to build upon itself, demanding that he remember what he was constantly failing to grasp. Each place he visited showered him with a fresh burst of nostalgia, filling his mind with vivid, life-like images of a past long gone by. Or maybe that wasn't the right thing to say. After all, Jed's past hadn't gone by. It was still with him, demanding to be understood.

The last place they visited was the courtyard, which was still pretty much the same. It was here that Jed had to bend down with his hands on his knees, sagging beneath the weight of so much time spent on that painted tarmac. He crouched for a few minutes simply feeling the breeze, his eyes washing over the empty chairs and marble benches scattered in the corner. If he focused hard enough, he could even picture his younger self seated at any one of those places, with Jeff, Mindy, and Rowan around him—all of them laughing.

Mathew cleared his throat politely. It was time to go back. Jed trailed him through the corridors he had just gone through, traveling out past those swinging double doors, and back into the reception area, where Linda stood, waiting. She looked at Jed and noticed the emotions bubbling across his face.

"I hope you had a good visit," Linda spoke cheerfully. "I'm sorry it was so short. If you can come back during the day, we can give you a proper tour."

"Thank you for having me," Jed told her in a slightly shaky voice. He gave her a sincere, grateful smile. "Coming here really helped. A lot. You should be proud of the way you're saving people's lives here." He bid her a final farewell, turning and leaving through the front door.

Back in his Jeep, Jed revved the engine and turned the radio's volume high on impulse. He didn't know why, but he suddenly felt lighter and cleaner, like his soul had just taken a shower. His mood was soaring over the skies faster than the nighttime wind, and his lips began to hum cheerfully along with the song on the radio.

He hadn't yet learned anything from his trip here, but that was okay. Jed knew that he would, and soon. His mind would fit the puzzle back together. He had complete faith in it. All he had needed to do was supply it with the right pieces, which he had just done. Now, it was only a matter of time.

The drive back passed quicker than he had expected. He drove in silence, listening to the music and the peaceful still-ness of his own mind. By the time he left the city's outskirts and entered its heart, it well past 3:00 AM. The sky was beginning to change from pure ebony to a deep, twinkling midnight blue. There was very little traffic on the streets—for a change—but that still didn't push him to gun down on the accelerator and drive fast. He didn't need to. For once, Jed was enjoying the journey, content with where he was at the moment—and where he was headed.

The call came at 3:37 AM.

Jed's phone rang in his lap, and he looked down with a frown, broken out of his tranquil reverie. When he saw his mother's name flashing on the screen, the calm curtain of his mind shifted sideways, and his earlier sense of foreboding peeked through it. Feeling a slight chill snaking through him, he answered the call and held his cell against his ear.

"Hello, Mom?

"Jed, help!"

"*Mom?*" Terror bolted through Jed. His hands clenched on the wheel, and his feet unwittingly stomped down, sending the Jeep shooting forward with a loud roar. "Hello, Mom?"

"Jed, please! Help me!" His mother's frantic voice cried out through the speaker. "He's here, Jed! C—" There was static, and the voice cut off.

"*MOM!*" Jed screamed, hearing his shrill cry mix in his ear with the Jeep's screeching tires as they swerved to a brake. "Mom, are you okay?"

There was more static now, crackling in his ears like a sputtering fire, and then Laurie's voice returned, even more frenzied than before.

"Jed help! Call the police! I've locked myself in the bathroom but he's ri—" There was a terrible banging noise that drowned out his mother's terrified pleas.

"*MOM!*" Jed screamed again, his vocal cords threatening to be torn apart with raw terror. He pressed down hard on the accelerator, and the vehicle shot forward with a tortured noise, its tires grinding against the tarmac and spewing curls of smoke upward. "Mom, can you hear me?"

Ten minutes. Her house was ten minutes away from where he was now. Just ten, that's all it would take. Or maybe five, in this traffic.

God, please let her be okay. Oh, God, please. Not my mother. Not her.

"Mom?" he shouted into the phone again, his heart curling and whimpering inside his chest. "Mom, are you okay?"

The terrible banging noise subsided. A moment later, his mother's breathless voice spoke again.

"Jed, please come quick. Call the police. I can't talk anymore; I have to hold the doo—" Another flurry of those awful banging noises. A cloud of static rumbled in his ears, distorting everything, and then it was replaced by dead silence.

The call had been disconnected.

No, no, no. Oh, God. Steering the wheel with one hand while his Jeep raced forward on the road, its tires barely maintaining their grip, Jed fumbled with the phone using his other hand. He tried clumsily to unlock it using his thumb and dial the police's number, but it just wasn't happening. His thumb was twitching madly, slick with sweat, and his phone's touch screen wasn't responding.

His phone rang again.

Jed looked down at it and almost couldn't believe his luck. For a small moment, he thought he was hallucinating. His mind had been pushed over the edge, and it had finally snapped.

The phone continued to ring.

Christie's name flashed on the screen.

Nudging his thumb gingerly against the screen, as if he was expecting this dream to break apart at the slightest touch, Jed answered the call and held the cell against his ears.

"Hello, Jed?"

No, he wasn't imagining this. It was real. Christie's voice was real.

"Hello, Christie?" He spoke in a high, panicked voice. "Christie, you need to send police officers to my mom's apartment. She's being attacked, Christie. Someone is in her apartment right now! I don't have time to talk. Please send someone over to her place fast."

"Oh, God! Okay, I'll—"

Christie's voice cut off midway as Jed disconnected the call and threw his phone on the passenger seat. He didn't have time to talk anymore. He had to reach his mother.

For the next five minutes, Jed drove like a possessed man, not stopping for a single red light and skidding around corners without braking, his tires squealing in protest as they were pushed to their very limits. His mind raced just as fast as his Jeep, filled with dark, dreadful thoughts, but Jed didn't pay any attention to it. He simply couldn't. He had no time, not even a microsecond to spare.

Finally, after a mad rush through the streets of the city, Jed arrived at his mother's apartment. He came to a grinding halt before the front doors and was out of the Jeep while there were still puffs of dust and smoke rising from its wheels.

Through the front doors Jed went, spotting the guard at the entrance sprawled out, unconscious, in his seat.

Oh, God, he knocked the guard out. Or maybe killed him. Please don't let anything happen to Mom.

Up the stairs he ran, taking them three at a time, his breath pushing through his lips in whistling pants. He reached the fifth floor and barreled toward his mom's apartment, noticing the door to her place standing slightly ajar.

Jed flung it open and charged into the living room, then toward his mother's bedroom on the opposite side. His feet stamped the floor like mad oxen hooves. The bedroom door also stood slightly ajar. Jed threw it open so hard it slammed into the wall and rattled on its hinges. He barged in, his hands curled into fists by his side, his nostrils flared, his eyes turned into the slits of a predatory animal.

There was a man standing in the room.

He had his face toward the bathroom door, which he was banging on and trying to unlock. The man's back was initially turned to Jed, but as Jed entered the room, he turned around to face him. His features were contorted by an insane rage. His lips were quivering with barely controlled energy. His eyes had turned into the beady, psychotic eyes of a rabid dog. And yet, despite this horrid transformation, Jed recognized the man. How could he not? He had spent his childhood with him, after all.

It was his father.

"You?" A geyser of confusion exploded within Jed, colliding with his anger and creating a chaotic mix that momentarily paralyzed him. He stood where he was, staring at his father's rage-filled face, not understanding. Had his mother called him here, too, to save her from the assailant? Or was h—

—Jed was given the answer by his father's bloodcurdling scream. It was a terrible, maddening banshee cry which tore past his lips and broke Jed's spell of paralysis. Jed blinked once and saw his father rushing toward him, a glinting silver object held in his hand.

He acted quickly, without thinking. There was a nightshade lamp lying to his left. Jed picked it up and flung it in his father's direction right as he was bringing his hand up with that strange, metal instrument in it. The lamp slammed into Richard's hand, and he let out a yelp of pain, his fingers opening, and the object gripped within them falling to the floor. Jed's eyes flicked toward it for a fleeting second, and he saw that it was a taser. There was no time to see anything more, then. His father was upon him.

Their bodies collided with a loud thud, and they both went sprawling to the floor. Richard Gray was a big man, strong and burly. He rolled over Jed and pinned his hands down with his own. Then, he head-butted him right on the tip of his nose.

Jed heard a slight cracking noise. A moment after, his face was engulfed in a blinding, searing pain. He cried out violently, raising his knee from the floor and slamming it into his father's groin. Richard shouted incoherently, more in anger than fear, and drew his head back to bring it down upon Jed's face again. This time, Jed turned sideways to avoid the incoming attack from smashing his nose to a pulp. But his father's rock-hard forehead still connected with his chin, and he felt another sharp stab of pain roll over him in a nauseating wave. Jed fought off the dizziness and brought his knee up again, this time connecting properly. Richard cried out once more, pain contorting his expressions, and momentarily faltered over Jed. Jed took advantage of the opportunity, sliding one hand out of his father's grip. He curled it into a fist and slammed it into the side of Richard's face, sending him toppling sideways. As Richard was trying to regain his bearings, Jed saw something in the corner of his eye.

But Richard wasn't done. He was a strong man, built like an oak tree, and Jed's blows had served only to infuriate him, nothing more. He rose to his feet, snorting like an angered bull, and turned around to charge Jed once aga—

—but fell to the floor.

Standing there with the taser in his hand, Jed looked down grimly at the twitching body of his father on the carpet. There was a thin line of drool coming out from the corner of Richard's lips. His eyes were wide open and frozen, and his limbs convulsed violently in the grips of the taser's current. He continued to lie there on the carpet for a few more seconds, shaking like a palsied patient, before going perfectly still.

There was silence.

Jed sniffed, and the simple act sent another blistering needle of pain piercing through his nose. It felt like it stabbed his brain. He felt blood slowly trickling down his upper lip and heard his heart's dull pounding in his ears, each pound accompanied by an ache from the blow he had received. Shuffling over to the bathroom door, Jed gripped the handle and croaked:

"It's okay, Mom. You can come out now."

At the sound of his voice, the lock turned instantly, and his mother came into view.

"Oh, God," she moaned, looking at his messed-up face and rushing toward him.

"I'm okay, Mom," Jed mumbled, speaking in a slurred manner to avoid moving his nose. "I'm fine. I just fractured my nose, I think."

Laurie looked down at the stationary body of her ex-husband lying on the carpet.

"He just barged in late at night," she whispered to Jed, her eyes unable to move away from Richard. "I was coming home from my friend's place, after a writing session, and I think he followed me here. I saw him rush into the building as the elevator doors were closing. H—he was so fast... I had no time." She shuddered. "I could hear his feet thundering behind me as I sprinted into my apartment, fumbled with its lock, threw open the door, and then rushed into the washroom, locking it behind me. If I had been even a tiny bit slower, I—I wou—"

Laurie broke off and shivered again, violently.

"Shhh. It's okay." Jed lay a comforting arm across her shoulder and pulled her toward him. "What happened to him? Why did he want to attack you? Do you know?"

His mother shrugged weakly. "Not really," she murmured. "I think... I think he just snapped, after the deaths. When I was locked in the bathroom, I could hear him screaming at me from outside. He kept yelling about how I had ruined his family, killing the two people he loved most. He kept pinning the blame on me, even though I didn't..." she trailed off, and Jed didn't urge her to speak more. He had heard enough.

They continued standing there, huddled over Richard Gray's unconscious form. A few minutes later, there was the sound of the apartment door creaking open, and then approaching footsteps.

Christie stepped into the room, followed by three armed policemen behind her. She glanced at Richard on the floor, then looked toward Jed standing with his mother, and understood what had happened instantly.

"Oh, God," Christie spoke, eyes widening as she took in Jed's face. "We need to get you to a hospital."

"Sure, in time. But I'll be fine until then." Jed nodded toward his father's form. "Just take him away so my mother can sleep in peace."

Christie didn't have to answer Jed's request. The police officers were already hauling a bleary-eyed and half-awake Richard Gray to his feet and dragging him away, handcuffs slapped on his wrist.

Jed tentatively touched the bridge of his nose and winced. The pain was still fresh.

"Come, Jed. I'll take you to the hospital." Christie absently reached for his hand, then seemed to realize where she was. She paused and looked at Jed's mother, really looked at her, taking in her entire appearance.

"I'm sorry we didn't arrive at the scene sooner, Laurie," she spoke with awkward nervousness. "It's really terrible that Jed had to handle this situation by himself."

Jed's mother shook her head. "It's not your fault, dear." She smiled a thin, tired smile. "Jed arrived less than ten minutes after I called, and he made quick work of his crazy father." She reached forward with one hand and affectionately ruffled her son's hair. Jed didn't shy away from it, nor did he look embarrassed. Jed opened his arms and embraced his mom. He hugged her, maybe a little too tight. He was so grateful she was alright.

"It is going to be okay, now. They took him away. He can't hurt you," Jed spoke softly as he held his mother at an arm's length and looked her up and down to confirm for himself that she was, indeed, unharmed.

"Thanks to you, Jed, I am okay. You need to go to the hospital and get patched up," Laurie responded as she looked at her strong son, knowing the young boy that had just subdued his father was still in there somewhere.

"Are you sure you will be okay on your own right now?" He carefully wiped away a smear of blood from his upper lip before giving his mother another quick hug.

Christie interjected and told Laurie, "I will make sure he is looked at in ER tonight. These officers are going to secure your apartment and let you get some rest. You can come in tomorrow to give us your statement."

Laurie grabbed a towel to wipe away some of the blood on Jed's face.

"Okay, okay. I'll see you tomorrow morning, Mom," Jed said as he took the towel from her.

Jed and Christie left through the front door, taking the elevator this time, too tired to make another run down the stairs.

Paramedics were taking care of the guard who had regained consciousness.

By the time they exited the building, Christie's comrades had already taken Richard away to the station.

Once they were inside Christie's Explorer and on their way to the hospital, Jed realized what he had been meaning to ask her.

"Hey." A frown creased his forehead. "Why were you calling me so late at night, when I was rushing over to my mom's place?"

Christie didn't answer immediately, and Jed saw her face tighten. A single finger twitched nervously on the steering wheel, and the streetlights illuminated the shadows dancing across her eyes.

"What, Christie?" Jed pressed. "What is it?"

Christie looked sideways at him. There was dismay on her face.

"Jack Stanley is dead, Jed," she told him, her voice heavy. "He died tonight in his cell. Hung himself from the window bars in the ceiling using a torn strip of his own clothes."

Jed fell silent upon hearing this. He found that he was not surprised to find out this news, but he was surprised at his own lack of surprise. It was a strange world.

"Are you going to say something?" Christie inquired, glancing at him worriedly.

Jed paused for a moment, gathering his thoughts. "It doesn't matter. His death holds no relevance for us now. He has already given us what we needed to know. It makes sense. He lived his life on his own terms, so he would want to die in the same way."

"But he didn't tell us the name of the person who hired him," Christie argued. "Not only that, we didn't get to find out why this Jack Stanley even agreed to work for that guy in the first place. What kind of sway does this man hold over people, to get them to become killers?"

"That's what I'm trying to tell you." Jed shook his head with firm certainty. "This was more than a simple contract killing. Whoever sent this guy had him dancing entirely to his tune. Trust me, whatever he told us during that first session was all the information we were going to get. No matter what we did, there was no way Stanley would have revealed anything more to us. He would have gone to his grave clutching his master's identity close to his chest." Jed paused, and a humorless smile graced his lips. "In fact, that is exactly what he did tonight, from what you told me."

Christie was silent for a long time. Jed could feel the gears in her head turning as she pondered his words.

"So, what now?" she finally asked. "Is that it? Is this case closed forever?"

"No," Jed answered softly. "The hint he gave me about my past was enough. I did a bit of digging around, and there's something important, something crucial to this case I should know but haven't yet realized. I will, though, soon enough. My mind will eventually bring it to the surface, and then we'll go at this mystery again. But until that happens, we have no choice except to wait and…"

"And what?" Christie asked, staring at him.

Jed smiled. It was a full and clear smile despite the pain it sent shooting through his broken nose.

"And solve some more murders. Maybe, finally have that conversation we have postponed."

Jed continues to search for the killer from his past when they are thrown into another case that will test his partnership with Christie. Read **Reflections of Gray** now to find out more! Visit the Series page with all the books in the series: https://books2read.com/ap/xe7Amo/Jodi-Walter

Want to learn why Jed was chosen for this partnership with Christie over any of the other qualified therapists? Claim your copy of **Origins of Gray** when you sign up for Jodi Walter's newsletter and learn more about how Jed came to know Ethan: https://dl.bookfunnel.com/qikjjxz4u7

Honest reviews of my books help bring them to the attention of other readers, who are more likely to read something from a new-to-them author if it has more reviews. You can quickly and easily leave a quick rating or brief review – visit this link to the book page https://bit.ly/JedGray3LegacyOfGray. Just scroll down the page and on the left side and select "Leave a Customer Review". Reviews are the lifeblood of little authors like me. Thank you! Or scan this QR code with your device:

ABOUT THE AUTHOR

JODI WALTER WAS BORN and raised in the Western Prairies of Canada. She spent her childhood enjoying nature and animals on the family farm. She continues to volunteer with animal rescues and has adopted two rescue dogs that she shares her home with today.

Jodi went through some difficult times in her early thirties when her marriage broke down and she became a single mom of a fantastic young son. After picking herself back up and succeeding in whatever challenge she faced, she became a firm believer that "we are never put in any situation we can not handle". Her newest endeavour is to write mystery thriller stories for you to enjoy. Delving into her subconscious, she creates characters she hopes will connect with you. Jodi has experienced a profound amount of catharsis by putting her pen to paper and releasing her characters into the world.

Jodi's website: jodiwalter.com or https://thirteen-pages-b txdiq.mailerpage.io/

Jodi's Facebook: https://www.facebook.com/jodiwalterau thor

Jodi's Email: author@jodiwalter.com